WRECKED UPON THIS SHORE

a novel

Kate Story

WRECKED UPON THIS SHORE

a novel

Kate Story

killick press
an imprint of Creative Publishers

St. John's, Newfoundland and Labrador
2011

© 2011, Kate Story

Canada Council   Conseil des Arts
for the Arts   du Canada

Canada

Newfoundland
Labrador

We gratefully acknowledge the financial support of the Canada Council for the
Arts, the Government of Canada through the Canada Book Fund (CBF),
and the Government of Newfoundland and Labrador through the Department of
Tourism, Culture and Recreation for our publishing program.

Cover design by Christopher Rouleau
Layout by Amy Fitzpatrick
Printed on acid-free paper

Published by
KILLICK PRESS
an imprint of CREATIVE BOOK PUBLISHING
a Transcontinental Inc. associated company
P.O. Box 8660, Stn. A
St. John's, Newfoundland and Labrador A1B 3T7

Printed in Canada by:
TRANSCONTINENTAL INC.

Library and Archives Canada Cataloguing in Publication

Story, Kate
    Wrecked upon this shore / Kate Story.

ISBN 978-1-897174-76-0

I. TITLE.

PS8637.T677W74 2011   C813'.6   C2011-905316-0

FSC
www.fsc.org
MIX
Paper from
responsible sources
FSC® C011825

Thank you

Over the course of writing this novel, I have received help from many quarters. Many thanks to many people, including:

JoAnne Corbeil, Ursula Pflug, Martha Cockshutt, Bill Kimball, the indefatigable Marnie Parsons, Tim Bowling, Prim Pemberton, Peter Sanders, Guy Ratchford, Diane Flacks, Jessica Harris, Deborah Root, Pippa Domville, Tim Haines, Curtis Driedger, Barbara Ratz, Dy Gallagher, John MacEwan, Simon Story, Lachlan Story, Em Glasspool, Lisa Dixon and all the staff at Black Honey, and Michael Morritt for the chess. Christopher Rouleau for a fabulous cover design. Robin McGrath and Jessica Grant. Charlotte Smith and Ryan Kerr, and especially Janette Platana and Joe Davies, for taking me through the home stretch.

Thanks to Donna and Pam at Killick Press.

And to all my other dear friends and family who have supported me in ways tangible and intangible through so much of what I do.

For a week Pearl has been sinking. But this morning she is buoyant. Her breath rattles strangely, high up in her chest.

"How are you?" Stephen asks his mother every morning, stumbling by her bedroom on his way down the hall.

"Terrific, I feel great," she says today, and it isn't until he reaches the bathroom that he realizes how strange her answer is.

He goes downstairs and gets some breakfast anyway; it's the routine. Mouse has made coffee and left it on for the both of them, the way she's taken to doing. She gets up so early and goes out on her runs, her heroically long runs, impressive in a woman almost fifty. Stephen drinks the coffee his mother's friend has made, eats some toast, eggs. Then he checks back in on his mother.

The room stinks of sweat, stale smoke, the overflowing ashtray. Her eyes burn in her face, blue, startling like the pale iridescent indigo inside a mussel shell. Her face is thin now, but her eyes shine. Cancer eyes.

"You hungry?"

"No."

"I'll fix some eggs for you."

"No, I said. I'm not hungry." She always says this.

"You should eat." He always tries.

The newspaper is scattered over the bed; she does not, he suspects, actually read it anymore, but she still likes to have it there. He lifts some pages and sits on the edge of the bed.

"Want me to rub your feet?"

Her breath rattles, in, out, in, out. Stephen wonders if she's heard him.

But then she says, "I need to see the doctor. I'm having trouble." In, out. In, out. "Breathing," she clarifies.

She looks at him and the panic in her eyes brings up the same feeling in his chest. Hollow, confused and cold, like... no, not like this, we'll drown. He looks up. Light, sky – look – humming above. Follow the sky.

But instead he plummets, cold, into the singing depths. All the careful preparations wash away.

His mind moves quickly – she isn't going to make it to the doctor's office – she needs to go straight to the hospital.

1

"I'll phone an ambulance." He makes the call fast as thinking and they're on their way.

His mother is struggling to sit up – "I've got to get some clothes on. And comb my hair, will you?"

He helps her take off her pajama top, put on a shirt. It is difficult. He starts combing her hair; great blonde hanks of it come out in the comb. He won't tell her – she's so proud that she hasn't lost her hair to the radiation treatments.

"You look fine. Now let's get you up, get some pants on you."

Standing is hard; he has to crouch down in front of her and link her arms around his neck, then heave up. They stand there, locked together, swaying like the last couple left standing in a dance marathon.

"Okay, okay," he murmurs. Her breath frightens him; he'll never be able to get jeans on her. "Maybe your PJ bottoms are good enough, okay?"

In reply Pearl begins trying to shuffle toward the bedroom door. Stephen hears the front door open downstairs – at first he thinks the paramedics have arrived – but then he hears "Hello!" and knows it's Mouse.

"Up here!" he hollers over his mother's head, and footsteps bound up the stairs. He is facing the door, his arms locked around his mother's waist, and as soon as Mouse sees his face, she stops dead still. Then she nods. Stephen knows that she knows – it's a profound relief.

"Come on, Mom."

They sway and step, sway and step, and Mouse hovers by the door, breathing hard from her run, cropped hair sweaty and skin glowing with blood and health. She smells of the outdoors, brings a freshness to the stale, sick dying in the bedroom.

Stephen gets his mother to the bedroom door. But she begins to buckle, he can't hold her. Mouse tries to help, but Pearl sags against the doorframe and begins to slide down it.

"I gotta piss. Stephen, Mouse, I gotta piss."

Stephen looks at Mouse. "Paramedics are on the way."

"Good."

Stephen is sliding down with his mother, her arms still locked around his neck. He can't see her face.

"Stephen, I'm pissing myself."

She sounds like a little girl. Her arms loosen, and he pulls back to see her face. He is vaguely aware of Mouse crying.

"Everything's going to be all right," he says; his voice surprises him with its firmness. Then his body begins to cry. She is sliding, falling on her side

on the floor, and her throat is working. Is she going to be sick? Is she trying to say something?

The rattle, the breath in her, has stopped. Mouse's hands help him lie
her down on her back, and he leans over and tries to give mouth-to-mouth
resuscitation. Her mouth reeks; he almost gags. But he keeps putting his
breath into her lungs.

The paramedics arrive soon after. They put circuitry on her, shock her
body a couple of times. He and Mouse hold hands over the body and he is
aware that they are both crying uncontrollably, holding so tight to each other
that later his hand is bruised.

One of the paramedics says, "We could keep doing this but she's gone.
We're just breaking her up inside." The paramedics stand over them for a
moment, then the same one speaks again. "We'll give you a minute alone
with her. Then we have to take the body to the hospital."

Stephen and Mouse crouch over the body. Their tears fall on her face.
Stephen touches her teeth – her mouth hangs open – he has never touched
her teeth before. They are white, even. He realizes that he had forgotten to
put shoes on her. Her beautiful feet are bare.

Pearl and Mouse are driving to the island.

Pearl owns a shiny red Chevy Malibu coupe, a reward for graduating from high school. They've got the windows rolled down. The scents of cedar and wet grass fight with the Malibu's gorgeous wine red interior; it still smells new. The sun keeps threatening to break through clouds.

They are not supposed to be speeding past cedar woods and farmers' fields in a brand new cherry red car. It is October and they should be in university and thrillingly are not, because Pearl's parents are rich and bribed their daughter to graduate from high school.

Mouse has learned a number of other interesting facts about her friend today.

One: Pearl drives horribly, and very fast.

Two: Her last name, Lewis, graces both a small town and a street in Toronto.

Three: Pearl did not hesitate to flirt outrageously with the young police officer who stopped them on Highway 7.

Four: Pearl's blonde curls are, in fact, a perm.

Being next to Pearl makes Mouse feel even bigger than she usually does. Pearl gives an impression of delicacy; Mouse is what her father back home in Newfoundland cheerfully refers to as "a big grand girl." Later in life Mouse will wonder why, in 1979, she suffered so over her imagined fatness; here in the car next to Pearl she is broad-shouldered and tall.

She and Pearl sing along to the car radio, yelling over the wind rushing through open windows. *Is she reely goin ow withim? Is she reely gonna take him home to-nite?*

Mouse figures the song means something different to her than to Pearl, or for that matter, to Joe Jackson. Mouse has recently emerged from what her mother described as "a high-school crush." A cute, dismissive word – *crush* – oddly enough, though, it aptly conveys the grinding mass of overwhelming feeling that took what Mouse knew of herself and reduced it to fragments, to stumbling longing. The friend in question allowed Mouse kisses and blazing hope, only to turn against her and immediately take on a series of performative boyfriends. *I'm not a fuckin dyke.*

"Pearl." The song is over.

4

"Hmm?"

Mouse is studying the ticket the officer wrote. "Pearl, he's charged you with carless driving. *Carless*."

"What?"

"He left out the 'e.'"

Pearl stares at Mouse for a moment, then back at the unreeling road. She throws back her head and snort-laughs.

"You know what you should do? You should take it to court." Mouse adopts a deep voice. "Your Honour, clearly this police officer is under a delusion. He was too busy staring at the defendant's tits to notice that she was, in fact, driving a bona fide car."

"Ah. That's funny." Pearl inhales, lets smoke out through her nose. "Dad'll pay it."

"You'll tell your parents?" Mouse's voice goes up in an unintentional squeak. "Jesus. I'd rather stick pins in my eyes."

Pearl shrugs.

"But... carless driving!"

"Gimme that." Pearl takes the ticket and studies it. "What a moron." She tosses the ticket out the window; it whips away on the wind, a white fragment. She throws her cigarette after it and lights another. Her blonde hair shines against her burgundy Danskin leotard, her army pants, her $2.99 canvas summer wedgies from Woolworths. She's slumming. She looks wonderful.

By the time they hit Havelock they are talking about masturbation and Mouse is blushing. "You don't. Mary mother. I don't believe you."

"Well, if I expect other people to get off on me, I might as well make sure I can get off on myself."

"That's so... so..."

"Usually as a slutty schoolgirl. That's probably from the goddamn private boot camp they sent me to, those uniforms, you know."

"You jack off to your own image."

"Well, I don't have a big picture of myself on the ceiling, if that's what you mean. Although that's not a bad – "

"You imagine yourself with someone else? Or you imagine yourself as the guy fucking you?"

"No, no, I just picture myself."

"Jesus Mary."

Pearl storms through the railway town, steering with her knee as she lights another smoke. "Which hand do you use?"

"What?"

5

"Well, you're left-handed, right? So which hand do you use?"

"As if it's any of your – "

"Don't be so prudish. Tell me."

"No."

"I use my right."

Mouse feels a giggle building up. "Thank you very much for that. That information. For which I did not ask. Mind putting your hands back on the wheel?" The car wobbles back and forth in its lane. A transport truck comes toward them down the highway.

"You tell." Pearl waves her hands in the air like a cheerleader.

Ever since coming to Ontario on her university scholarship, Mouse has been trying to read people. Everyone here seems so different. They all have more money, or something – they are cooler, she thinks, so every moment she asks herself *Is this how to be? Is this what to say, how to say it?* But Pearl, now, Pearl is right off the radar. Pearl makes Mouse feel hot and reckless in a way that frightens her a little, in a way she has quickly found she doesn't want to do without. The truck is almost on them, the coupe straddles the lanes.

"Hands on wheel, Pearl, hands on wheel," Mouse begs, trying to sound cool.

Pearl will play chicken just to get Mouse to confess which hand she uses to masturbate.

"Right! I use my right, okay!"

"Why?" Pearl takes hold of the wheel and cruises past the blaring truck. Hot wind shudders the car.

"I don't know why."

"Maybe you're ambivalent about masturbating."

"Shut up."

Some time later they are in another town with more of those exotic red brick Ontario buildings, eating lunch at a hotel made of stone. "I love places like this," Pearl says.

Mouse looks around. Excepting the mainland accent of the waitress, which lends her a confusingly upper-class, educated air, the place is nearly identical to dives back home: smoke-stained walls, a carpet with history, air heavy with grease. "Why?"

"They're so… authentic. They're not trying." Pearl stuffs her mouth with French fries. "I can't wait to swim," she says thickly. "It's still warm enough. I brought three different swimsuits."

"Lah-di-dah."

"You're funny. I like that: lah-di-dah."

6

"I," says Mouse, very pleased, "brought a single suit. Which will not get wet."

"Why the hell not?"

"Because, my lovely Toronto brat, I do not swim."

Pearl stares. "As in, you can't? Or won't?"

Mouse takes a big bite of hamburger. "A little of both."

"Mouse is an even better name for you than I thought. Mice don't swim."

"I don't doubt I'll be stuck with it for life." Mouse puts weary skepticism into her voice, but she's been pleased ever since Pearl named her. She's had nicknames before: boys, of course, dubbed her *Dog*; and more lastingly, because she's always done well at school, *Brain*. Not a compliment. *Mouse* is better.

Pearl has a gift for naming people. Uncle Tod: the director of the production of *The Tempest* in which they are both involved is barely two years older than they are, but "uncle" suits Tod Owens's beard, the affected way he wears sweater-coats and loafers. Garage Bob: Robert Smith, who plays Antonio, lives in a garage. And Mouse: Mandy, stage manager, is brown (her hair, her eyes, her summer skin); her last name is Brown; and facetiously, she is Mouse because she is big and loud. They will all keep these names in the years to come, and they will remember Pearl because of it.

After lunch they head south through rolling, rocky countryside. The towns have names that chime like bells: Springbrook, Stirling, Belleville (although Bonarlaw leads to an elaborate scenario where perpetual erections are legislated on pain of death). Pearl takes a ramp onto the 401. Mouse remembers the late-night flight to Toronto, falling asleep against a bus window and waking up cold. Over a month ago; it seems like years.

The cherry red coupe gets attention from guys with mustaches who race alongside the girls.

"Our marina's near Gananoque," says Pearl. Gananoque could be a town, a mall, or a swamp; Pearl says the name like Mouse should know what it is. "The boat will still be in the water. I think."

"You think?"

"Well, family *tradition*," the word is slow and bitter, "is that dear old dad and mom go up there on the last weekend of September; Dad's birthday, you see. Then Floyd shuts up the cottage and the big house for winter, and once he's done, the boats come out of the water. But I don't think he'll have done that yet."

"What if he has?"

Pearl waves her hand and says nothing.

7

"Great. What did you have in mind? A brisk swim down the mighty St. Lawrence River?"

Pearl squints into the hazy distance, east. "I'm coming, island," she sings under her breath. "Here I come." There's a sweetness in her voice that makes Mouse's breath catch.

They're off the highway, and Mouse catches glimpses of water. The grass is so green, and oaks tower over the winding road; autumn has set the tips of trees alight, burning against grey sky. The air smells spicy, the stands of sumac tropical; dusky green leaves surge gently beneath calyxes of red fur, rising and falling, soothing as waves.

Suddenly Pearl twists the wheel and leaves the road, lurching over the shoulder and across a green field, sliding from side to side. Mouse screams. Clots of dirt spin up behind the car. Pearl swerves around a stand of trees, and brings the car to a halt.

"Jesus Christ, Mary Mother of Holy Jesus god fuck are you insane?"

"Calm down." Pearl turns off the ignition and checks herself out in the rear-view mirror, scrunching her permed curls with one tiny, perfect hand.

Mouse gets out of the car, legs trembling. A breeze reaches her and she can smell water on it.

"Can you see the road from here?" Pearl calls from the car.

"What?"

"Can you *see* the *road* from *here*?" Pearl addresses Mouse as though she is a retarded child.

"Jesus. No." Mouse looks. "Not really."

"Go out a bit and see if the car shows."

"Fuck." Mouse ducks under a branch, stomping partway across the field. Bits of red car gleam through the leaves, and tire tracks cut a telltale track through the soil. She stomps back into the grove, where Pearl is now out of the car slinging bags over her shoulders, mouth down-turned to secure her cigarette. "Tracks are a dead giveaway, and the red shows through."

"Rip off some branches and camouflage it."

"Yes, your Highness." Sometimes Mouse feels like Han Solo to Pearl's Princess Leia. "Immediately, Your Worship." Or maybe more like Chewbacca. She doesn't ask why they are doing this.

They cover the car in torn branches. Then, loaded with bags (Mouse takes most of them), and carrying two cases of beer each, they set off across the field and down a green slope.

Mouse is used to the business and noise of an industrial ocean harbour, great tankers with Japanese and Russian and Portuguese names, smaller boats making do along the waterfront. Pearl leads her toward a long, low, corrugated-metal building painted dark green. No one's around. There is a parking lot – only two cars in it, old beaters – and a grassy verge, green and soggy. They walk into the building and in the dimness there are wooden docks and rows of boats, each with a watery parking spot. Mouse breathes in the musty, wooden, watery smell, hears the hollow licking of the water.

Pearl dumps her bags and skips down the dock, springing up onto a biggish boat and disappearing into a cabin. Mouse follows and swings a bag up onto the deck, but Pearl reappears. "Naw, I won't take the Lyman." She jumps back down to the dock. "The Montauk."

The Montauk is a smaller boat with no cabin. Mouse watches as Pearl steps onto the white and wooden boat, strokes the wheel on a centre console.

"Well, come on," says Pearl. "Load her up."

Mouse doesn't like stepping across that gap of water; she's afraid she'll fall in. She swings the bags one by one over the metal railing, and last of all, hands Pearl the precious cases of beer. Pearl starts the engine; the key has been left in the ignition. Noise and the smell of gas fill the space.

"Get aboard!"

"Aren't there any life jackets?"

Pearl shrugs, rummaging around. "Here."

By the time Mouse has negotiated the tippy, swinging boat and that strip of water, Pearl has untied the boat. "You want to drive?" she asks suddenly, as if offering a treat.

"No! Never driven a boat in me life," Mouse shouts over the motor.

"But you're from Newfoundland." Pearl says *New-FOUND-lind*, just to irritate Mouse, who has taught her the right way to say it.

"I'm a townie, not a goddamn bayman."

Pearl shrugs. "Suit yourself."

They rumble backwards, out into the air. Pearl turns the boat around, and they are off, across the water.

Boat words, river words, cottage words: *slip, painter, Boston Whaler, red right returning*. Mouse cannot imagine why this fiberglass Montauk thing is called a Boston Whaler, they being neither in Boston nor whaling. "Are there whales in the St. Lawrence?"

"Never thought about it."

The channel is muddy, and there are reeds and ducks. Pearl says the water level begins falling in September, and continues to fall until it freezes; in places the water will be less than a foot deep. Rocks lurk.

9

"You know the channels, though, right?"

"Sure. And then of course there are the gummint boo-eys."

"The who whatsit?"

"Gummint boo-eys. That's Thousand Island talk for government buoys."

They come out onto open water. It's the first time in a month Mouse has felt this strength of moving air on her body, wind that has come across water, the force of that. It awakens a longing in her for home, an ache.

Islands: small, furry, woolen things. Jack pines, and Canadian and American flags. Islands crusted pink and white around the edges like the rim of a Caesar. Crenellated treetops rising and falling, outlined against the sky. Fairytale buildings, lace-trimmed, pink and green and red, storied houses, turrets.

"You call these *cottages*?"

"Yeah, some of them are mansions." Pearl is adorable standing behind the wheel, wind combing her long blonde hair.

"Does every island have a cottage?"

"Hmm?"

"Does every cottage have an island?"

Pearl considers, squinting across the water. "No. Some islands definitely have more than one cottage. Houses. And people live on Grindstone year-round. They have *cars*."

"How long has your family had your island?"

"So many questions." Pearl flashes her smile.

"I'd like to be armed with a little knowledge as I surge forward into unknown and possibly hostile territory."

"Well, since my great-grandfather for sure."

"My God, a dynasty. He built it?"

Pearl is laughing now, and Mouse is pleased she has made Pearl laugh. "Well, he didn't build it himself. He had people do it."

"Naturally."

"He bought the island in 1905 from a farmer, and the big house went up in 1909."

Pearl points out islands, naming them: Wolfe, Hickory, Black Ant Island. "Weekly square dances on Grindstone in summer," Pearl says. Mouse looks a question at her friend. "Anything to escape my goddamn family," Pearl answers.

"You *square dance*?"

The boat bangs across waves and the engine rumbles and whines. By the time Pearl points and says, "There it is," Mouse has started feeling just the tiniest bit queasy.

The island is green, she sees. The water grey blue. Pearl takes the boat around to a dock, and a large boathouse, and acres of unmowed lawn. And, "Are those *tennis courts?*" But it's what unfolds behind the tennis courts that really arrests Mouse's attention. Stately trees and gardens, gables and six chimneys, bow windows, sweeping porches, and upper-storey windows nestled beneath the many roofs.

"That's the big house," says Pearl. "Don't worry. We don't stay there."

Down by the water is a smaller version of the mansion. Green, with a shingled bell-cast roof, and curved upper windows hard as eyes.

Cold darkness pours out the door like water.

They walk in; vision adjusts. A rampart of round grey river stones resolves into a chimney and fireplace; gleaming darkness at the opposite end is a dining table, surrounded by sixteen carved chairs. Pale boulders are chintz-covered armchairs gathered around a black bearskin rug, and a wooden staircase leads to what Mouse assumes are bedrooms under the gables. There's a sideboard full of pink rose china, framed nautical maps on the walls, and a couple of taxidermied deer heads with dusty, slightly misaligned eyes.

When Pearl invited Mouse to come stay at the family cottage, she'd pictured a small, neat house, the sort of place where Snow White would cosy up to the dwarves. She wanders into the dimness. A narrow hall opens into a kitchen, and Mouse is relieved it's human-sized. There's a stove and a round-edged fridge, an ordinary wooden table with ordinary chairs around it.

"Maria used to sleep there." Pearl has followed, pointing to a door off the kitchen; Mouse perceives a tiny bedroom. "She did all the cooking, looked after us kids. She ended up marrying Floyd. The caretaker."

Mouse is astonished at the ease with which Pearl acknowledges servants; it seems decadent, from another era. She puts her beer cases down in front of the fridge and heads back into the hallway.

Rain gear all the colours of the rainbow hang there: red coats and orange, yellow and green, boots lined carefully on rubber mats beneath. The coats and boots seem as much a part of the place as the dark wood floors, the slightly musty smell, the light off the water: iconographic rain gear, it belongs. Light pours through windows from the porch, and the water is bright. Mouse blinks, and blinks again, dazzled.

They lie on the dock in the late-afternoon sunlight, drinking Blue and smoking. It's warm, here in the shelter of the boathouse. Mouse drinks her first beer of the day too fast and gazes at Pearl's perfect, brown pink feet.

11

"Put lotion on my back." Pearl props herself on her elbows, untying her bikini top with one hand. "I know you're looking, Mouse, so don't even pretend."

"I'm not."

Mouse makes a show of hunting around for the Coppertone. She had looked, and who wouldn't with those perfect milky breasts right there? She squirts too much lotion onto Pearl's back and starts rubbing it in.

"Calm down!"

Mouse tries to calm down, to apply the lotion the way she imagines Pearl would like it – slow, gentle circles. There's something about Pearl that reacts to something inside Mouse, creating light, like exposing phosphorous to oxygen. She wants to laugh at herself for the eager way in which she wants, always, to please Pearl.

"Princess."

"Got the part, didn't I? God, for a minute I thought Uncle Tod was going to give it to that redhead, that disaster, what's her name?"

"Well, you got it."

"It's going to be good. I think it's going to be a good production. Do you think it's going to be a good production?"

"I just see lists of things to do." Mouse gently slaps Pearl's back. She lies back on her towel with arms crossed over her face, palms smelling of Coppertone, of Pearl.

"Come on. Tell me I'm good. Tell me I'm the best Miranda ever."

"You're the best Miranda ever."

"Dr. Livingstone makes a pretty hot Prospero."

Mouse registers a tiny flare of jealousy; the professor playing Prospero is handsome and flirty. Already Mouse has seen him linger with his hand on Pearl's lower back, too low.

"Better learn his lines."

"You're such a stage manager." Pearl tips her bottle, pouring beer delicately down her throat. "A virtuous stage manager."

Mouse suddenly finds the feeling of her braid under her shoulder blades irritating; she pulls it out and around, flinging it sideways on the dock. "I like getting things done." Mouse loves everything about stage management: being on book, procuring props, bossing the director when necessary, the endless lists.

They lie on the dock in silence. The waves lap, the breeze picks up and it is chilly. Two mallards fly overhead, quacking, splashing faintly as they land in the river.

Pearl swings her legs around to sit up. She looks down at Mouse with an amused expression.

"What?" Mouse squints at her friend. The blue sky around Pearl's pale head renders her impossibly lovely.

"I want to be Prospero." Pearl leans in, whispers. Mouse is intensely aware of Pearl's breasts, almost touching her. "I want to be Prospero." Pearl is mocking, deadly serious.

"Be Prospero, then. Be my guest. Go ahead." Mouse's smoke, forgotten, has extinguished itself.

Pearl laughs. She rolls onto her back and stretches out, arms flung over her head, the full length of her. She arches her back like a dolphin.

"My island!" she yells. She springs to her feet and runs to the end of the dock, shouting to the sky, the empty river. "My island! Mine!"

It gets cold when the sun goes down. They drag their sleeping bags and a case of beer to the fireplace, lie on the bearskin rug. It's like a picture in a magazine, Mouse thinks – the soaring chimney of rounded, many-coloured stones, the bear with claws and head, the fire licking and licking at the blackened mouth of the fireplace. She can hardly believe she's here, in this picture-perfect place: something has gone wrong. She doesn't belong here, mechanic's girl, *Newfie*. She imagines the upper-class mainland bear suddenly rearing up and devouring her.

She remembers her first class at university a few weeks ago: a small tutorial, the professor reading down the list of names and coming to hers, looking up with a smile. "Mandy Brown, our scholarship student from Newfoundland." Some in the class stirring, staring at her.

A girl spoke. "You've come a long way."

"You've come a long way, *baby*," a guy said, quoting the cigarette ad, raising a general laugh.

"Say something," said the girl.

"What?" Mouse stared at her.

"Say something in your accent."

Mouse felt heat rising in her cheeks. "You'll get to hear me talk soon enough," she'd said, carefully erasing any hint of accent from her speech. It had earned her a reputation as a hard-ass. Mouse is a smart girl and has always stood out that way. She remembers her grade three teacher making her stand up to repeat for the whole class *Three times three is nine* because she'd said *Tree toimes tree…* That woman, Mouse thinks now, had a thicker accent than she herself. She'd never have been punished if she hadn't been a *Brain*. Too smart for her own good.

In places, the bear has begun to go bald. Behind them, through the window – black tree trunks shivering against silver water – the moon shines down; but they aren't looking to the moon, they're staring into the fire and drinking. The deer heads look down on them.

"Your father shoot those?"

"The deer? I don't know. He shot this bear, though." Pearl picks up a front paw of the bear and waves it at Mouse, growling softly.

"You ever go out with him?"

"Hunting's for men, don't you know. He takes along his entourage, his lackeys. His fucking lawyer. Mr. Pleasant just *loves* hunting with *daddy*. Or he takes his rich asshole friends. They talk about money, that's all they talk about. Fucking money, and how to make more of it. And how much it costs to send their bad daughters off to boarding school. Fuck."

Mouse watches Pearl carefully raise her cigarette to her lips, blow smoke, her head jerking to the side in an exaggerated gesture of disgust. Pearl, suddenly it seems, has hit the wall and is drunk.

"When did you go to boarding school?"

"Who cares. Three years. Went to Jarvis, but Pearl was a bad girl so they shipped me off to Bull Shit School with all the other poor little rich girls. Send for me at Christmas, and buy me cars when I graduate. Ballet camps in the summer. Thousands, tens of thousands. Hated that school. Asshole."

"Why didn't you refuse to go?"

Pearl jerks her head toward the fire, pouting. She throws her cigarette into the flames, lights another.

"If you hate him so much, why take his money?"

"It's what he loves most. I'll take every fucking penny I can."

The beer case is almost empty.

"The last bottle is calling me," Pearl sing-songs, and opens it. She can barely find her lips with the bottle. "We are such stuff…" she begins, and belches. "We are such stuff as dreams are made on," she begins again, "…an' …an' … our little life… is rounded with *sleep*. You wanna sleep, Mousey? I'm passing out." And Pearl puts her head down, hand still clutching the bottle, a lit smoke between her fingers.

The fire is burning down. Mouse takes the smoke from her friend's fingers, throws it on the fire. Pearl's mouth is open, her beautiful face is flushed. She is breathing – Mouse checks – yes, she is breathing. Where has Pearl gone? The sleeping are like the dead, she thinks. Yes, like in the play, where the villain tries to convince the brother to murder the nobles asleep on the beach. *Say, this were death that now hath seized them; why,*

14

they were no worse than now they are. Except then you don't get to wake up. Mouse takes the beer from Pearl's fist; she moans softly, settles.

Mouse's parents drink steadily, daily, grimly. It is nothing like Pearl's wild extremity, drinking to oblivion, drinking almost to the point, Mouse thinks, of death. "Here lies your brother," Mouse whispers. The actor playing Antonio can never remember his lines; she's had to be on book for him so often that the words come effortlessly – "here lies your brother, no better than the earth he lies upon. If he were that which now he's like, that's dead."

The fire burns low, and lower still. Mouse's head sinks down until her cheek rests on the rough-furred skull of the bear. Poor bear, she thinks, stroking his snout. Poor bear, poor little monster, what'd they have to go and kill you for? As if by way of answer, a grating noise fills her ears. It is faint, but cuts through the air, through the soft pop of the dying embers and the swish of the wind outside, a rhythmic grinding. It stops for a moment – was she imagining it? – no, there it is again. Her heart leaps and she sits, trying in the near-dark to see. A wild thought that it's the bear passes through; she wonders if it's coming from outside but the noise is right here, next to her.

It's Pearl. The sound is coming from Pearl. She is grinding her teeth as she sleeps, her jaw working back and forth. She is engaged in a struggle, some terrible thing is trying to get out from between her clenched teeth. Mouse watches, and after a time she reaches out and places tentative fingertips on her friend's jaw. She massages gently, and after a time, the grinding stops.

Mouse pillows her head on her arm and watches Pearl's face in the changeable firelight. Gold unfolds into gold. There are vast rooms; treasures; paintings of a family not hers. Mouse wanders through the grand old house. She comes to a bedroom. Lying on brocade is a baby wrapped in a thin silk blanket, pale blue. She doesn't know what to do. The baby's eyes stare. What to feed it? Milk? The baby's another treasure wrapped in this house, but it will die. Water? Her own mother fed her canned milk with water, she knows this, but that might kill this baby.

She leaves it lying there, roams through the house to find someone who might know. But the house is empty. Once there's a flutter of silk: a woman from one of the paintings dressed in black, pale, going down a staircase but she doesn't stop and Mouse can't speak. The baby will die.

She goes back to the bedroom, to the little blue creature lying on its parents' grand gold bed, huge fire burning in a marble fireplace but the room's cold, cold. Painting of fruit red as rubies, she'd reach through the frame if

15

she could, pluck one out, keep this baby with her and raise it on pome-
granate seeds and water. The baby's eyes stare up at her. She doesn't know
what to do and the baby will die.

The fire burns down, and Mouse dreams.

The bookstore is almost beautiful at this time of day. Winter sunlight blooms across the big front window, dispersed by frost and grime into a warm glow. It lights up the bookshelves – the friendly orange and green spines – illuminates the chessboard, pieces gleaming white and black.

Normally Stephen likes these late afternoons, the day narrowing toward the end of his shift and home, or maybe an evening at the bar. That's all changed, since the accident.

Today has been busy, which is good – less time for his brain to boil uselessly in his skull. And just as it looked like things were emptying out, his friend Dieter came by to hang out and play chess. Stephen has even managed to win a few games, but now, as the day starts to close off, his mind is spinning again. He looks at the board and suddenly sees the trap Dieter has laid. It's unwinnable, and he groans.

"I can't believe I didn't... You sure you didn't move things around while I was ringing up that old guy?"

Dieter flashes his perfect trust-fund-baby grin. "Aw, come on."

Stephen rubs his hand over his face. "The way I'm playing, you could cheat me and I'd call it a fair game." He stirs, checks the clock. "Guess I should cash out."

Dieter gathers the pieces and unfolds himself from his stool. "You want to come out for a beer?"

"No, thanks."

"Listen, tomorrow we're having a big piss-up over at the house. Come if you can."

"What's the occasion?"

"It's my birthday, buddy," Dieter reminds him. "The big three-oh."

Stephen stares, then busies himself with shelving a book. "Jesus, I forgot. Sorry."

Dieter's been talking about turning thirty for months now; Stephen can't believe it slipped his mind.

"Hey, no worries. You got a lot going on." Dieter shoves his hat over his ruddy hair; the bookstore is so cold he's not bothered to remove his coat. "How's your mother? Still in hospital?"

Stephen nods. "She's furious. She has to go outside to smoke." The clench has come back to his gut. Pearl has been in hospital for three days, now.

"They find out what caused that stroke?"

"They did tests. We don't know yet. We're waiting to hear."

It's weird, this *we*; it isn't a way he has ever spoken of himself and his mother.

"Hold on a sec." Stephen turns to a shelf and runs his finger over the spines. "Somewhere… yeah." Stephen pulls a thick paperback off the shelf, *Galaxy*, yellow letters glowing against red. "Published the year you and I were born, my fine friend." It's an excellent collection of short SF published in *Galaxy* magazine between 1950 and 1979, with an introduction by Frederik Pohl – he knows Dieter will love it.

"Hey – this is great. Thanks!"

They thumb through the book together, agreeing that the cover art is terrible. But back then was when writing was really exciting, things were really happening.

"It's like pre-1950, science fiction was still caught up in the American Dream. Problems existed to be solved and all that."

"With gadgets," Stephen agrees.

"But the good writing, like these stories… it looks at what comes after."

"Yeah, the worm in the apple. They really had the fire in them then." Stephen pictures Frederik Pohl pounding away at a typewriter late at night. The sound is brave, mechanical; it flings pieces of light, bright against the darkness.

"I picked up a typewriter at Value Village today," Dieter says.

Stephen looks up from the book. "You're reading my mind."

"Why, you want one?"

Stephen laughs, shakes his head. Dieter collects typewriters; he writes poetry on them.

"The real old kind, an Underwood," Dieter says. "It feels good, you know? The action."

"Yeah." Stephen used to collect typewriters too, and he still has three or four: gathering dust under his bed, in his closet. He used to love the heavy solidity of them, rough coldness of black and grey metal, imprint left on paper. The smell of ink, the swinging return. A couple of years ago he was working on something, not sure if it was fiction or a journal entry, and his mother came by his apartment. She saw the page curving out of the machine and made one of her remarks: *Me, I don't miss typewriters one goddamn bit,* she'd said. *Goddamn retyping every essay. You're lucky you've got computers, your generation. Typical to imagine typewriters are real or better or something. It's just romancing.* Somehow the collection, and his attempts to write on the machines, felt juvenile after that. "Happy birthday."

Dieter leaves and Stephen putters around, putting books back on shelves, sneezing in the dust of the art book section, and it isn't until he catches himself trying to scrape crud from the computer keyboard that he realizes he is avoiding going to the hospital.

He stands in the winter dusk, sun sunk now, oppressed by the noise of passing traffic. He forces himself to put on his coat, hat, gloves. As soon as he steps outside, the wind hits; he ducks his face into his coat collar and quickly locks up the store.

The cold air brings the smell of smoke to the surface, soaked into the wool fabric of his coat. On his morning visit to the hospital, it was so cold that nurses turned a blind eye to the patients huddled in the porch of the north entrance, and in consequence his visit consisted of standing in the enclosed space, air thick with the exhalations of several sick smokers. At least it alleviated the awkwardness of a visit with his mother; he made small talk with the other patients instead. He suspects his mother hates his visits. His solicitousness reminds her something's wrong.

The smoke has clung to his coat all day, like when he was a kid. The other students thought he smoked; he never had, he just stank of it. The others got on the school bus in a clump, a mass, a grinning tribe of bullies, stinking with that sweet, sick smell. The boys smacked him on the head on their way to the back of the bus, one after another. Striking the back of his skull, his ear.

He survived school by reading: on the bus, during lunch break, anytime he could dive into a book. He remembers clearly learning how to read; he was four years old. Pearl had this British kids' book. *See Peter. See Jane. The ball is in the tree.* The ball was red, against a blue sky. Pearl must have read the book to him, but he doesn't remember this. What he remembers is sitting on the floor in a hallway. It wasn't the hall of the house he spent most of his childhood in; it must have been in the apartment Pearl has told him they shared in the early years. He remembers sitting on the floor with this book, looking at the pictures, and he remembers *ball.* The red ball. *B,* he made the sound of letter *b* with his lips. And then *a,* and *l,* he knew his alphabet, he knew the sounds belonging to those letters. And suddenly it was there, incandescent. Ball. He was reading. Ball. It was a word. Ball! And then he could see *d-o-g, dog.* And *tree.*

"Tree!" He shouted the words. "See! See the ball! See the dog!"

He remembers running to Pearl in the kitchen; she was reading a paperback novel and smoking.

"I can read too!" he shouted to her. "I can read!"

But surely he isn't able to remember that. It was too long ago. Stephen walks, wind cutting through his coat. He must be making it up. What's the earliest a person can remember? Five, maybe. Kindergarten. He remembers Kindergarten. The class had its own "library," a set of three wooden shelves forming a U-shaped enclosure. Stephen read all of the books, starting from the upper left-hand corner and working his way right and down. Sometimes other children would come in, grabbing books to read out loud to each other. Stephen would make himself round and hard when this happened, hunch over his book. He'd concentrate and the noise would disappear, he would go back into the world of the book.

One day something was different, something was wrong. It was quiet. Slowly, still half in the dream of the book, he stood and looked out of the shelf-U. No one was there. What had happened? Had school ended? Had everyone gone and left him? Something else too – he remembers now – the pants he'd been wearing, they wouldn't stay up on their own, the elastic was gone or something. So he stood there holding onto his pants with one hand, the book in the other. Panic – was he alone and locked in the building? Where was his mother?

But then he heard, muffled below, singing voices. *O Canada*. He remembered: the teacher had told them that today there was a school assembly. Stephen dropped his book and, holding onto his pants, began to run to the door of the classroom – he should be with the other Kindergarten kids in the front row of the gym, singing "O Canada." Then he stopped short. Going into the assembly now would mean walking past all the teachers, and all the kids: scary Grade Sixes at the back, down the aisle to the Kindergartens at the front. Holding onto his pants.

He retreated into the U, sank to the floor and tried to resume reading. He couldn't concentrate. The assembly went on a long time. When would the others come back?

Something was creaking rhythmically up the hall. It swished. It came closer. He shrank back against the shelves. Past the classroom's open door came a giant bucket on wheels and a mop, pushed by the janitor, Mr. Lavery. Mr. Lavery was tall and stooped; hair grew out of his ears and nose. His hands were big. He was strong as a troll in a fairytale; once, Stephen had seen him pick up the rear end of a parent's stuck car, pick it up off the ice and shove it on its way. Mr. Lavery was mopping the hall floor. He paused and flicked his mop over the entrance to the classroom, back and forth. He looked up and saw Stephen.

Stephen froze. Mr. Lavery opened his eyes and his mouth wide, and his tongue emerged. It was yellowish, there was something wrong with his tongue. He waggled it at Stephen, jerking his jaw up and down. He made a sound, *ai-ah-ai-ah-ai-ah*. Stephen didn't move. His heart beat so fast he thought it would rise up out of his chest, up into his throat, and choke him.

Mr. Lavery's tongue went back into his mouth. He looked at Stephen a moment longer, then shoved his bucket out of sight with his mop. Stephen heard the creak of the wheels and the swishing, growing gradually fainter as it went down the hall.

When Stephen heard the noise of students returning to their class-rooms, he stood awkwardly by the mouth of the library U, clutching at his waist. He wanted Miss Lefranc to see him, he wanted to know if he'd been bad. Stephen stood there as the other children flooded the room, reaching for toys and games interrupted by assembly, Miss Lefranc following behind. She didn't notice him.

Finally he approached the teacher. He tugged at her skirt with his free hand.

"I missed assembly," he said. He was so quiet that she bent at the waist, asked him to repeat himself. He had to tell the truth, it was important. "I missed assembly."

"Did you? Where were you?"

Stephen pointed wordlessly toward the U-shaped library.

"Well, what a surprise."

Miss Lefranc walked away. She didn't care. Stephen wasn't going to be in trouble for missing assembly. He started toward the bookshelves again, then stopped. He turned around and sat with some other kids, careful to conceal the trouble with the pants; it'd be okay, they were sitting down, playing with Lego. He didn't want to go into the bookshelves anymore today.

A few blocks from the bookstore Stephen cuts across a frozen park. In the centre of the park is a tree he always notices, an old pine; twisted, its trunk is as thick as three men. It should be tall, but the top's been blasted off – lightning, maybe, or wind. Today a girl stands under it, a young woman, bundled up in a black wool coat with a scarf over her head. She rolls a baby carriage back and forth, back and forth, across icy footprints in the snow. Stephen likes babies; he smiles and tries to catch her eye, swerving so his good ear will be next to her in case she says something as he passes. But her eyes are empty; the pine creaks in the wind. The carriage seems to contain only a bundle of blankets. No sound, no movement from any baby.

He lowers his head and hurries on, feeling sad and, for no reason, guilty. A little way off he turns and looks back. The girl still stands there, rolling the silent carriage, her figure dark and thin, an ink drawing against the snow. The pine arches over them both.

He comes to a street crossing and, waiting, takes out his phone. Laura has texted him twice: *Great spirits meet calamity greatly. Aeschylus.* She's full of quotables as usual; Stephen almost smiles. And the second: *Home 10ish xoL.*

He is about to text her back when his phone buzzes. His hand jerks; he knows, somehow he knows, that it is his mother. His hands are almost shaking but still he takes his time, removes a glove and puts it in his coat pocket, hits *talk*. He is methodical that way, always has been – a distressingly methodical child, his mother says, I don't know where the hell you came from.

"Hello," he says. "Hello, Mom? It's me."

It's a half-hour walk to the hospital. This is good, he tells himself, it gives him time to think.

Lung cancer, and it has overflowed. It has spread through her chest and into her brain.

That's what that "spell" was. Not a "stroke," not a "turn"; those were what they thought it was, back in the good old days when the bad things were the constant drinking and the head games and the contempt, when bad things were a minor car accident and a mild stroke.

He realizes he is having trouble with the word "metastasize." That's odd; he never has trouble with words. But as he walks he tries to say it, and he can't see it, it melts away, stutters there on the end of his tongue: *miss… tata… size? Mata… messasize.*

He is walking as fast as he can, almost running. He stops, takes a breath; she isn't going to die yet, he tells himself. She is not actually dying at this very moment. He needs to compose himself, to be there for his mother. He begins to walk again but he can't help it, he walks so fast his lungs burn.

It wasn't a stroke, it was a malignant tumour, and being malignant, a thing with dark intention, it disintegrated itself a little, only a little; it dribbled off into her bloodstream in small, floating, pernicious pieces, fragments of self-replicating garbage, and thus it has traveled through her body. Taken root there, and grown.

"They say I could go because my lungs stop working," she told him over the phone, "or because my heart stops working, or because my brain stops telling my body to keep breathing and pumping."

22

She has been given between one and six months.

They have put her on steroids and prescribed a series of radiation treatments on her brain. The radiation may shrink the tumours enough to extend her life a very little. To Stephen's surprise, she has agreed to go ahead with the radiation. That isn't like her, he thinks. It feels meek, and also like a decision made by someone in love with life.

He walks through the main doors of the hospital. His mother has been moved since his visit that morning. It seems long ago. He doesn't know the room or floor number, but there is a long line-up at the reception desk and a man is yelling at the reception nurse, banging one fist into his palm. Stephen goes forward into hallways and tries to make sense of the signs. One elevator and several wrong turns later he finds himself in a hall lined with gurneys upon which patients sleep and stare. Nurses rush by. He goes through double doors labeled "X-rays." Surely there is a desk, someone to ask directions of? He passes a packed little waiting room and finds his way to a closet-like office with a line of people against a wall, waiting. He gets in line; it takes twenty minutes. Stephen sweats in his coat, frustration at himself building; how hard can it be to find his mother's damn room? Finally he gets to the X-ray receptionist; she is nice, thank God, and sends him down the hall and up another elevator, around a corner – would he remember that? – good boy, there you go.

Her face lights up when she sees him. She looks surprised, she smiles. "I'm on steroids," she announces. "I feel terrific." She shows him the faint blue-green line they've tattooed on her head, a relief map along her temples just shy of the hairline, showing them where to radiate her. Her eyes are bright, wild; they scare him.

"How long are they going to keep you here?"

She stares at him coldly, then snorts. "How long? As long as it takes." She breaks into a coughing fit.

Are you going to die here? – but he can't say it.

There is something different, something he can't put his finger on – it feels too personal, too vulnerable, maybe. What is it? He swallows it down. "Is there, ah, well, anyone you want me to call?" He has to say it.

"What the fuck."

He has promised himself, on the walk here, that he will say it. "He might want to know."

"What do you think? You think I want you to call him?" She coughs again. "Have you ever, ever in your life, seen or heard me call him?" The coughing takes over and she can't speak any more. She sits bolt upright in the bed, coughing.

23

He waits for the fit to subside. "This is different." He keeps his head down.

"Look at me. Look at me, damn you."

He looks. She is fierce, white around the mouth.

"If you fucking think for one minute that you get to do whatever you want just because I'm dying…" He realizes then what is so different: there is no cigarette in her hand, her mouth. There is no smoke between them. "You don't even have the number."

"But you could – "

"It's my decision." She slaps her palm on the sheet. "I don't want him getting to you."

"But – "

"You don't know what he's like. Dammit!" She stirs. "I want a smoke."

"Go have a smoke, then."

"Not until you promise me you won't call him."

"Mom," his heart races, "you're his only – "

"Shut up."

"Oh, go have a smoke."

The fight goes out of him, he sags, defeated. It never works, trying to have at it with her. His mother struggles with the covers and he reaches to help her. She slaps his hand away, gets her legs over the edge of the bed, then sits there, breathing heavily, bare legs mottled in the fluorescent light.

A nurse comes in, medications in hand.

"What are those?" His mother's head rears, the fight back in her. "Those aren't antibiotics, are they? Because I can't have any antibiotics."

Stephen stirs, miserable; she's exaggerating again.

"Mom, you're allergic to penicillin, but that doesn't mean… She's allergic to penicillin," he shifts to the nurse, suddenly anxious. Has his mother remembered to tell them that? She never wears her medic alert bracelet; maybe they don't know.

"The last time I was in hospital I got given… Oh, I can't remember what it's called, but I got c-dif. C-dif! That'll be the end of me if it happens again. Everything I ate poured out my asshole." She starts coughing again.

"She got c-dif a couple of years ago," Stephen says to the nurse; he can feel the smile, that stupid, subservient smile stretching across his face. "But she's not allergic to every single antibiotic – "

"Who's the doctor here?" His mother's voice cuts through her coughing. "Are you a doctor? Are you? Last time I checked you worked part-time in a second-hand bookstore selling fucking science fiction."

"C-dif is serious," the nurse says to him. "Very serious. Your mother is right to be concerned."

"Of course." Panic and frustration nag at him. "But if she has to have surgery and you guys believe she can't have any antibiotic at all, like she says – "

"Shut up, Stephen," his mother says. And, to the nurse, "I'm not having any fucking surgery."

"Okay, okay," he says, trying to soothe. It never works; he can never argue with her, and especially now he shouldn't. "Go and have your almighty smoke."

Pearl slides down off the bed like a kid being given permission to get a cookie from the jar. She shuffles into slippers and grabs her jacket on the way out, fishing a pack of cigarettes out of the pocket with one hand, flipping it open and taking a smoke out with her lips even as she walks through the door.

"You don't get clostridium difficile from antibiotics. Right?" he can't help asking the nurse.

"No," she agrees.

"I've told her that," he says in a low voice.

"Your mother's very ill, you know. Don't be hard on her."

The bad son, he is a bad son, and the bad son says, "Sure."

He stares at the backs of the nurse's shoes as she pads out.

He sits alone in the hospital room, his hands open, palms up on his lap. The rage inside swells, indistinguishable from terror, an animal thing, a hard thing. It's too much for him, pushing and pushing to get up out of his throat. But just when he thinks it will burst him, the fog arises. It's almost like sleeping, this fog, and he drifts, Stephen drifts away.

It is strange to walk through the door of Pearl's house knowing she isn't there. He uses the key he always carries on his chain, even though he never needs to use it. He never drops by, only arrives when summoned.

Heat and smell hit him, the dankness of smoke. Kicking off his slushy boots, he walks straight through to the kitchen. He leans his palms on the edge of the sink and stares out into the tiny snow-bound backyard, stainless steel cold beneath his hands. He fumbles with the window latch, slides it open. The sound of traffic comes through; somewhere, a single bird calls.

Stephen methodically opens every window in the house. There is a guilty pleasure in the act, cold pouring through staleness. The storms aren't on; he was supposed to do that, he remembers with a start, but he'd forgotten and she hasn't asked.

25

He goes around and dumps the overflowing ashtrays, one in every room, even the fucking bathroom, even down in the tiny unfinished basement. He ends up back at the front door and, leaving it wide open, he stands on the front porch in his coat and sock feet.

Stephen remembers the day they moved into the house; he was about five. Women helped, friends: moving the furniture, voices ringing and laughing, keeping him out from underfoot. His mother cracked her first beer at noon, sat on the front porch of the house using her cigarette as a pointer as the women carried things from the rented van.

But he can't remember that, can he? The move, and where they lived before, dwell in the backward dark, in the abyss of time. Like imagining he could remember learning how to read. He is adding things, picturing the scene from far off, like a dream.

He wonders where she got the money to buy a house. It would have been relatively cheap, certainly, in the mid-eighties, on this street, to make a down payment on a small house. But her job at the seniors' facility didn't pay much; she'd worked there Stephen's whole life and stayed because there were benefits. Still, she bought the house somehow, and then, over the years, never really managed to move in. Fleshy beige wallpaper blossoms with the cold blues and pinks of the eighties; a border of pallid ducks marches across the kitchen wall. Stained carpet in the bathroom.

His own room was a baby room, and as a teen he covered every inch of it with posters: fantasy and sci-fi. And music: Radiohead, Ween, and Primus; Cyprus Hill, Beastie Boys, Sonic Youth; Zeppelin, of course. Pearl Jam because he nurtured (and still does) an almost secret admiration for Eddie Vedder's perfect voice. Later he'd gotten into Modest Mouse and System Of A Down – like his ability to drift between groups of friends at school, his musical tastes ranged pretty wide. Bad posters, but he left them up when he moved out and they are still there.

His mother had put up some prints from her student days; they sag on the walls (Munch, Egon Schiele, a Picasso in the bathroom). In her bedroom she tacked up a poster of the Artemesia Gentilischi painting where Judith is severing Holofernes's head from his body. Stephen wonders how the men she brings into the room interpret that. Pearl says she likes it, likes that it was painted by the daughter of a famous painter; and the light in it, the elegant streams of bleeding on white sheets, the red velvet coverlet. Artemesia Gentileschi was raped at fifteen, was tortured and jailed, Pearl had told Stephen. Pearl has a red velvet cover on her bed.

She started stripping the wallpaper, intending to paint, but never finished. There are no plants.

The driveway is empty, snow drifting across cracked pavement. His mother's car is still at the shop, recovering from the collision. It is a small grey Honda Civic with fuzzy dice hanging from the mirror because Pearl thinks that's funny. The ashtray belches butts and ash. Stephen wonders if he should call the mechanic, tell him not to bother fixing it now.

No. He can't make that kind of decision yet.

They were on a shopping trip in Toronto when it happened – Stephen commandeered to help his mother – driving down Jarvis Street. Pearl was handling the wheel in her usual fashion, while Stephen clutched at the door handle and occasionally cried, "Look out!" as his right foot spasmodically struck at the floor. "Ghost Brake Lewis" she called him, and thought it funny, as funny as fuzzy dice.

She fixed her hair in the mirror while she drove. She was always fussing with it; it's thick and blonde, and she says she knows it makes her look younger, an antidote to "these damn bags under my eyes," and the grooves scoring the skin around her mouth, between her eyebrows. She always wears clumpy mascara, and Stephen remembers how that day some of the makeup speckled black under one eye.

They were heading back home from the city and its mounds of dirty snow. They were looking for something, a place to eat, Tim Hortons or Horny Tim's as Pearl calls it.

"I'm sure there's one at Dundas… is that it there?" she shouted over the roaring radio, the car heater.

"How the hell do I know?"

"Don't swear at your old mother, ha ha. Shit, I dropped my lighter." She leaned over and rooted around on the floor.

"Jesus, Mom, look where – fuck!"

And they'd rear-ended a sleek black Audi sedan.

When the tall grey-haired man got out of the car, unfolding himself with weary grace, Stephen sensed his mother's body go still. She stared, stared at the man, her smoke fixed in her mouth like a thermometer.

"My God," she breathed. "Jesus." And looked wildly behind her and seemed ready to throw the car into reverse, to escape.

Not stopping to think, Stephen sprang from his side of the car and started babbling introductions to the man, breath steaming in the cold.

"Pleasant, David Pleasant." The man shook Stephen's proffered hand. He was really very tall.

"Fuck, Stephen, get back into the fucking car." Pearl glared through her open window, her face white. At her voice the man looked at her. His hand spasmodically gripped Stephen's, enough to hurt. He dropped the handshake.

"Miss Lewis?"

"What the hell."

How did the tall man know his mother's name?

Pearl didn't look at the man – she stared straight out the windshield.

"You... haven't changed," the man said.

"Yeah. I still appear as a sudden bolt from behind."

"Are you all right?"

"But then, you always liked it from behind, didn't you, David?"

"Are you injured?"

Stephen had the wild thought that Pearl was going to bite the man's face.

"Mind moving your fucking car out of my fucking way?"

Stephen jumped in. "I think we should, you know, pull over to the side of the road."

Cars behind them were starting to honk; a Hummer roared past, nearly colliding with traffic head-on. Stephen was oppressed with his usual confusion, and something else pulled at him, a sense that his mother's fear was going to deprive him of something essential. He spoke impulsively to the man, apologetic, insistent.

"I'm her son."

Mr. Pleasant really looked at him then. Stephen had a feeling of things, large things, falling into place in the man's mind. A sense of destiny? – or was that him remembering now, adding to the dream, like with the scene of moving into the house when he was a child?

He does remember the way Pearl gunned the engine, remembers how she almost side-swiped the two of them as she squealed over to the side of the road. Her front bumper fell off and rattled on the pavement. She leapt out of the car and leaned against it, smoking and tapping her foot, arms across her chest, while the man walked to his car, restarted the engine, and smoothly pulled over. Stephen picked up the bumper and brought it over to his mother, then put it down on the sidewalk, uncertain. Traffic swirled around them like an angry sea.

"What the hell d'you think you're doing?" Pearl hissed at Stephen as they waited. She wrapped her arms around herself, cold, angry. "Making introductions. To the manner born you are. Jesus."

"I'm trying to be polite."

"I can," she broke into a coughing fit, speaking between gusts, "... see that."

"But who *is* he?"

"David Pleasant. I thought you'd gotten that much from your polite introductions."

"Oh, come on. Who is he to you?" he said, but Pearl exhaled, looking suddenly older, tired. "Are you okay? Did you get banged up in there?" He was suddenly aware that his own left knee was hurting, had struck the dash in the collision.

She rubbed her collarbone. "I'm fine. He's my father's lawyer." Her mouth quirked. "The family retainer." She said this loud enough for the man to hear as he approached them.

There followed a brief conversation where the man indicated that there was absolutely no need to claim any of this on insurance, that the damage to his car was minimal (indeed, it was invisible to Stephen's eyes) and that Pearl need only send him the repair bill and he'd take care of it. Pearl refused to look at him, laughing when he mentioned covering repairs. She looked like an angry teenager, and the helpless rage and longing in her eyes drove Stephen to load the lost bumper into the hatchback – a temporary, useless escape.

When he came back the man was handing Pearl a white business card. "He wants to see you. He wants to meet his grandson." He didn't look at Stephen as he said this, quite deliberately, and it worked, Stephen felt his heart leap even as he saw the man's theatrics. "It's time to re-establish contact, don't you think, Pearl?"

"That's Miss Lewis to you," Pearl snapped. "And I have no desire to *re-establish contact*." She stuffed the card in her purse and threw her cigarette down on the pavement. "Now please fuck off." She started to open the door of the car, but the man stood in the way.

"He's old, now, Pearl. He may not have much time. Come and see him."

"Get out of my way."

"You and your son have a lot of money coming to you."

"It's mine, is it? Well, they're only a custom of law, inheritances, aren't they? I don't owe him for that. For unloading sperm into my dead mother?"

The man didn't flinch. "Inheritances aren't a right. They're a gift, under the law. A gift, a privilege."

"Then it's a privilege I've lived without for this long, and I can keep living without it. If you don't get out of my fucking way I'll rip off your balls and stuff them into your mouth."

The man stepped aside and Pearl got into the car, slamming the door and starting the engine. Stephen met the man's eyes. The man handed him a white business card too.

"Call me, any time." And: "Your grandfather would like to meet you."

Pearl spoke through her open window. "Get in the goddamned car, Stephen."

He stammered a goodbye and ran around the vehicle to get inside. Pearl peeled off so fast he jolted against the door, and the man had to jump out of the way. This pleased Pearl. "Fucker."

Stephen studied the card: *David Pleasant, Q. C., Barrister and Solicitor.*

And then Pearl snatched the card out of his hand and threw it out the car window. It sailed down Jarvis in the wind, a bit of brightness, gone.

On the highway home Pearl had to pull over at the Fifth Wheel Truck Stop because she wasn't, she said, feeling well. And then in the restaurant she had a sort of seizure. A nice waitress called an ambulance.

Stephen followed them in his mother's car, the detached bumper rattling and sliding in the hatchback. It's a stroke, she's had a stroke he said to himself all the way up the 115 – past his favourite field with the cows and the white sweep of land against the sky, across the high plateau where there was always so much snow, down into the valley and town. She'd sagged in her restaurant chair, one side of her mouth pulled down, she'd been confused. It was the smoking, she'd had a stroke at the age of forty-nine from smoking so much, that's what had happened.

But, no. Cancer, spreading from her lungs. The seizure was the first sign.

Now he remembers little things. Even before the accident, he had noticed her dropping objects – a can opener, her lighter – as if her hands weren't able to hold them. She was confused at times, and a couple of months ago he'd found her sitting on the staircase in the house. "I just needed a rest on the way up," she said, and he'd thought only that she was drunk. But she wasn't, the certainty fits into him like bricks in a wall. Also she came home early from work a few times; how many? Because, of course, he only knows for sure about once or twice when he phoned, counting on her not being home so he could simply leave a message, and she surprised him by being there. He wonders if there were more times, more incidences that looked like little strokes. He wonders how they could have missed the fact that her chest was full of cancer, so full it had to squeeze up through her body and start filling her brain. He pictures the tumours like leeches, twining through the tissue of his mother's body.

She works in the dining room at the seniors' facility, bringing out three meals a day and also delivering trays around to the apartments; it's a semi "independent-living" scenario with full-time nursing care. Stephen remembers how she'd come home in the evenings and fling herself down into her kitchen chair.

"Good thing I went to university," she says, lighting a smoke and kicking off her shoes. She puts her feet up, tells Stephen to get her a beer from the fridge. Sometimes she cradles the cold bottle between her feet before opening it; sometimes she gets Stephen to rub her feet.

At some point, when he was about thirteen maybe, he stopped thinking of her as "Mom." To her face, he keeps calling her that; he couldn't face the inevitable blow-up if he'd started calling her by her name. "What, I'm such a lousy mother I don't even rate the title?" Something like that. But in his mind, almost always, she's Pearl.

She keeps an ashtray on the table, a burnished copper bowl, a little crucible with rows and rows of white butts in obsessive lines. She strokes her cigarette across them, leaving trails of ash, stroking over and over and Stephen imagines they flinch from the touch of ember.

For years her coughing has punctuated every conversation, as if her lungs are trying to tear their way out of her ribcage.

He finds himself back inside, sitting in his mother's place at the table. The house is icy; his feet cold. He pulls his coat around him and puts his feet up on the table. He knows what he looks like: grey wool coat, old black jeans, grey woolen socks. One has a hole in it. His feet are big; Pearl would slap them off the table if she were there. He held out hope until he was twenty years old that he would be tall, with feet as big as these. But he's just sort of average.

Under the copper ashtray is Pearl's customary pile of papers, bits and pieces – grocery lists, to-do notes, some scribbled phone numbers. He thumbs through them, wondering if the numbers are those of new boyfriends; Pearl started picking up men rather often as soon as he moved out, almost fifteen years ago now. Her purse slumps on the table too; Pearl had sent him home with it after taking what she wanted (smokes). He hefts it – what the hell does she keep in there, a hammer? He begins pulling items out, adding them to the collection on the tabletop: old receipts, three pairs of sunglasses, lip balm, eyeliner, a paperback novel...

David Pleasant's business card.

He takes his feet off the table.

He dials one of the numbers on the card, a mobile. A deep voice answers. David Pleasant is glad to hear from him, and David Pleasant thinks Stephen should call his grandfather. David Pleasant chats for some time and gives him his grandfather's home number. Stephen doesn't tell the lawyer about his mother's cancer. But he writes down the number of this man, his grandfather. His hand shakes as he writes and the writing does not look like his own. After he and the lawyer hang up, he sits holding the phone in his hand for quite a long time, hearing the whine of the dial tone change to insistent beeping, then silence.

The cottage is full of little spots of colour.

Mouse hadn't noticed these right away; the place is wood and shadows, dark-stained floors, dark walls rippled with reflected light from the river. But today, in the hazy afternoon light, she sees the macramé wall hangings in bright yarn with wooden beads and twined driftwood; needlepoint cushions; knitted afghans thrown over faded chintz; hand-knotted rugs.

"My mother," Pearl says. "She gets them from kits."

Pearl lies on one of the rugs, spirals of red and pink-orange radiating out like a psychedelic halo. She blows smoke into the air. Mouse still feels a little sick from drinking on last night's empty stomach. She'd cooked them a breakfast of eggs, toast and coffee, and Pearl had opened a beer. She has one at her elbow now. The smoke rises slowly, spinning in the sunbeams.

"Get yourself a beer, Mouse."

"Sure, I guess."

Mouse goes to the kitchen, to the fridge which yesterday Pearl plugged in and loaded with Blue.

"She made homemade sausages once. And once she tried to make shoes for the whole family," Pearl calls from the living room. "It was carnage."

"She made *shoes*?"

Mouse re-enters the main room, beer in hand, and sinks into an armchair.

"And sausages."

"I was going to ask about those later. The shoes alone are mind-boggling enough."

"Mind-buggering." Pearl laughs, drains her beer, and rolls the empty across the floor. "Get me another, will you?"

Mouse's breath catches in her throat. Why does Pearl do this, continually push at the limits of patience?

"I think you can get it yourself."

"Fuck."

Pearl saunters to the kitchen. She is graceful, tiny and insolent; little blonde hairs flicker like light running over the surface of her tanned arms and shoulders. It hurts to look at her. She disappears into the kitchen and Mouse hugs a needlepoint cushion to herself. Strange animals in an impossible garden, tails forking and curling: a smug leopard sits amongst giant bell-like flowers with an ornate collar enclosing its neck; a goat-cat turns its head over its shoulder like an owl. It makes Mouse sad.

"Unicorn Tapestries." Pearl has returned. "She went through this phase we called her Medieval Period. That's when she made the shoes too. Heavy peasant clogs, and she made us eat bulrushes and dandelions. And the fucking sausages. My God, you should have seen it. She made me help. Like stuffing raw meat into condoms."

Mouse doesn't particularly like it when Pearl talks about condoms.

"My mother wanted to bleach the floors, paint some walls. The family put the lid on that pretty much right away." Pearl sucks beer, wipes her mouth with the back of her hand. "They had a family meeting about it. My Great Auntie Dragon goes, *That's not how we do things here. My mother Pearl Lewis decorated this cottage and so it stays.* Mom cried."

"You're named after your great-grandmother then?"

"So Mom was reduced to crafts. She reads craft magazines. Great Aunt Dragon can make anyone cry."

Mouse feels the dark walls close. They slept late and haven't ventured outside today at all.

"Pearl, want to go for a walk or something?"

Her accent comes out strongly and Pearl imitates her, grinning. "Want to go for a walk or something, wha'?"

Mouse stands. "I'm going down to the dock." She deliberately flattens her voice into mainland intonations.

"Make dinner when you come back."

Down on the dock the sun is desperately trying to cut through the autumn haze. The river laps against wood, a hollow sound. Mouse looks out over the water, the safe river, tideless.

It was a mistake to come. Pearl is going to drink and treat her as a personal slave the whole time. Why did she come? The answer arrives: because Pearl asked you to. Because of this feeling inside your chest, in your throat and stomach whenever you think of Pearl.

"Well, I'm here now."

Mouse sits on the dock, trying to love the sunset, the calls of birds, the trees and the hollow sound of water. It's impossible.

There is a burning up the green slope behind her in the cottage, a heavy fire, the wild, inescapable thing inside Pearl.

Mouse isn't the only one who sees it. Boys look at her, eyes heavy with sexual longing, mixed sometimes with clumsy tenderness. She's out of control, they say, they want to fold her in their arms and fuck her and make it all better. Pearl gets beyond drunk and takes them. Mouse isn't the only one who sees it, but she is, she believes, the only one who can make it better.

Her residence room and Pearl's are next to each other. She was the one who found Pearl the night she got so drunk that she tore her room apart, literally tore it to pieces, holes in the walls and fluff from the pillows, clothes out the smashed window.

Other people said, "That's just university, having a little too much fun, eh?"

It wasn't. It was like dying. Pearl had passed out on the mattress and she would have choked on her own vomit if Mouse hadn't been there to roll her over, clear the puke from Pearl's mouth with her own fingers.

And I with my long nails will dig thee pig nuts; show thee a jay's nest, and instruct thee how to snare the nimble marmoset.

Lines hang on like little bulldogs in her mind: *I'll bring thee to clustering filberts, and sometimes I'll get thee young scamels from the rock. Wilt thou go with me?*

No, that was wrong; it is Pearl's island, and Pearl is Miranda, not Caliban.

Two boats drift out on the river, rods affixed off the back of them, trawling for some river fish or other. A scattering of wet blooms on Mouse's arm. Is it going to rain?

When she gets back up to the cottage Pearl is actually doing something: laying a fire in the fireplace. And she announces her discovery that the phone is not working.

"I've got you alone up here," she says, and laughs like a movie villain. "And look what else I found."

She reaches behind a mantel clock and pulls out a flask of Dewar's scotch.

"Hey, I found one of those this morning," Mouse says.

"Where?"

"Under the seat cushion in the armchair."

"Where is it now?"

"Under the seat cushion in the armchair."

Pearl crouches back down and observes the fireplace. "Dad's. This here is one lit fire."

Mouse makes chili from beans and tomatoes in cans, and they wonder what "without" is in Spanish, for they have no meat. Pearl deems things too

35

quiet and pulls a transistor radio out of a cupboard, but the batteries have been removed for winter.

"Here's another mickey," Mouse says, standing on a chair looking for batteries on a high shelf. Pearl, below, is rooting through drawers. Mouse takes the flask off the shelf, sniffs it. "Dewar's again."

"Dad's. No batteries here."

"That makes four. The chair, the bathroom cabinet, behind the clock."

Pearl stands and sucks her thumb like a child. "Did you see any batteries in the fridge?"

"No. Why would there be batteries in the fridge?" Pearl opens the fridge as Mouse climbs off the chair. "And why does your father stash booze? I mean, it doesn't make any sense. He has a fully stocked liquor cabinet, and it's his house. Why hide mickeys everywhere?"

"Eureka!"

"Batteries?"

"Only my mother would store batteries in an unplugged fridge. She read somewhere that they last longer in the cold. God, she is so stupid."

"Well, at least we found them."

"He stashes booze," Pearl sits down at the kitchen table and starts inserting batteries into the transistor radio, "because that's what he does. He's always done it. And he keeps track of them too. I stole one once and did I ever catch it."

"But – "

"Why?"

Mouse wonders if Pearl will suck her thumb again but she just scratches her neck.

"I think he's hiding his alcohol from himself."

"But if he knows where they are…"

"Not literally. I think it's some kind of compulsion. A manifestation of his denial about how much he drinks. Or something."

Mouse thinks of her own father, the inevitable beers after work, the heavy slurring mixed with the scent of unwashable oil, the sarcasm. But he doesn't hide it. He doesn't hide anything like that. Pearl's father is incomprehensible to her.

Pearl flips the *on* switch of the little AM radio. It takes a second for them to recognize the tinkling little tune.

"Fuck! 'Musicbox Dancer'!"

Pearl whips past static. They come up with someone talking about the tornado in Woodstock ("God, they're not still on about that, are they?"), the Bee Gees ("No, please no disco,"), the Village People.

Finally they settle on a station playing Donna Summer. Pearl takes the radio under her elbow, grabs Mouse's hand and her drink, and drags her through the door. Out under the sinking sun, a blurry piece of moon.

Donna Summer croons, aching, girlish. *Ooooh, luv ta luv ya baybeee... ooooh...* Pearl and Mouse reach their arms to the sky. The sun stretches out fingers toward a pale moon, a vivid shell pink greeting. *They're like sisters*, Mouse thinks, the sun and moon, and she wouldn't be caught dead saying that out loud and they are so beautiful she feels tears coming to her eyes.

"It's a beautiful sunset!" Pearl calls from the end of the dock, swaying.

"Very."

Rod Stewart, more Village People, it's all disco out here but they stop caring. Mouse is suddenly completely happy. They mimic disco moves and fall down on the dock laughing. Mouse imitates one of the jocks at university, the way he dances drunk, pelvis thrust forward, mouth slightly open and idiotic.

Pearl shrieks, "Okay, oh my god stop my stomach hurts! Okay, here's my trick! Look, look at me, it's my trick."

Mouse sits and drains her beer. "Shoot."

"It's the only trick I can do." Pearl kicks off her shoes and lies on her back. Then she arches and pushes her body up into a bridge, and starts walking like that down the dock.

"Watch, watch!" Her hands have come to the very edge of the dock, her legs and stomach glimmer pink in the setting sun.

"Okay, here it goes." Pearl kicks her legs up and is suddenly in a handstand, there at the very end of the dock. She holds for an instant, gorgeous, a statue. And then she springs off her hands and goes feet-first into the water. A splash, the dark water. She swims around the dock, sleek as a seal.

Her face open and happy.

"It's smaller than at home."

"How can the sky be smaller?" Pearl ducks under a branch and holds it back for Mouse, whose hands are occupied with a beer case.

"I don't know. It just is."

"But it's the same sky. Is it the trees?"

Mouse looks up. Trees tower above, obscuring the faint moon and shredded clouds.

"No. It's not that. I just..." and she has no words for that huge sweptup whirl of Newfoundland sky. "Maybe it's the wind."

37

Pearl laughs. "Wind can't make the sky bigger."

She leads Mouse through the growing dark, past a tumbledown barn, over vast fields of goldenrod and raspberry canes, under big soft trees that Mouse has never seen before and that Pearl tells her are cottonwoods.

"It's just down here."

In the last greenish light leaching from the horizon, they emerge into a rocky little cove with a small expanse of sand that the water laps against. An immense pine tree towers above a ring of blackened stones. They drag branches out of the undergrowth to make a fire there.

"We always came down here as kids," Pearl says, "with Mom, to roast marshmallows. Then when we got older we'd come here to drink and smoke up."

"With your mother?"

"No, Mouse, not with my mother. God. The idea of Mom smoking dope is just... Hand me that branch thing."

She peels bark for kindling.

"Who's *we*?" Mouse is curious; Pearl hasn't mentioned any siblings.

"Me and my cousins. We're all about the same age."

Pearl lays the dry birch bark underneath the pyramid of sticks she has made, and fishes in her pocket for her lighter.

"Boys or girls?"

Pearl sets the bark alight. She leans into the flames, concentrating, blowing gently; the warm light flickers over her face. The bark is consumed almost instantly and flames lick over twigs and sticks. The fire catches.

"Boys. Two of them." She sits back on her heels. "First guy I really had sex with was Mark, the older one."

"You had sex with your *cousin*?"

Pearl lights a smoke. "Yeah." She stares into the fire. "What's wrong with that?"

Mouse splutters. "Well, I think it's illegal for starters. And he's, well, your goddamn relative, for the love of God."

"It was this weekend my parents were off in Kingston, and Jim was at camp or something." Pearl drags smoke deep into her lungs, exhales. Mouse feels suddenly, sickeningly, anxiously jealous.

"Well, how was it? I mean, was he any good?"

"I didn't have much to compare him to." Pearl looks at Mouse sideways. "I was thirteen."

"Jesus!"

"We did everything. Fuck, suck," she lowers her voice, "anal sex – "

"Oh for crying out loud."

Pearl starts laughing. "Hey, you know that chick Anna? The one down the hall?"

It takes Mouse a moment to switch her mind to their university residence.

"What about her?"

"The one who got engaged during intro week to that rowing guy?"

Mouse vaguely remembers something about this; Anna doesn't interest her very much. "So?"

"Marjorie across the hall? She told me she was partying in the room next to Anna's the other night, and Anna and the guy were, you know, having sex, and they could all hear and were trying not to, and then they hear Anna saying, clear as day, she says, 'But baby, I don't want to have anal sex. Can't we save something for when we're married?'"

Pearl laughs and laughs, rocking back and forth, and finally Mouse starts laughing too.

"Save something for when we're married!"

Mouse decides not to ask all the questions burning in her mind about the cousin. Images of Pearl getting screwed by this faceless teenage boy lodge in her imagination; she's vaguely aware of being aroused by this, and disturbed.

"Anna's a real romantic."

Pearl stops laughing. "Yeah."

She looks out into the night, at the darkness of water, and falls silent. Mouse watches her. Pearl sits nestled between two immense roots of the pine; in the firelight her hair is like a pale flame flickering over the rough bark. Behind Mouse water laps gently, a light slapping sound, and the air smells sweet, heavy with the scent of pine and the woods behind them.

It is all so different from beach parties back home. Driving from town always in some guy's car, fast around curves with the dark cliffs dropping down to the depths on one side, the immense rise and fall of hills. Falling out of the car into gravel, cold air hitting you like a hammer. Crossing the ridge of smooth rocks, past the creek writhing among stones, plunging across the lacy litter of high tide – seaweed and shells and old tin cans – onto the beach, to drag driftwood into a pile, the flames reaching up into the night, sparking, crackling green with salt. People downing beers, yelling, laughing. Waves pouring across the rocks, the rhythmic click and suck of that. Always someone daring you to plunge in, the water instantly freezing you into a full-body ache.

"Hey, aren't we a little close to the edge?"

"What?"

"Aren't we a little close to the edge? The water?"

"No, why?" Pearl gazes at her across firelight.

"Where's the tide right now? Because…" Mouse looks around, trying to see the tidemark on the stones, "if it's low, we're going to get right into it when it rises…"

"Mouse, Mouse honey, we're not by the sea. This is a river. A big river, I grant you, but…"

Mouse stares, then starts giggling. The tipsy feeling hits her; she's had a few, she realizes. "I forgot."

The stars shine brilliantly overhead, they pick out constellations together. Big Dipper, Cassiopeia. They try and fail to find the North Star, the Little Dipper, although Pearl insists she knows where it is. She keeps pointing to a star, a different one each time.

"There. That one. I'm telling you!"

The great tree overhead sways in the breeze, branches creaking with movement. The bushes at the edge of the woods rustle.

"What kind of animals live here?" Mouse wonders. "Besides birds. Deer?"

Pearl stands. "I'm going to get more wood." She walks toward the woods, turning back to say, "Well, that bear for one. The one Dad shot," and then she pushes her way into the undergrowth.

Mouse is not sure how big the island is. It's conceivable that all kinds of animals live here, although she finds it hard to believe bears would. But they can swim. Maybe bears from the banks of the river swim out sometimes, looking for deer?

The pine creaks. The fire flickers.

From the woods comes a terrible scream.

"Pearl!" Mouse jumps to her feet. "Pearl!"

Pearl screams again, and bushes thrash.

Mouse grabs a burning branch and is just about to plunge up the slope when Pearl tumbles out into the firelight. She grabs Mouse by the shoulders.

Mouse realizes she is laughing.

"You should see your face!"

Mouse drops the branch onto the fire and sits, knees weak. "Jesus, you scared me."

"I should have spun it out longer."

"I'm glad you didn't." Mouse doesn't know whether she feels angry or relieved.

"Ah, your face! You would've set the whole island on fire."

"I thought it was a bear."

"There are no bears here! Or deer…"

Mouse's heart is beginning to slow. She opens another beer and drinks deep.

"If I was a bear I'd live here," Pearl says. "You ever see a bear?"

Mouse rolls onto her side and lets the hot flame-breath beat against her face.

"Lots of times." She is lying. She's only seen a bear once, and that at a distance.

"In St. John's?"

Mouse laughs. "Yes, Pearl, bears regularly walk the downtown streets." She pauses. "Although there was this one time a moose came across the harbour, when it was frozen. Saw himself reflected in the glass windows of a bank and charged himself."

"Exciting."

"I saw a bear near Terra Nova, when we were hunting with Dad."

"What did your dad hunt? Deer?" Pearl yawns.

"We don't have deer. Caribou."

"Aren't caribou deer?"

"They're a kind of reindeer, I think. Bigger than deer."

"Oh." Pearl tosses her bottle into the bushes and makes clawing motions at the fire, growling. "Caribou, caribou…"

"He went every year. Usually for caribou; once he got a moose license. Grouse."

"… I am going to eat you, caribou."

"The hardest part was getting the animal out once he'd shot it."

Pearl and Mouse fall silent. The flames roar softly, and the trees hiss and swish.

"Usually he'd go out with his buddies."

They'd drink unbelievable quantities of rum, eat nothing but meat (liver wrapped in bacon, steak wrapped in bacon, whatever they shot wrapped in bacon), get what they called "the horrors" and consume bottles of Tums. But one year her father had an affair, so Mouse's mother wouldn't let him out of her sight after that.

"So he had to take me and my mother and my younger brother Clancy along on the trip. No buddies. Less meat. More rum."

Mom had gone on the hunting trips in earlier years, before the kids were born and she and Mouse's dad still liked each other; so this year, the year of infidelity, she knew how to prepare. Separate bunks for her husband and her (*I don't want no smelly blood-covered man snoring next to me in my*

41

bed, thank you very much), the kids sharing the double in the camper, (even though Mouse and Clancy were fifteen and thirteen, respectively). A planned daily menu. A giant Rubbermaid container; kettle after kettle of river water boiled on the propane stove to fill the thing; bubble bath (yes, scented bubble bath) and a bath every night in the Rubbermaid, for Mouse and her.

Even though Mouse didn't want to bathe, and Clancy, although he wouldn't say it, did.

Even though already, at fifteen, Mouse was really too big to fit into the Rubbermaid.

Even though Mouse, although her mother didn't know it, wasn't really in her heart a girl.

Get in there, Mandy, it's time for your bath, her mother would say. *Time for your bath, Mandy me love.*

Her father got his animal their last day out. Mouse was back at the camp helping her mother pack up. Every nerve in her longed to be at the Spot. They'd spent every day of the trip up there, her father pointing out eagles, a black bear with her cubs far off on a hill, his eyesight keen. Mouse watched years drop off him, cares fall away, out here in the air, away from that job in the garage and the boss who hated him.

He spoke to Clancy of caribou, how they are attracted by movement (he spoke to Clancy but Mouse listened), how if you're upwind of them you can wave them in, just wave your hat or your hand and they'll come closer and closer, fascinated. He told the story of the biggest buck he ever shot, how it had already been shot in the gut by some arsehole incompetent, some guy who didn't know how to finish the job. The cow he stalked through the woods for two days, how he knew that she knew him. *It wasn't me that shot her, it wasn't my skill nor my power. It was her that decided.* He rubbed almost angrily at his cheeks. *That was the hardest thing I ever did. Shoot that animal with her looking at me.* Mouse shivered, feeling it, the power of that moment.

Her mother snorted, her brother looked uncomfortable. Her father pretended he'd been coughing, wiping his nose on his sleeve and disgusting her mother.

But no caribou came anywhere near them on that trip.

Are you praying them away, Mandy? which was unfair; if anyone would do that it would be Clancy. No animals came near, until that last day when Mouse wasn't even there. They'd long since finished packing and Mouse's mother was getting angrier.

Then a great dark shape appeared, a lurching creature smelling of blood. Mouse almost screamed until she realized it was her father, and her heart filled with a rush of love.

Where's your son? her mother demanded, at the same time as Mouse screamed, *You got one! You got one!*

Mouse's father swung the shape down off himself. It was the hind quarter of a caribou, paunched, parallel slits cut into the skin to act as straps for carrying. The smell was so strong, animal, Mouse felt saliva rush into her mouth. The skin had a silvery lining, bloodied.

Last I saw Clancy, he was face-down in a bog with a quarter on top of him.

You left *him there?*

Mouse's father caught his breath. *I says to him, you say you can't go on. Well, you got to go on. Yeah, I left him there.*

Is he following you?

Mouse's dad looked at his wife. He looked behind him, theatrically shadowing his eyes with his hand. *Not that I can see.*

Jesus, Matt, go back there and look for the boy!

I'm going back to get another quarter.

Jesus Christ!

Mouse broke in. *I can carry a quarter. Look!* She heaved the meat up with desperate strength, holding the thing like a giant gore baby.

Her mother: *You're getting blood all... you're worse than your father.*

Her father: *All right.*

They ran up the old stream bed to beat the light, rocks rattling behind them like phantom rapids.

Mouse was surprised, and a little hurt, that she hadn't known intuitively when her dad shot that animal. She thought she should have. *They have a bond*, that's what her mother says; one day he fractured two bones in his hand at work, and at that very moment, in school, she was suddenly crippled with pain in her right hand – the one he'd fractured. Surely she should have known about this animal.

But at least now she was with him – she was hunting, she was with her father! – and he even joked a little as they went, about how he hoped they wouldn't have to carry Clancy too, and she said she'd carry Clancy and the quarter together, just see if she wouldn't, and her father laughed. When they got up to the bog the light was still in the sky and they saw him at once, sitting next to the piece of animal.

I'm not carrying this fucking thing one more step, he yelled across the bog.

Mouse's dad stepped from rock to tussock across the shaky bog. Deep mud quivered; Mouse followed her father. He made his way up to his son and dispassionately slapped him across the side of the head.

You get up and get that animal on you and you walk. And watch your language, and Dad strode on by.

Mouse saw that her younger brother was trying not to cry.

Fucking dyke. But he got to his feet.

The Spot was a smooth, grey dome emerging from the bog. Lines of quartz glimmered in the fading light like the raised-up veins on the back of an old woman's hand. They crested the rocky dome and went down the other side.

And there was the head of the animal, and front half of the body cut in two, four severed forelegs, guts. Her father used his knife to cut into the hide to make straps. Mouse knelt next to him. With a heave her father lifted the quarter and held it at her back. She was to put it on like a backpack.

Swallowing, she fished her hands through the gory slits. She closed her eyes.

It's a cow, see? her father said. *A real big one, too. Came right up here, right to the foot of the hill. Part of a herd, but the rest of them stayed near the trees. Not this one – she was curious. No calf. A barren doe, maybe. They've got the best meat on them.* He was talking to calm her down, distract her; she took a deep breath and shoved her arms through the skin up to her armpits.

That's the way. Her father offered his hands, Mouse staggered up. It was heavy, but she could stand. *Good girl.*

Mouse got her quarter back to the campsite. Clancy made it too. Mouse and her father caught up with him at the top of the streambed and wordlessly they filed down in a straggling line: Mouse first, then her brother, with their dad taking the rear.

It smelled like her period but worse, the heavy, unwelcome blood. Coming down the streambed was hard – Mouse was afraid she'd lose her footing on the rocks and fall. Her legs were trembling and her breath was sobbing in her chest when she got back to camp, but she made it.

She remembers her father bear hugging the still-sullen Clancy. And the hug he gave her, so hard it almost hurt. The sound of her father's heart pounding in his chest, her ear pressed to him as he held her. *That's my girl. My girl. My lovely, my girl.*

"Your father had an affair?"

Mouse stirs, looks away from the flames. Her face is hot. She has lost herself in the telling, is slow coming back.

44

"Yeah. With some younger woman, I guess. I don't know much about it."

Pearl moves closer to Mouse, leans against her. Mouse feels Pearl's shoulder against hers.

She wants to put her arm around Pearl.

"Your mother must have been steamed."

"She got every piece of their wedding china and took it outside and she smashed it. Threw every plate and cup and wine glass against the side of the house and smashed it."

"Dramatic."

"Then she spent the next morning picking up the shards so no one would hurt themselves."

Mouse shifts so more of her body rests against Pearl's.

"How about you?" Pearl's head sinks down to lie on Mouse's shoulder.

"What about me?" Mouse's heart beats strongly.

"Your dad had an affair. Fucked some other woman. How'd you feel about that?"

"Well, hell, doctor, I guess I didn't feel too damn good about it."

"Yeah?" Pearl's voice is a murmur.

"I don't know. Really, I don't. Don't remember."

The towering rage of her mother, the monstrous hurt, filled the house. There hadn't been room for anyone else's feelings. She remembers huddling with Clancy on the carpet of the living room, seeing her mother walk out the front door carrying a large china soup tureen with a lid; remembers the sound of smashing against the wall of the house. She and Clancy lay on the floor with their hands over their mouths, trying not to laugh. Her stomach had ached with holding it in.

"What happened to the head?"

"Hmm?" The fire spins a little. Mouse puts down her beer.

"The caribou head."

"Oh. We left it there. Dad took the heart and – "

"Why?"

"You eat it."

"Christ." Pearl shifts away and leaves the side of Mouse's body cold. She lights a smoke. "Left the head, though. I thought men always stuff the things they shoot and kill."

Mouse begins to giggle. "Men: they stuff the things they shoot and kill," and after a moment Pearl drains her Blue and laughs.

A cold wind has started to blow. Trees murmur over their heads, then lash around. Mouse realizes with a thrill that the stars on the horizon, over the water, have been blotted out. Light flickers, warm inside the distant clouds; the great pine leaning over them groans, sways. More stars disappear, and more; a great darkness is sweeping their way.

"It's a storm!" Pearl cries. Their fire is bending, wind picks up, the fire shifts within its ring of stones.

They kick at the fire, send most of it into the great river's edge. The roar and hiss of rain come across the water, this thunderstorm out of season. Waves.

Taking hands they run, stumbling across stones and under trees, across fields, laughing until they can hardly breathe. The rain hits them just as they get to the dock, soaking them in seconds. Mouse has never seen a storm come up so fast, with so little warning. Pearl runs down to the end of the dock and flings her arms out to the sky.

Mouse follows her.

She reaches Pearl, and Pearl turns to her and wraps her arms around Mouse, and she kisses Mouse, full on the lips. Rainwater runs over them, they sway together in the wind; their lips are warm, and Mouse's heart beats until she thinks it will burst.

$\mathcal{I}$t's the third day since the diagnosis, and Stephen's visit is not going well.

"What do you mean, you didn't think?"

He half-sits on the painted heater, leaning against the window. "You asked me to check on things at the house. You didn't mention picking up clean underwear."

The warmth plays over his legs, dancing on the surface of the bone-deep cold from his walk to the hospital. The glass is a long hard chill through his overcoat, against his spine.

"Well, fine." She coughs. "I'm asking... you now..." she goes on through the hacking. "Some new books – I've read all these," and she gestures at a stack of crime fiction paperbacks. "Oh, and bring them back to the library, I don't want to be paying any goddamn overdue charges. There's another bunch in my bedroom at home."

"Library books?"

She coughs once more, decisively. "Of course they're from the library. What do you think, I got a whole personal collection of this crap?"

Stephen shifts his weight. The cold has wound its way around his muscles and he can't stop shuddering; he feels terribly tired all at once.

"And I need more cigs. You know the kind. They only sell them at the smoke shop on the Parkway." She coughs again, thin body shaking. "So, what the hell did you do at the house, then? Sit at the kitchen table with your feet up?"

"Yeah." He thinks of his phone call to the lawyer, hugs his coat around himself. Almost he feels she will read his mind if he keeps thinking of it. "Yeah, I sat at the kitchen table with my feet up."

Pearl glares at him. "Beats me," she says, "where the hell you came from." Her eyes spark, bright blue. "You've always been like this."

"Like what?" She's often able to disorient him with her swift readiness to fight, but today she's ramped right up. He wonders if he should just let her go at him. He wonders if he can take it, today.

"Like this! So bloody elusive. You know you didn't even cry as a baby? I thought you had brain damage or something. You just looked at me – like you're doing right now."

"Mom…" but she begins coughing again and shoves at the sheets. One shoulder slips from her nightgown and he is shocked by the thinness of it, the way bone pushes at skin. He comes forward. "Let me help."

She slaps at his hand. "Oh, for Chrissake, I can get out of bed alone."

A nurse comes into the room, and Stephen backs away from his mother like he's doing something wrong.

"Hey, Mrs. Lewis!" the nurse says. "Hey, is this your son?"

Pearl changes at once, grins at the nurse, her charming smile. "Hey yourself. And it's just Pearl, no missus here."

"How are you this evening?"

Pearl's up on her feet now. "Going for a smoke." She winks at the nurse. "I mean, to the north entrance for some fresh air."

The nurse winks back. "I never heard nothing. You bundle up now, it's a cold night."

Stephen stumbles forward a half-step. "But I just got here."

Pearl turns her eyes on him. "And I am going for a smoke."

He thinks of following her, then gives up. "I'll wait for you here."

"You won't come outside for five fucking minutes?"

"Sorry… I'm really chilled, and – "

"God. What a wimp. I've got a wimp for a son," Pearl says to the nurse. "Why do you bother to visit then?" she switches back to him. Stephen opens his mouth to say something but she surges ahead. "And don't even start about the smoking."

"I wasn't – "

"It's too fucking late now! Can't you get that through your head?" She grabs her dressing gown and shuffles out of the room.

Stephen sits on the heater again, rubbing his eyes with his fingers.

"Hey," says the nurse. "Don't take it personal." Stephen looks up at her. He can't take it, no, not more criticism, but the woman's eyes are kind. "It's the steroids, you see. Makes them cranky."

Ah. "It's been kind of rough," Stephen says, then winces at the self-pity in his voice. "Well, but," he rushes on, "I guess, under the circumstances…"

"Thing is," the nurse says, "they get to do it their way."

Stephen stares, then realizes what she means. "Yes," he says. The dying.

Stephen always enters the apartment quietly, in case Laura is phone counseling.

Tonight she sits in the living room, fake-wood-paneled walls rising above her, a woman's voice buzzing over her phone. The apartment is always too hot, the thermostat being controlled by the pasty, paranoid little guy in the basement unit. Laura's wearing a pair of plaid boxers and a white singlet that, with a small surge of surprise and pleasure, he recognizes as his own. She has small breasts and pointed shoulders, her legs are folded up under her. She gives him a half-wave.

"It's not about that, Cheryl," she murmurs into her phone. "It's about learning not to hold on to feelings that hurt you."

He goes through to the kitchen. On the table sits a small open box filled with business cards; Laura's gotten them back from the printers, then. He helped her with the design; he was the one to suggest soft colours (Laura'd wanted red and black) because the majority of her clients were women. *Dreams into Action*, the cards proclaim. A futurist-style human figure stands in heroic profile. **Laura Leonard, Professional Life Coach.** Her contact information beneath including, Stephen's heart sinks to note, a website. Laura doesn't have a website; she wants Stephen to build her one. He puts on a kettle for tea. *Affirm your Power*, the cards conclude. They look pretty good.

"Look, Cheryl, I *was* honest with you. What did I... I don't recall any promises!" Laura's voice rises, startling Stephen. That never happens when she's counseling. "Cheryl just... Can I please finish just one sentence?"

He moved into the apartment six months ago, and it still feels like Laura's place. At first he didn't really mind the feeling of surfing through. He knew her from around town, and she sometimes came into the bookstore; he'd always thought she was a lesbian. When he saw her Facebook appeal for a roommate, he thought that would be fine.

Then she'd jumped him. Over a cup of herbal tea.

She'd explained that she was an ethical polyamorist. *You know, consensual non-monogamy. I don't want to own you, Stephen. As long as we're honest and open with each other...* He'd thought it all sounded a little just-graduated-from-Women's-Studies, but she meant it. And she was so pretty.

"That's it. Okay. No, that's it, I said. Goodbye. Fuck!"

Wow. The kettle boils and he pours water into the pot. Laura stamps into the room, managing to make a lot of noise for a small person with bare feet.

"Nice cards," Stephen says. "They look really good."

"Oh – thanks." Laura sits at the table, tugging at her blonde dreadlocks. "Did you get any of that?"

"What, the phone counseling?"

"That wasn't counseling. That was psycho Cheryl. The one I slept with last Saturday."

"Cheryl?"

He'd known Laura had hooked up with someone, but hadn't paid attention to the name. Stephen feels his gut lurch and leans against the counter with his arms folded over the feeling.

"Not... not drunk Cheryl? The real estate cougar?"

"Yeah. Drunk Cheryl. Well, I was Drunk Laura at the time, so we're even."

Cheryl was a woman with a reputation for drunken pickups, hard not to make a joke of her face on real estate billboards and bus stop benches. Last week Stephen had tested the reality of her existence in the third dimension by buying her some drinks. She'd come home with him; definitely three dimensions. It was a bang, thanks, I'll go home now kind of thing, but it left him feeling good; now there's a whispering suspicion that much of what had prompted him to pick her up was trying to prove something to himself about this thing with Laura. The non-monogamy thing, the thing that makes him a stranger to himself like some jealous boyfriend in a movie. The sinking feeling in the gut, the high note of panic, the stirring rage in his chest, hating himself for it. Why does he put up with it? He clears his throat.

"I didn't think that she was a – that she slept with women."

"Neither did I. But you know how it... Well." Laura flashes her self-deprecating, charming grin. "It was okay. She had these... unexpectedly beautiful breasts."

"Yeah," he says.

He hadn't let Laura in on the fact that he'd slept with Cheryl, thus breaking the consensual non-monogamy rules. And he isn't about to tell her now.

"Straight women are kind of your specialty." He wonders at the bleakness welling up. "She in love with you or something?" he hears himself asking.

"In love with me?" Laura looks startled.

"You have a tendency to underestimate your effect on people."

She shakes her head. "I'm just her first woman. She'll get over it. God. Can I have some of that tea?"

He gets two mugs down from the cupboard.

"So you thought I was counseling, eh? That's funny." Laura leans back in her chair; Stephen tries not to stare at her nipples showing through the thin fabric of his singlet. "You know, that's really funny," she goes on, "because lately I've been thinking I've had it with all this touchy-feely supportive... Some of these people need a kick in the ass." She pulls the box toward her on the table. "Yeah, the cards do look nice. You were right

50

about the green and lavender – way better for the chicks – I mean, my exclusive clientele."

"Thanks."

Laura examines a card then throws it onto the table, uncharacteristically restless. "I'm never going to make this work."

"What?"

"This whole counseling thing." She covers her face with her hands. "I lost another client today."

"So?" Why is she so volatile tonight? "You'll get more."

"She said she had to stop because of the economy," Laura says through her hands. "You know, counseling is a frill or something. It was a choice between me and getting her hair done."

"Oh, come on," Stephen protests. "There must be millions of half-alive, lonely, fucked-up women yearning for your guidance." He pauses. "Like Cheryl." He hates the resentment in his voice, lowers his head and pours their tea.

"Maybe."

He reaches out, takes her hands from her face. She looks drawn, her eyes puffy.

"Hey, are you okay?"

"Oh, I'm fine." She shifts. "My mother phoned today."

"You serious?" Laura's mother is a murky figure, living in Stephen's imagination as a troll under a bridge. "I thought you were estranged."

"She's not all there, you know?"

"She's delayed, you told me."

"Borderline retard is what the social worker told her when I was a kid."

"Nice."

"Yeah."

"Why'd she call you?"

"She wanted something, of course."

"What?"

Laura shifts, looking away from him. "Her latest boyfriend is in jail and she wanted me to bail him out."

"Jail? What for?"

"That's what I asked her. And she says, He beat me up. But I've changed my mind, I want him back."

"Christ."

"I asked, how bad? And she says, he broke her arm and her nose, and burned her breast with a cigarette, and she had to go to the hospital…"

"Laura, Laura…" It feels good to be talking about someone else's problem; he feels his mother in the hospital fading into the background, almost manageable.

"So I said, Mom, I'm really sorry but I can't bail him out. Not if he's doing that to you." She rubs at her eyes. "And then she called me a cunt face and… well, anyway."

"Do you know the guy?"

Laura shakes her head.

Stephen knows he can't fix it, not the nameless abusive boyfriend, not the reality of Laura's mother. He feels again his admiration for Laura, swelling like tenderness – her survival, her creativity and resilience.

"Well, at least I won't hear from her again for a good while. She never calls when she's mad at me."

He hands her a mug of tea, caressing her hand.

"Thanks." They both sip. "How's your mother?"

His mother. Pearl and her illness reassert their place in his life with a surge. "Fine. The same."

"They know when she can come home yet?"

"No."

"Have they started the radiation treatments?"

"No." His gut is churning again.

"I still don't understand why they're giving her radiation if, as they say, it won't change things."

He shifts in his chair. "I don't know. I guess they just like to do something."

"But it's all so weird. First the car accident, then they say she's had a stroke – do all these tests – then they say, whoops, cancer." He wishes she would stop talking about his mother. "And they're keeping her in there and they won't say how long?"

"Well…"

"You know what you should do?" He shakes his head and tries to think how to change the subject. "Get her car from the shop." He didn't expect this. "It's a long walk to the hospital – and it's winter, and you're there every day."

The feeling in his stomach swells; he takes an unguarded glug of tea and burns his tongue. "Mmm. I suppose."

"You've really been through it, Stephen." Laura leans forward and wraps her fingers lightly around his wrist. "Look, I'll pick up the car for you. It's too much; one more errand."

"But… how will I pay for it?" The sensation in his gut has turned to pain, the sick feeling, like being on the yellow bus on the way to school.

"It'll work out." She strokes his wrist lightly with her fingers. "I'll pick it up tomorrow."

"Well... thanks." He sips his tea, trying to swallow down the feeling in his gut.

"Just get them to bill your mother," she says, and laughs; Stephen winces.

She quiets. "You're a sweet man, you know. Looking after your mother like you do."

He remembers the rage he'd pushed down at the hospital. "Sweet is one word for it."

"No, really. She is so untender, yet you stay connected to her." Her voice gains strength; she loves this emotional analysis stuff. "Maybe it's because there's only the two of you, so you aren't able to separate – "

He snatches his hand from hers. "Don't, please."

She lowers her eyes. "Sorry."

He feels dull remorse. "I didn't mean to snap."

"But you don't need someone analyzing your enmeshment with your mother right now."

"Probably not." He pauses. "Enmeshment? What are we, fishing lines?"

"Emotional enmeshment. As opposed to being differentiated. Accepting emotional drama in lieu of real connection."

"Ah." He doesn't want to think about it. "How's your book going?"

She gives him a look that says she knows he's changing the subject. "Okay. I'm almost done. But when I put it online, on my *website*," and she strokes his palm now, sending a thrill down his wrist to his body, "I'll need that software, whatever it's called, so people have to pay to read it. You know. All those people desperately seeking information on how to harness their emotional intelligence and realize their full potential."

The topic is safely turned. "Emotional intelligence," he murmurs. She writes with humour and passion; there are too many quotations from famous people, but overall he thinks it's shaping up to be a good book of its kind.

"I need more money to do it right," she says. "Set up professionally. That's always the issue with people like us – money – isn't it?"

"You're telling me."

"I want to help people articulate their own story, to begin to heal. Is that so unworthy?"

"Of course not."

She casts him a wary look; he used to tease her about the new-agey aspects of her work. But once he learned more about who she was and is, the flake factor began to seem more like an act of heroism.

"How can you heal," she says, "if you don't own your story?"

A sudden cold thread winds through him, cold thought: money. For the first time he has that part of his story. He has, maybe, money. Doesn't he? *I could write a letter to my grandfather. My grandfather Lewis.* For some reason it presents itself in this old-fashioned way, a handwritten letter on paper, sent through the mail; not a phone call or a text. No, this is too important, too ancient a thing.

"I'm sorry," Laura is saying. The kitchen is too quiet. "I was going on."

He shakes himself. "No, I was listening."

"With all you're going through."

"Hmm?" Stephen can't quite hear her.

Laura gets up and moves around so she sits on Stephen's right side, his good ear. "I sat in your usual chair. Sorry."

"S'okay."

They sit slurping tea for a while. Stephen likes this about Laura; they can sit together in silence, she is sort of like a guy this way. She also claims to be psychic, and sometimes Stephen thinks maybe she is – sometimes she senses the needs of another person by the way, she says, her own body feels.

"You're pretty sad in there," Laura says.

Oh no. She's fixing him with a penetrating gaze. "What?"

"You want to talk?"

"Not really."

She looks down at the table. "You sure?"

"What do you want? Some kind of emotional outpouring?" He makes his voice cold.

Laura sits back in her seat. "No, no, Stephen. It's okay."

"Look." He takes a deep breath. "She's just... really difficult sometimes. Really, really difficult. And I'm tired."

Laura looks at the wall above Stephen's head. "She really picks on you sometimes, eh?"

"Fuck, yeah." He puts his head down on his arms.

Laura's voice goes on, slightly muffled, almost comforting. "She hates her father, right? Cut him off. I mean, you've never known him, right?" Stephen looks up. God, it's creepy when Laura picks up on him in this way, as if she knows that he was thinking about his grandfather. "So the way I see it, she's never truly been a woman, an adult. Something is stuck there."

"An eternal girl," he says.

"Something like that."

"What does that make me?"

Laura looks at him, considering, for a long time. "I don't know."

They sit, the kitchen clock ticking between them. The comfort of silence has left Stephen; now he feels the tug of things, longing and resistance. The ticking gets louder, magnified, ringing in his skull. *You didn't even cry as a baby. I thought you had brain damage. You just looked at me, like you're doing now.* Sometimes he plays a game with himself: this isn't really happening, his mother is not dying, she doesn't hate him. He thinks he can imagine what his mother sees: this hesitant, blinking kid, always hanging back, lost. He feels his body sitting in the chair and loathing for it fills him: his thinness, the weight of bones, deaf ear, bad eyes, nodding head. He hates it. It's a wave breaking over him, overwhelming, he can't keep feeling this way, he blinks. The walls waver, the room becomes insubstantial. His hated body fades away, or is the room leaving him behind? This feeling has dogged him all his life, that the world isn't real, or else he isn't. The feeling flows through him like water, he is a jellyfish, a bit of weed, washed along, thin, transparent. Drifting is fine, but beneath he senses panic, beating at him from inside, it could beat him to pieces, this fear.

And then there's a warm weight. Laura's hand is on his shoulder. "Hey, darlin'," she says, and Stephen floods back into his body, ducks his head, ashamed of the moisture that pushes at the corners of his eyes. Tired, I'm just tired, he thinks. Laura's grip on his shoulder is an anchor to the room.

"Where did you go?" she asks.

"What?"

"You were sinking there."

As into water. "No, I'm just… tired…" He almost drowned once, he was about four years old. His mother took him to an island. There was a wooden structure of some kind, high up. His mother was with some other adult on the wooden platform, the person was a stranger, Stephen remembers. He hadn't liked the person. "There was a dock."

"A dock?" Laura looks into him with her strange eyes.

"Aw, come on, Laura. It's creepy when you do that."

"You wanna talk about it?" Laura pats Stephen's shoulder, a friendly, almost maternal pat, then grips it again with her long-fingered, bony hand. The touch reassures Stephen, for no real reason he can think of.

"No. Okay. Yeah, so this dock."

"You're scared."

"I didn't know how to swim."

"Who's there?"

"My mother. She's drinking, for a change. Up on the dock with some guy."

"What are you doing?"

"I'm wading." Stephen can remember the little swimming trunks he'd had, yellow, and he'd been wearing his special water shoes, old sneakers for wading. "And the water feels cold at first, but then it's not so bad. And it's up to my knees, and then my thighs. My right hand is on the side of the dock. It's rough; I'm afraid of getting splinters." Stephen remembers the way the adult voices rang out above his head, laughter. He'd taken another step. The touch of cold – he'd taken his hand off the dock to cup his balls, shivering with mingled delight and fear. Another step, and another.

And then it fell, it was falling. There was no rock under his foot. "The bottom disappeared."

Stephen remembers the sudden slipping under the surface. Looking up, seeing bubbles rising in the brown, toward the bright surface of the water. He falls away from the brightness, his knee hits cold rocks, he sits helpless on the bottom.

"Did you go under?" Laura's voice is in a controlled panic, and Stephen feels strangely calm because Laura is doing it, doing the feelings for him.

"Yes." He remembers being inside the green brown mumbling light, the water filling his nose, his ears. The chill walks through his body, taking him. And then he hears it. Sweet, light and airy, like music. It *is* music, harmonies and twangling instruments. A voice soars, aching in its beauty. Yellow, green, blue this music, singing careful syllables, a guitar? And he hears a deeper noise, hollow, confused and cold, like… And then the world shatters.

"A big dark shape in the light. It crashes in."

"A person?"

Stephen keeps his eyes closed. "She saved me."

"Your mother?"

"No."

"Who is it?"

"The man. No, a woman," with a surge he remembers, "it was a woman on the dock."

"She saved you."

"I'm on the dock, then, a towel around me. And I'm crying, I can't stop crying."

"Is your mother there?"

Stephen pauses. He can't see.

"Is it your mother?" Laura's voice is yearning, soft, almost a child's.

56 .

"No." It is a hard word to say.

"Where is she?"

"She's sitting on a chair. Drinking. Screaming, *Stop crying, you're okay, you hear me? You're okay, quit that goddamn noise.*"

The kitchen is quiet. Stephen realizes his eyes are still closed. Carefully, he opens them. Laura is bent over as if in pain, her hand slipping from Stephen's shoulder. "Ah," she says. "Ah."

They sit in the kitchen, letting the clock tick.

The small grey Honda Civic buzzes loudly. Pearl's fuzzy dice swing in spirals from the rear-view mirror. Stephen hasn't driven a car in over a year; he keeps turning on the wipers when he means to signal, and his foot hesitates over the brake. A guy in a pickup tailgates him for a block, tearing past at an intersection. Stephen rips off the fuzzy dice, throwing them into the glove box and slamming it shut.

Pearl's sitting up, playing solitaire on the tray table. The room's rearranged: the big chair that had been on the right side of the bed has been moved to the left, and the curtains are drawn around the second bed.

"Hey, Mom. You got a roommate?"

Pearl glances up, then back down at her cards.

"How are you?"

She breaks into a coughing fit, not covering her mouth. "Why the hell are you whispering?" she hacks, flipping cards from the deck.

He jerks his head toward the drawn curtains.

"She's gone for a constitutional or something. You bring the cigarettes? And the books I asked you for? And the underwear?"

Stephen hands her a plastic bag containing the requisite items. He runs his hand along the chrome railing on the side of her bed; it reminds him of something, the handrail on a boat perhaps.

"Sit down, will you? She's a real bat." Pearl rummages through the bag. "Stephen King. Good. She kept me awake all night, snoring and screaming."

"Screaming?" Stephen walks around the bed to sit. He has to twist sideways on the chair so his good ear faces his mother. "She in pain?" Automatically he tries to nudge his mother toward compassion.

"I don't care." She goes back to her cards. "Black seven. My nerves are shot." She coughs again. "She's a piece of work. Red five. Lures every unsuspecting passer-by to talk about her daughter; I've heard the routine about fifty times by now. How wonderful her daughter is, how intelligent, how beautiful, how many prizes she won in high school, her scholarship to university, her perfect marriage, and she goes on and on until the hapless victim asks, And what is your daughter doing now? And then she goes, She's *dead!*" Pearl imitates the woman's crying. "Ah, ha, hoo, hoo...!"

"Oh, God, Mom, that's mean." But he can't help laughing.

"She got me right off the top. Can't believe I fell for it."

"You seem good today. Really good."

"Yeah, real good. Had my first radiation treatment today."

His stomach lurches. "How was it?"

"Piece of cake. Hey, how come you're wearing those glasses again?"

"Glasses?"

"Yeah, glasses. The ones on your face?" Her voice sharpens.

"Oh, you know." Stephen stares at the wall. "The contacts never really worked for me."

"What do you mean, they never really worked?"

"Well, they always made my eyes sort of sore and red – "

"You looked fine in them to me."

She's trying to pick a fight, Stephen realizes. He won't rise to the bait. "Well, I didn't feel fine." He needs to change the subject, thinks of the car. "I got the car from the – "

"Those glasses are so ugly," she interrupts. "If you insist on wearing glasses, why can't you at least get decent frames?"

"Because I can't afford decent frames."

"Another reason to wear contacts. I'm not going out on this one." Pearl deftly gathers the cards. "You've got nice eyes. I think you just want to make yourself ugly." She glares at him. "You've got *my* eyes."

"No, I don't. I've got nearsighted eyes. You can see perfectly, as you are fond of reminding me." As soon as the words come out of his mouth he wishes they hadn't. He tries again to change the subject. "I got the car out of the shop. Or rather, Laura offered to and – "

"For God's sake, just don't come in here looking so terrible. I sit here all day with nothing to look at but dying people and then you come in like yesterday's corpse. What are you wearing, for Christ's sake? You look like a street bum. And I hate, hate, hate those fucking glasses."

She glares at him like it's all his fault. Stephen is conscious of the shabbiness of the coat, the frayed cuffs of his pants, of the answering anger rising in him even as he tries to swallow it down. "Maybe if you hadn't picked a myopic loser for my father, I wouldn't have to – " He cuts himself off, gets up and starts dragging the chair around to the right side of the bed.

"What the hell are you doing?"

He won't, won't, won't fight with her now. The years of learning to hold his own aren't going to work; he has to find a new way to talk to her. "I'm moving this chair." And besides, it's the steroids, and everything. She's dying, he reminds himself.

"I liked it where it damn well was."

He looks down at her, bolt upright in her bed. "I can't hear out of my left ear. You know that."

Pearl thrashes at the blankets, shoves the tray table with enough force to spin it on its castors. "Look, if you're just coming in here to fight with me – "

"I'm not fighting, I just want to move this chair." She's struggling with the blankets, the bed is too high, she might fall. He reaches out, trying to help.

"I just want to move this chair!" Pearl does a whiny imitation of his voice and slides to the floor. She brushes his hand away and leaves the room, grabbing her coat and smokes on the way out. He can hear her coughing all the way down the hall.

He carries the chair back around to where it had been when he first entered the room and slumps into it, staring out the window at a dismal view of brick wall. Should he wait here for her return, or would she rather find him gone? He can't tell. He'll wait, wait for her to come back.

The scene between them plays itself out in his mind; he sees how pathetic his announcement about picking up the car was, the way he was longing for her to say *good boy*, like he's a child, like she's a mother. His dig at her about the *myopic loser* of a father, the longing to know something under that. He despises himself. He waits for the pain of hating himself to become sufficiently sharp; then it will submerge reality in the convenient fog. It's a trick he learned young, like a trick of the eyes, pulling something close at hand out of focus. He wills the fog to sweep over him as it had with Laura in the kitchen, but it doesn't come. He sits there, his body unoblivious, heavy.

You can't skip over the feelings he's heard Laura say. But she's wrong; you can. And he wants to. He might pay with a piece of himself each time, but he's not sure that matters. Laura's gone so far as to call it a form of passive suicide. In that way, as in so many others, Stephen feels the shadow of his mother. But Pearl's gestures toward self-annihilation, unlike his, have always been active.

He remembers one particularly vivid incident, coming home and finding her at the kitchen table with her drink, bottles of pills lined up in front of her.

"You going to take those?" he asked. He was in high school, he remembers, maybe fifteen.

"I thought I might. You don't need me anymore, and I'm pretty sure no one the hell else does."

She'd threatened suicide before, usually after too many drinks, and that's how he thinks of the incidents: as a threat, a dare to him.

"Take them," he'd said, and left the house again. He walked around all night wondering if she'd die, picturing what he'd find when he got home. He walked until his legs were lead. He came home at dawn, went into the kitchen, heart hammering so hard it pounded up into the root of his dry, thick tongue. She wasn't there, slumped over the table like he pictured. The bright plastic pill bottles were still lined up, tiny as toys.

He found her asleep on her bed, fully clothed. He'd shaken her gently awake to be sure. She was fine, just drunk. Just drunk. He put the pills away and got detention for sleeping in class the next day.

Pearl's deck of cards lies askew on the tray-table, fanned out like a ragged nautilus shell. He straightens the table, taps the deck into place; he puts the things he's brought his mother back into their plastic bag, slings it over the bed rail. He shakes out her blanket and smoothes the bed. It's warm where she was sitting; good, she'll be cold when she gets back from smoking.

The room fills with the noises of the hospital: voices in the hall, a phone ringing, someone moaning in another room. An old woman shuffles by the open door with a walker; two nurses hurry past, one of them laughing. On Pearl's pillow stretch two long pale hairs. Something coils in the pit of his stomach.

She will be gone. That's what the doctors said, gone; it seems impossible. But that's what will be. Cards left like that, sheets tangled where she'd been. But they are still warm, he puts his hand under the blankets to feel. Yes, she's just been there, yes, but later, and then, she's all I have, he thinks. She's all.

All she's told him about his father amounts to nothing, to bribes. To lies.

"Go to bed and in the morning I'll tell you," she said, when he asked her as a little boy. Or, "Pick up your room," or "Mow the lawn." Then there'd be something, a detail. Brown hair, it was once, he remembers. Tall. He had tanned skin, freckles. He worked on the water. Always one detail at a time, and the images sharpened and were made small by his longing. As the years went on Stephen caught her in contradictions. The hair colour changed, the eyes, perhaps. He was in his twenties before he realized that the list wasn't ever going to add up to anything. How humiliating, he thinks, to be that slow to figure it out.

60

He sits there in the empty hospital room for nearly an hour. He remembers the important thing he'd hoped to discover on this visit – have the doctors told his mother how long they are keeping her here? They've started the radiation treatments – when would they let Pearl go home, what kind of care would she need there? He dreads knowing. He thinks of going out to the nurses' station and asking his questions there, but he slumps, looking out the window at the brick wall.

An older woman shuffles into the room, wearing knee-high nylon stockings with her slippers. She stops at the sight of Stephen and gives an elaborate start, hand fluttering to her chest.

"Hello," says Stephen in what he hopes is a reassuring tone. "My name's Stephen." Her face stiffens as though he'd just said, *I'm here with my spaceship to abduct you to Betelgeuse.* So he adds, "I'm Pearl's son."

The woman makes her way slowly to the curtained bed, draws the fabric aside and sits down. "Pearl's son," she repeats. "It must be nice to have a son. Me, I had a girl. I'm not complaining. You never saw such a sweet-tempered baby, and she's been that all the way through. Sweet! And smart. You never saw such a wonderful – "

Stephen cuts to the chase. "And where is she now?"

It is dark by the time he gets home. Laura's on the couch, bathed in the light of her laptop monitor.

"Hey."

"Hey." He flings his coat on a hook, dumps his scarf and hat on top.

"Find out when your mother's coming home?"

"No."

Laura looks up, pale blue as an elf. "How's the car behaving?"

"Fine." Stephen kicks his boots into a corner, then feels a pang for his bad temper. "Thanks for picking it up for me. The walk to the hospital was starting to get really old." He sits next to her on the couch, runs his palm over her dreadlocks. "You wanna go out for dinner or something?"

"Naw. There's soup in the fridge from yesterday." She pulls her laptop onto her knee. Stephen glimpses a red sunset, a picture of the seaside.

"What's that?"

"I'm researching other life-coach sites. This is the sixth site with the ocean. And the seventh with a person silhouetted against a sunset."

He leans in and looks; there's a man with raised arms against a sea and an orange sky, and words scroll across the screen: *Let Me Take You Where You Want To Go...*

"Not to mention the constant use of ellipses. And inappropriate capital letters."

"We could do puppies," he says, and her mouth quirks; she punches him on the arm. "Hey!" he says, pretending to be hurt.

"Oh, I'm so done with this anyway." She snaps the laptop closed, snuggles into him and drapes her arm over his thigh. Stephen feels himself stirring. Last night he'd been watching TV, trying to numb his mind enough to sleep, and she'd come home. They'd started fucking there on the couch, and then he'd lost it. He hadn't been able to stop thinking – about some stupid thing a customer at work had said that day, about the fact that Cheryl had phoned Laura again, about the car sitting out there on the street – would someone key it, steal it? His brain wouldn't shut off and he'd gone limp inside her. She said she didn't care, was nice about it, which almost made it worse. Maybe she was so okay with it because she'd just gotten laid by someone else.

They'd started sleeping together first and talked later. Setting the ground rules, that's what Laura called it. She mostly slept with women but liked screwing men too. As long as they *communicated*... Yes yes, he'd nodded, lying in her bed, his body still slick with her sweat and his own. Sure, that sounded okay. Six months ago that was, and he's never really gotten used to it. It still makes him feel sick, the way you feel when someone punches you in the gut, the times he comes home – knowing what he'd find because she's told him in advance – her bedroom door closed, sounds coming from behind it; or the times he thinks he can smell someone else on her. It isn't an open relationship – it isn't a relationship at all. Fuck buddy, she calls him.

He lifts her chin and kisses her, and she kisses back, but perfunctorily; she isn't in the mood. He has an instant of wanting to force his tongue between her teeth, to push her back and pin her, make her small body do what he wants. He gets up, feels her hand fall away from his thigh. "Tea?" He moves to the kitchen.

She follows him. "Those sites are all so touchy-feely. I want something different." Stephen puts the kettle on. "What people need is to learn to take charge of themselves in the present, to create a future. People chronically underestimate the importance of looking ahead."

"Sure." He thinks of his own failure to ascertain the hospital's plans for his mother; remembers how Laura asked him about that the second he walked through the door. Has he failed some obscure test; is that why she doesn't want to have sex tonight?

"Yeah, the future. Five, ten years. Long-term goals."

"Is this a primer for me when I'm, oh, say, setting up your website?" Stephen takes two mugs down from the shelf.

"If you have long-term goals you'll thrive under pressure, earn more money, have happier and longer-lasting relationships." She counts on her fingers.

"Really. Let me get my pen and pad."

"Really."

Her voice is a challenge, and he looks at her. "Do I have to believe that to build your site?"

"What's not to believe?" She sits at the table, legs sprawled. "What have I just said that's not believable?"

"Like you're into long-lasting relationships."

He's pleased when she looks away. "That's not the point." There's a silence, and he watches her decide not to take issue with his dig at her. "I thought the site might open up to a series of questions. People love quizzes. Like, *One: what's the most exceptional thing you've done this week?*"

"Drive my mother's car without an accident."

Laura giggles. "*Two: what's the most exceptional thing you'll do next week?*"

"Ah, drive my mother's car without an accident. No, scratch that – not throttle my mother."

"Well, ideally you'd have positives."

"Yeah." The kettle rattles. "That's good," Stephen says. "You're right. People will like that."

"And they'll read it and think I have all the answers."

They are both laughing now. Stephen strikes a pose, one eyebrow raised. "You'll be their guide to their own tomorrows."

Sleep moves further and further from him. Stephen lies tangled with Laura on her bed, trying to hang on to the fuzzy, golden contentment, trying not to think. She'd climbed onto his lap in the kitchen and twined herself around him; his thought that she only ever wanted sex that she initiated soon disappeared into his want. The memory of his temporary flash on the couch, of wanting to force himself on Laura, is unreal now. *I was a guy in my last life,* she said to him; it was like that, the way she knew his body, how to do things. She'd lain on her back, him kneeling up between her legs, and she pleasured him with her hand that way; *it's like it's my cock,* she said, *like I'm jerking myself off*. She didn't accept any pleasure in return. *You're always so attentive; you're totally the best guy lover I've ever had. You are! Let me…* It had felt like mercy sex.

How would he be different if he'd had a father? he wonders. Would he even know Laura?

Would a Stephen with a father be in this relationship?

She's curled on her side under the sheet, head nestled into his neck, half-asleep. He often feels like he's missed out on the how-to-be-a-guy handbook. Women consist of two X chromosomes, men are XY; Stephen thinks of himself as some weird amalgam of the two. XXY maybe. His father, the man he's never met, the phantom, maybe a superhero, YY. And his mother's father?

"I have a rich grandfather," he blurts.

"What?" She looks sleepily at him.

"I just found out. My mother's father."

"You mother's father?"

His heart races. "I guess the guy is filthy. That car accident in Toronto, Mom hit his lawyer."

She sits up, rubbing her face. "But that's... what are the chances of that?"

"She's cut off from him."

Laura stares. "Yeah. She disowned him, you told me." *Disowned*, the desolate finality of that. "She must have had good reason."

"Not that she'll tell me."

"Does she want to contact him?" She meets Stephen's eyes. "You know. Now that she's..."

"No."

Laura lies back down, reaches up to touch his face with her hand. "God, Stephen. That's huge."

"Well, never mind." It is his turn to sit up.

"Why not?" Her voice rises, quivering at his back. "God, if I found out who my grandfather was – "

"It's not like that!"

"Not like what?"

He looks over his shoulder at her where she lies. "I'm not all misty about it. My mother, she'd kill me if she had even the ghost of a suspicion that I was thinking about contacting this guy. So my feelings don't matter."

"She doesn't know you know?"

"No. I called the lawyer after she went into hospital. No, she doesn't know."

Laura sits up too, staring forward, considering. "And given the circumstances..."

"Yes."

64

They sit side by side. Stephen feels the familiar sickness in his gut, growing. Finally he speaks, his voice coming out as if through someone else's throat. "You said it. *Given the circumstances.* She's dying. I can't call him." He looks at Laura. "Can I?"

Laura's eyes are big, like an animal's. "Do you want to?"

Excitement rises in Stephen, hard, like he's about to get into a fight. "Do you want me to?"

Laura simply looks at him, but her breath quickens.

"He's got money, you know. He could set you up. Your website, your book, without even thinking about it." He tries to picture it, the extent of the wealth. "He's rich."

"Shut up. Shut up." Laura twists the sheet around in her hands. "This isn't about me."

"But it could be. One call and – "

"Stop it!"

Stephen stares.

Laura goes on more quietly. "Stop it. You're trying to make me make the decision for you."

Stephen shoves the sheet away. "You're right. I… I don't know what to do."

She rubs her palm across his shoulder blades, soothing. He wishes he could decide, be clear, let all this uncertainty wash away. He can't stop his mind from running along the same channels, over and over.

"I just… it'd be against her wishes, you see? Against more than that – against her whole life."

He takes Laura's hand, can't look at her. Looks instead at the wall: plaster stained from the leaking window the landlord has done nothing about *because it's winter*; the old wall-to-wall carpet Laura has tried to cheer up with a little rug she found at Value Village. Someone like his grandfather has probably never even been inside a place like this. Someone like his grandfather would believe that anyone who lived here did so because of some fundamental personal failing, because they lacked something inside themselves.

"She came from this money, and she turned her back on…" Stephen's throat constricts. "She's dying. How could I push it, now?"

"Yes." Laura leans gently against him.

"Except…" Where are these tumbling thoughts coming from? "I keep thinking it happened for a reason. You said it. What are the chances of hitting that guy? It's like a ship lost on the ocean, coming across a… a tiny island, one of those coral atolls or something. The chances… Like it was meant."

"You don't usually talk like this."

"No, but I've never had anything like this happen to me."

A feeling flashes through him, a morning feeling. It was long ago: Grade One. Pearl with her housecoat and cigarette; him in the middle of the room and the air was ringing. *If you don't like the goddamn school lunches I make for you, you can goddamn well make your own!* And he'd said, *Fine.* Sugar-and-margarine was a favourite, or ketchup on white bread. So then Pearl didn't really need to get up in the mornings any more, unless she was working an early shift at the retirement home. He could walk to the corner to catch the school bus by himself; it wasn't far, and there were always a couple of mothers slumping exhaustedly against the telephone pole. Pearl didn't need to be there. He didn't need her.

The first time walking to the bus alone, he'd been completely terrified. He hadn't told his mother. He'd just done it.

And this is the feeling now – the excitement of defiance and independence racing over the sick stomach of having made Pearl mad, again. Always.

"My mother is dying." And the lonely mornings rise up in him. "I've just discovered that her father, whom she hates, is living nearby, and is rich. She doesn't want her own father to know she is dying. And she doesn't want me to know him."

"What do you want to do?"

"I want... to... I want to call him." He speaks against the tightness in his throat. "But I don't feel I can, not now." Another pause. "But wouldn't he want to know she's sick? I've told you what she's like. Maybe he's not as bad as she thinks."

Like him, Laura only has her mother as family; the thought strikes him, and he feels guilt for bringing all this up with her. Pearl's a peach compared to Laura's mother.

Besides, there's no right answer. No matter what he does, some part of him will believe it is the wrong thing.

Lying in Laura's bed that night Stephen feels his chest tighten, feels again something pushing against his throat, his clenched jaw. He can picture his mother's small body lying in that hospital bed, screaming, snoring roommate beside her. She seems so alone there; it makes his heart twist within him. Maybe she can't sleep, maybe her body is wracked with coughing. Softly, so as not to wake Laura, he gets up, pulls on his clothes, and goes out to the car.

The streets are empty; it is three in the morning. When he arrives at the hospital all is dark and strange. He half expects that someone will stop him, but the night-desk nurse simply keeps working and scarcely seems to notice him. It's like when he was a kid, pretending he wore a cloak of Loth-lórien which granted him near-invisibility, if he was careful.

The room is an underwater version of itself, lit only by fluorescence seeping in from the hall, reflections rippling from the parking lot lights out-side. The roommate does indeed snore, but Pearl is asleep. The hospital bed seems to float, a glimmering whiteness in the shadows. Stephen draws the chair closer to the bed, sits quietly. Her breath comes harshly, and it stinks – is it the corruption in her lungs? – but she isn't coughing. He won-ders what the radiation has done to her insides. He pictures photographs of Hiroshima victims, pictures the way radiation would fry the cancer, sure, but it has to fry everything around it too, meat, deadness. She lies spread out on her back, mouth open. One of her hands rests outside the covers, and he reaches for it, draws it toward him. Her pale hair spreads out across the pil-low, one edgy collarbone protrudes from the neck of her nightdress. He sits with her in the blue-dark of the room, the two of them, under water together.

It's an evening game of pretend, out drinking in a bar with human be-ings. He can feel like that person before the diagnosis, before the accident, be Stephen again. Alcohol helps; only every now and again does the sud-den grief, the long sliding writhing feeling, assert itself, rendering Stephen impossible.

He'd finished up at the bookstore early and gone in search of a game of chess. He used to do this pretty often, going to the legion where the old men have a chess club, or to Dieter's vegan café The East Wind; he can usu-ally find someone willing to play him, and Stephen is a pretty good chess player. There are four or five opponents he plays on a regular basis, Dieter one of them. Stephen likes to win, but even more he likes to play with someone willing to analyze the game – go back over a series of moves and see where the traps were laid, share analyses of great games past. On evenings when he finds a game like this he feels good; there is a glow, in-tellectual and even, he thinks, spiritual.

He hasn't found any chess buddies this evening except Dieter, and Di-eter has been drinking all afternoon and so isn't any use for chess. But he buys Stephen a pint, and another pint, and then Stephen returns the favour. Funny how drunk you get on an empty stomach.

"How's things at the Wind?" Stephen asks. "The new bartender is work-ing out, obviously, else you wouldn't have been drinking since noon in this rival establishment. Or are you drowning your sorrows?"

"No, she's working out great. It's good not to have to be there all the time, I can tell you. Not that I don't love the place…"

"Half the time I go in there, it's like everyone is dying of malaria. What's up with that?"

"Come on, I've got a youthful clientele."

"All those facial piercings. And tattoos."

"Old Granddaddy Lewis," Dieter laughs.

Stephen shivers, gulps his pint. Granddaddy Lewis. He considers, and rejects, the notion of trying to talk to Dieter about the grandfather thing. Too hard, and he's too tipsy right now. Still, it's an interesting notion. He too could be a trust-fund baby, like Dieter. He could do something with his life, open a business or travel; he could be free. Stephen remembers meeting Dieter, ten years ago now; how he'd noticed without being quite conscious of it how superior Dieter was: his white, straight teeth, his clear eyes and skin; a big guy, tall and fit, and straightforward in his feelings and motivations, a superior being. Stephen had been almost disappointed to discover that Dieter came from wealth, that his dad was involved big-time on Bay Street. Always had the best of everything growing up, and it shows. Stephen wonders for the first time why Dieter lives in this town, why he's doing what he does instead of following the path no doubt intended for him. He never speaks of conflict with his parents. They seem to get along.

"Hey, how's your mom?" Dieter's asking. His face is open and concerned, like a worried Saint Bernard, and Stephen feels a flash of anger. He doesn't want to leave this pleasant evening yet, doesn't want to feel the long dark slide into pain.

"She's dying, Dieter." Dieter ducks his head and Stephen instantly regrets it.

"I know, man, I know."

Stephen tries to make up for it. "She's in pretty good spirits, actually." He's got to do this now, be the person whose mother is dying, be brave. "She's on steroids. Seem to really cheer her up."

Dieter's eyes gleam. "Really? What kind?"

Stephen grins at him. "Like I'd tell you. You'd go up there and steal the steroids out of my dying mother's hand."

Dieter grins. "Awwww…" His smile dies away, and he stares into the surface of his pint for a moment. "I'm really sorry about… Really. Let me know if I can do anything, right?"

"Sure, sure."

Someone puts on the Stones; Mick struts around through the air. "How's Laura?" Dieter asks.

Stephen knocks back half his pint. "Laura?"

"Yeah. How's things?"

"Oh… okay, I guess."

Dieter orders two more pints. "You always get the great-looking girls."

"I do?" Stephen's heard this before and he always finds it strange, like a description of someone else; however, when he thinks of the girlfriends he's had, it's true, he's found them all beautiful. "Yeah, but so do you."

Dieter is the town catch, but he shakes his head. "How do you do it?"

Stephen shrugs. "My animal magnetism."

The pints arrive.

"Cheers."

"So it's like you got to skip the whole will-we-move-in conversation and went straight for the home run."

Dieter's still talking about Laura, Stephen realizes, and feels compelled to tell the truth. "We're not really… *together* together."

"How's that?"

"Laura's into the open relationship thing."

Dieter's eyes widen. "Um. Because she's bisexual?"

"I suppose so. That, and striking a blow against patriarchy."

"Does she bring other people home?"

"Sometimes."

Dieter gulps his beer. "I'm tempted to make some kind of crass and joking comment, but to be frank with you, I actually think I'd kind of hate that."

"It's not always easy."

"Man."

"Yeah."

"She's so pretty, too," Dieter muses.

Stephen feels a jolt. "Hey, are you… you know…"

"No. But man." Dieter puts his hands on either side of Stephen's head, brings them gently forehead to forehead. He whispers, "Don't think I haven't thought about it."

He bursts out laughing, and Stephen can't help but join in. But he makes Dieter buy him a shot of Jameson for that.

Before leaving the bar he texts Laura, *Going to hospital, where r u?* She texts back almost at once, *Home.* Good. She's home, he knows where she is. Somehow his satisfaction makes him feel obscurely dirty. But then she follows with another text, *Maybe out later.* He wants to demand that she be home when he returns. But that would be breaking their rules. He wants to break the rules, wants to know she's his, and the force of this longing surprises him. He shoves his phone into his pocket.

It's cold and long dark, after seven o'clock. Stephen moves easily through the early dusk, the yearly tilt of the world. He walks. Yesterday, driving home from the hospital, he skidded out on some ice and clipped a parked car. No damage to the Honda, but the other car's wheel well crumpled over the front tire, like tinfoil. It looked familiar, an ancient lima green Mercedes Benz. Stephen battled an urge to flee the scene – the street was dark, no porch lights even, no one would know – but he stopped and put a note with his name and cell number on the windshield. He apologized. *So sorry I hit your car,* he'd written. His mother's insurance would go up even more now – two accidents. So today, he walks, as he would have had to anyway, being drunk.

He quickens his pace and rounds the corner onto a busy street, the long slow slope that leads up to the hospital. Traffic zooms by, headlights bright, everyone rushing home for the weekend, or downtown to go out. He catches himself in the familiar imagining: everyone driving past him is married, hurrying home to husbands and wives. Kids. A house. Or on the way to a hot date. The traffic is too loud, too fast. He turns off the road to take the long way around, through the quiet of the fancy part of town.

Big, silent houses sit far back from the street, old trees arch overhead. Signs warning "Community Safety Zone Begins." And two blocks later, "Community Safety Zone Ends." He and Laura have a running joke about getting a sign for their neighbourhood: "Community Danger Zone Begins!" He wonders what Laura's up to at home. Working on her book?

They could be business partners, he thinks suddenly. They could work well together. They already *do* work well together. He could handle book distribution, organize things, reading tours and such – where Laura would speak, flirt, and sign copies. Laura would be good at that. Women would come in droves to hear her read – men too – her message of self-empowerment, coupled with her twist on self-help, held an appeal for both genders. The way she herself did: a sexy woman who thought like a guy. It could work, it would really work. With a little start-up money Laura could publish her book on the web, make money on the web readers, then find a publisher. Stephen feels sure of it. He stops under a street light, takes out his phone. He wants to tell her… what? No, better wait until he thinks it through more. Better wait until he's actually contacted his… Strange, hard thought. That old man, the sinister, shadowed old man. Surely he is not anyone's grandfather.

Street lights spring into life overhead and up the block. A pool of illumination about three lights away bathes a woman with a baby carriage. A

70

sad, dark figure, it's the girl he saw before in the park, the one who stood rocking the carriage back and forth. The street light catches her through the soft needles of a pine tree, ancient, grown into a hoop, leaning protectively over her; he doesn't recall seeing this tree before, so big, so old. It sits on a palatial front lawn, a mansion rising up dark behind. The girl's clothes are shabby, dark, and the carriage is obviously some old thing from the seventies picked up second-hand; she doesn't belong here any more than he does. She stands still, one mittened hand on the handle of the carriage; unlike the first time he saw her, she stands perfectly still, not rocking the carriage. No sound comes out of it.

Maybe there is no baby, he thinks. Maybe she's crazy.

He gets closer, and suddenly her arm begins to move, rocking the carriage back and forth, back and forth on the rutted sidewalk ice. Her back is to him; maybe he could just cross the road and not have to deal with her at all. Christ, there are a lot of crazy people in this town; do they ship them up from Toronto or what? Is the whole town a sort of immense halfway house for the broken and the damned? Most everyone he knows is lost in some way – alcoholics, abuse victims, wannabe artists – people Toulouse Lautrec would have liked to paint. The girl's head is bowed. She wears a black scarf wrapped around it, a street girl in Paris. She should be wearing fingerless gloves, a shawl maybe, but her mittens are blue, her coat a grey polyester fill. He's almost on her now. He mutters hello. There's a mound of blankets in the carriage, he sees that much. Nothing moves.

"He doesn't cry," she says.

When she speaks he almost slips on the ice. "Sorry?"

"But he loves trees. So do I."

"Sure."

"We are all trees."

Either his bad ear isn't hearing her, or she's a nutter. Her face is sort of familiar. She's young, maybe twenty; he wonders if he's seen her at Dieter's café or something. Young to be a mother.

Police sirens come from behind, making him jump. When he looks toward the blare, he sees two dough white faces inside the car. They flash by, red and blue. Light sweeps in a circle, illuminating the Community Safety Zone: winter trees, white lawns, beveled glass porches and dark roofs set back from the road. Over and over.

He turns back but the girl and the carriage have disappeared, lost in light blurring across his eyes. He takes a few steps and thinks that maybe he hears the squeak of wheels beside the vast old house with the curving pine; but he can't see anything. The rhythmic squeaking disappears into the wind.

"What the *fuck* is your fucking *problem*?"

She sits up ramrod straight. Stephen glances over at the roommate; the woman huddles in her bed, mouth open, eyes gleaming with pleasure.

"Do you mind keeping it down?"

Pearl is so mad her lips have gone white, she is shaking. "Don't take that fucking *reasonable* tone with me! I hate that. Jesus, what a moron!" She slaps at the sheet with her palms.

"All I said was I wonder how you'd feel if I just, you know, called him – ".

"Pretty fucking goddamn violated, that's how I'd feel! And I think it's a bloody dirty trick to be bringing this up now. You can't wait until I'm dead!"

Stephen clenches the arms of the chair. "Now that is unfair. That is really unfair."

"I mean it! And that's a good idea, come to think of it. Wait until I'm dead! Then you can call him all you like. You'll get along with him. He loves sycophantic hole-lickers."

Stephen throws his hands up. "There's no talking to you when you're like this."

Pearl stares into him, burning him. "Don't you think," she spits, "that if he was interested in you, he would have tried to find you by now?" She breaks into coughing.

Stephen twists in his chair. "I... I know. You're right, he hasn't." He feels himself go small and stubborn inside. "But I can." It reminds him of a hallway, a winter hallway. He didn't want to go outside, he didn't want to put on his snowsuit. Something like that. He makes himself round and hard and small like a marble. "Try to find him, I mean."

"If he wanted you, he'd have found you. Believe me." Pearl hacks out each word. "He doesn't want you. And you can thank me for that."

She knows how to reach inside of him, grab hold of his beating heart, how to squeeze. The man doesn't want him, never did. Stephen looks at her from under his brows, his glasses framing a line between her and him. "If you would just tell me why you cut him out, it'd help. Can't you just tell me?" He hears his pleading tone and knows that to her it just sounds like whining.

"He'd just use you to get to me." She turns her face away and his conscience smites him. Is she crying? But she whips around again. "And don't think I don't know that you're drunk."

72

"Oh, for – "

"Coming in here, asking my *permission* to call your grandfather." He ducks his head but the words keep coming, the venom. "You're pathetic."

Stephen doesn't look up. His hands clench each other, the knuckles white. "Actually, I don't need your permission – "

"That's right! Do whatever you goddamn please for once in your pathetic life…"

He keeps talking, low, determined. "… and actually, I already called him."

Pearl shuts up. Silence, finally there is silence.

"You what?" Her voice is soft like a little girl's.

Stephen meets her eyes, and keeps lying. He never lies; it's exciting, he's making a new world in which he decided, on his own, to contact his grandfather. "I already called him. We've talked." Her eyes look purple when she's angry, he thinks. Really remarkable. His body is numb, words come from somewhere as if he has been summoned by an external power to speak. "He seemed all right, actually." He tries to sound light but it keeps falling, his voice is rough, cracked. "He deserves to know that you're… He deserves to know me."

What she does then hurts more than anything. She turns her head away and stares at the wall. His words echo in the air, in his head. *Deserves.* He doesn't know what this man deserves or doesn't deserve. When Stephen pictures him it's ridiculous: an old man in a cloak, a black cloak that billows in the wind; also long white hair, a beard. He is a cipher, a presence that looms over Stephen's entire life, defines it; and Stephen has lied just to hurt his mother. She is dying. It's ridiculous.

"Mom, I…" What is he going to say? "Look, I didn't do it, okay? I didn't call him." She keeps staring at the wall. "I don't know why I said that."

She won't speak to him, she refuses to answer him no matter what he says. After a long time of this, over and over, the gaping roommate loving every minute of it, he just gets up, he walks out.

Instead of going home he goes back to the bar. Maybe Dieter will still be there; but he's gone. The walk and the fight have leached all the booze out of him; he thinks he'll order another beer but then realizes how hungry he is. He turns to leave and almost sideswipes a middle-aged woman. "Whoa!" she calls out, and then says, "Why, it's you!"

It takes him a moment to recognize Cheryl.

"Oh… hi."

"Took you a minute." She has her coat on; is she leaving or just coming in? "Funny to run into you; I was just going to call you."

"Yeah?" He doesn't remember giving her his number.

"About my car."

"Your car?"

She laughs, a throaty sound, sort of forced, a laugh that is supposed to signal *I'm a woman who has a really, really good time, all the time.* "Yeah. You hit my car. Nice of you to leave the note, though."

That had been *her* car? He'd forgotten she drives that green Mercedes. Stephen sits down on a barstool, rubs his head. "God, I'm so sorry. It's my mother's car. I spun out on some ice..."

"Ooooh, driving mummy's car. I bet she's pissed."

He suppresses irritation. "Do you know how much it'll cost? I mean, I'd rather settle just between us, if that's, you know, okay. I'd rather avoid the insurance thing..."

She eyes him up and down. "What are you up to this evening?"

Stephen thinks about his evening thus far: getting drunk with Dieter, jealousy over Laura, the desolate fight with his mother – the phantom woman under the pine.

"Nothing."

Cheryl gives him another look.

"Actually, I was thinking of grabbing a bite to eat. Maybe a drink?" He slides his hand under her arm.

"Well, well, well, well, well." Did she never find an off-switch? "Now you're speaking my language."

They eat at a new, not-so-good Thai place, pad thai too sweet, almost sickening. They go to one bar, then another – dives, places neither of them normally go – Stephen doesn't want to run into Laura.

One bar has grubby padded armchairs; they pretend they are in an airport lounge, make up stories about where they are traveling to. Cheryl wants to pretend she's never met him before and is seducing him there in the airport, on the way to Khartoum. She calls him Bill, runs her hand up his thigh. She leans forward and makes sure he's looking at her cleavage.

She arouses him. He doesn't even like her and yet she arouses him; a strange thing, and he takes off his glasses and kisses her on the mouth. It feels so different from Laura – Cheryl likes to open her mouth wide and her lips are fuller, sloppier.

They walk to her house in the cold, bumping against each other. Stephen's questing hands find gaps in her clothing, places he can touch her: under her top, down the waistband of her skirt as they stand, swaying, waiting for a light to change. She is slick under his fingers, breathes sharply when he finds her there. He draws back his hand, and she leans into him, lips sucking his neck.

They have sex in her living room full of animal print cushions and big silk ferns and a giant flat-screen TV. He can see the two of them reflected in the screen; it's kind of hot, turns him on and makes him want to laugh at the same time, the cliché of it. She keeps her eyes closed and the sounds she makes are theatrical; he tries to ignore them, concentrate on the taste of her, the delicious feeling of her body. Her thighs and stomach are plump, soft, generous. "You're so good, that's good, baby…" She comes quickly, and then he brings her there again. They fuck. It is distant, drunken, the gap between them. But when he comes, suddenly he is crying – he is horrified to find himself crying.

"Shit, I'm sorry, I'm sorry," and he feels himself almost trying to get away from her even as he comes. She grabs him and holds him tight against her, inside her as they shudder together.

"What is it, baby? It's okay, God that felt good, what is it baby?" Murmuring, babbling.

He hides his face in the soft hollow of her neck as she strokes his back. He holds one of her perfect breasts in his hand.

Pearl and Mouse take a boat trip into Gananoque, for groceries and excitement.

"Pop. I want pop, Mouse, honey," Pearl says, so Mouse leaves her sitting on the curb and goes into a gas station convenience story.

She picks two Pop Shoppe bottles out of the cooler, lime green and incandescent orange. As she pays for them she has a sliding sensation, a slight dread that the big man behind the cash will somehow know that she has kissed Pearl. He takes her money, goes back to his newspaper. Safe.

When she emerges, Pearl is talking to a tall young guy, a long-haired smoky sort of guy, a guy wearing jeans and canvas sneakers. He's wearing big sunglasses and he's standing too close to Pearl, all tall and lanky, nodding his head constantly, *uh-huh, uh-huh, uh-huh, yeah man*. He's putting his hand into his hip pocket and Pearl is reaching into hers. A transaction of some kind. *Uh-huh, yeah man*. Mouse surges forward but the guy drifts away, still nodding, still smiling. *See you later.*

"Yeah, see you later," Pearl sings after him. Her voice is high and soft. A musty smell trails behind him like smoke.

"Who's that?" There is something about the way the guy stood over Pearl, like he owned her, that makes Mouse's stomach jump.

Pearl takes her hand out of her pocket and waves a little plastic baggie of weed in front of her face.

"Put that away; are you nuts?"

Pearl laughs, tucking the baggie back into her jeans.

They walk along King Street drinking pop. There's a park with a pond, and swans, and a fountain spewing water. They get ice cream cones and sit on a bench to eat them, huddled in their jackets. The sky, after the storm, is clear with streaks of cloud running across – the wind smells clean – fall has truly arrived.

The feeling of the guy, his smell, fades. Mouse lets one hand fall on Pearl's thigh – thrilled when Pearl doesn't stop her – is thrilled too by the illicitness of touching a girl in a park, in public. She can feel the heat of Pearl through her jeans.

A woman walks toward them, and Mouse pulls her hand back. She's wearing a neck brace, one of those high plastic collars.

"Looks like those costumes they want us to wear in the play," Pearl says. "The Elizabethan collars or whatever they are." Mouse stares at the woman, touches her own throat. "I don't want to wear that thing," Pearl is saying.

"Yeah."

"*You* don't have to wear one! Unless the designer's completely insane and wants you to lurk backstage in full period regalia – "

"I mean, it would make me feel like choking. If I had to wear it."

The neck-brace woman is almost level with them now, walking serenely across the grass. Something about the brace, the way it makes her hold her head, gives her a regal air.

"Mousey," Pearl says, cocking her head and looking up at Mouse, "do I have to wear that dress she's cooked up for me? I mean, really. The collars make us look like fucking circus clowns."

"I'm not the director."

"And that fur thing, that little cloak or whatever. It's the same colour as my *hair*. It washes me out."

Mouse thinks Pearl looks enchanting in her costume. The designer brought in some pieces in-progress for the main characters to try on, and Pearl walked out from backstage burning cold in metallic embroidery, shoulders encircled by a pale mink capelet, ragged around the edges. She'd stood next to Prospero, him in a black silk green-edged cloak. All water-stained, every edge shredded, evoking years of exile on the island – the two of them like sunken treasures frilled with seaweed and coral – Elizabethan collars proud and frayed, reminders of past grandeur.

"I liked how you looked. It worked."

"Well, I think I look like shit. Can't you talk to Uncle Tod about it? I can't wear that thing."

The neck-brace woman is past them now, and Mouse sees that the woman has put her ponytail through the hole in the back of the brace. Pearl sees it simultaneously and her hand flies to her mouth.

"Oh, my God."

"And the ribbon." The woman has encircled her ponytail with a big pink bow.

"Somehow it just makes it all worse."

The two of them begin to laugh meanly, helplessly.

Mouse drops her ice cream cone on the ground and of course it lands upside-down and this only makes them laugh harder, falling against each other. Hardly knowing what she is doing, Mouse flings her arm around Pearl, and then she is kissing her. Her lips taste of ice cream, they're cold and sweet and thrilling. Pearl goes soft, her mouth opening under Mouse's lips, her head sinking back on her neck.

Blood surges into Mouse's belly and between her legs like a tide, an opening flower; she longs to rush into that softness, surround it, submerge it with her want. She slides her hand under Pearl's T-shirt and up her ribs, touches the soft roundness of Pearl's breast. She wants to pull Pearl into her, twine their bodies into one.

But they are in a park. Mouse tears herself away from the kiss; you can't kiss another girl in a park. She looks around in a panic – have they been seen?

An elderly couple walks through distant trees.

There are the swans.

No one else.

Pearl lays her head on Mouse's shoulder and looks up. There is no expression in her eyes.

Is this how Pearl looks at the men who grope her?

Mouse gently pulls away, shifting down the park bench. She puts her head in her hands.

"What's the matter?" Pearl asks.

"Did you – do you – want that?" Her voice is rough, a bit too loud.

"Do *you*?" Pearl moves closer to Mouse on the bench. It suddenly frightens Mouse.

"Not if you don't."

Mouse stands up. It is impossible. Pearl doesn't want to kiss her. Pearl isn't gay. Pearl has slept with more guys in one month at university than most girls do in a lifetime; dykes don't sleep with guys like that.

When she was eight years old she saw Trudeau on TV talking about the bedrooms of the nation; her parents were uneasy, her father cracked a joke about fags, and she knew, even at eight, she knew there was something wrong with her. She knew to keep quiet.

There's something else, but Mouse can't articulate what. Something about the flatness of Pearl's eyes, the way kissing her makes Mouse feel like a drunken frat boy. Touching Pearl makes her feel too big, too rough, loud; she is afraid of frightening Pearl, or hurting her. She is going to walk away, she will not touch Pearl again.

And then Pearl reaches out her hand and pulls Mouse down next to her, and all of that is forgotten because there is only this yearning, taste and tongues and gasping hunger, flood of feeling in the body.

They walk holding hands, Mouse not caring who sees it.

78

Her heart is singing. They will go back to the cottage and they will make love. She will finally see a woman, really see and feel and taste Pearl, as she has longed to, the way she has imagined it.

She remembers the one girl before this, her high-school crush, thinking she wanted the kisses and touching; then the rejection, name-calling, threats to tell. This time it will be different. Pearl isn't afraid. Mouse looks down at Pearl by her side and her heart swells. Pearl isn't afraid of anything.

The town is pretty and a river runs through it, crossed three times by bridges.

Pearl stops at one at the head of the swan pond, bends over the balustrade and looks down. The water flows beneath them; hypnotic, flowing water. Shapes appear and dissolve, always almost but not quite the same; there are smooth places, swellings like sleek muscles, and there are places where it foams on the surface so you can't see down through it. The water surges and ebbs, Mouse thinks, but it never really changes.

"You want to get going?" But Pearl keeps looking dreamily down at the water. Traffic at their backs. Mouse paces a little. Chill seeps in.

"Come on, Pearl, let's go."

Pearl reaches into her pocket. She throws coins into the air, bright discs, followed by a hair elastic.

"What are you doing?"

"Throwing things in."

Pearl's hands go up to her ear, she unhooks a gold stud.

"I can see… hey, not your earring!" But the small hard thing flashes in the sun and disappears into the water. "Why did you do that?"

"I don't know. I like it."

Pearl's voice is dreamy. She plucks her sunglasses from the top of her head. Mouse makes a grab for them but they're gone.

"Okay, that's enough."

Finally Pearl lets Mouse drag her from the bridge.

They go to the A & P for groceries – oranges, bread, cheese, chocolate bars – and Pearl wants to go to the liquor store for more beer, but Mouse points out, "A: we have no I.D., and B: we have five million beers back at the island."

"No we don't; we have one case."

"Which is more than enough," and Mouse drags Pearl back to the marina.

They cross another bridge on the way and Pearl stops at the apex, taking out her second earring and throwing it into the river.

"Now you're symmetrical, very good." Mouse hopes Pearl will be satisfied but no, she unbuckles her expensive wristwatch and tosses it high into the air.

"Look," Mouse says, adjusting the grocery bags she carries and trying to muster some firmness and wit, "you may find this amusing, but as you have nothing left to throw to oblivion save our apparel and yourself, I suggest you follow me to the boat."

She walks away and is relieved when Pearl trails after.

They reach the marina. Mouse steps onboard the boat, and that's when Pearl suddenly bolts.

"Hey!"

Pearl can run surprisingly fast for such a little thing. Mouse follows her through town, gaining on Pearl with her long legs. Pearl takes reckless corners, almost bowling down a fat woman; she is heading back into town, the park; she is headed for the bridge where it crosses the river, that obliterating tumble of water.

Pearl runs to the centre of the bridge. She flings one leg over the balustrade. Mouse flies, grabs Pearl, and throws her to the sidewalk, pinning her.

They stare into each other's faces, panting. Pearl laughs.

Mouse gets off Pearl, angry, terrified. Pearl slowly stands. She suddenly feints, making another lunge for the balustrade. Mouse grabs her from behind. They struggle. Mouse lets Pearl go, and Pearl reels around. They face each other.

Pearl slaps Mouse across the face.

Mouse cannot move. The shock freezes her. She watches Pearl walk down the bridge back the way they have come, back toward the boat, the water, the island. Pearl walks away with her head held high.

She staggers a little, once, but she keeps walking.

The broken voice cries out the words, spitting the rhythm. *Tell me why, ah dun like Mundays! Tell me why, ah dun like Mundays! Tell me why, ah dun like Mundays! I wanna shoo-oo-oo-oo-oo-ooo. The ho day down.*

Pearl won't stop singing.

"It's not even Monday," Mouse says through gritted teeth. "God, I can't get it out. Shit."

"I wanna sho-oo-oo-oo-oo-oot... It's really stuck. Maybe I can find some pliers somewhere."

"Well, hurry."

Mouse's jeans are rolled up, her feet are in the water. She sits at the edge of the dock, one hand pressing an orange behind her ear, at the lobe. A tea towel with a fistful of ice sits in a puddle by her side, and a safety pin is pushed half-way through her earlobe, against the orange for resistance.

She and Pearl are stoned. The pot buzz resonates through her body, the pain from her frozen and now rapidly thawing, half-pierced ear is traveling through her in waves. "I think I'm going to puke."

"Look, this is silly. We have to be able to get it through…"

Pearl makes a motion toward Mouse's ear and Mouse jerks away.

"I don't care about through. I want it *out*."

Pearl sits back on her heels, looks at Mouse. She begins to giggle.

"Wonderful. That's wonderful. I'm glad you see so much humour in my suffering, *schadenfreude* girl."

The thing on the bridge in town had ended, finally, at the boat.

Mouse followed Pearl, Chewbacca behind the princess again. All she could think was *how can I leave now, how can I get away from this?* She wanted Pearl and feared for her, but it was breaking her – she could feel it – this would break her.

Pearl had clambered onboard and she'd stayed on the dock. "I'll hitch-hike," she'd said. "I'll hitchhike back home."

"All the way to Newfoundland? Get in the goddamn boat."

Pearl walked to the console and started the engine, just like that, a pale ring around her wrist where her watch used to be.

"Come on. It was just a joke." She'd looked up at Mouse, eyes flat; was she pleading? "Let's go back. Let's go back to the island."

They'd sat on the porch of the shuttered, only-used-at-family-reunions Big House and smoked some of the pot that Pearl had gotten from that guy, the tall long-haired guy with the sunglasses. It soothed Mouse. She felt okay now, she didn't need to worry about Pearl. It had all been an act, a drama, on the bridge, and that guy, he was just a dealer. It was okay. *Uh-huh, uh-huh.*

She feels the pain in her ear, heat rushing through. She'd been able to penetrate the skin with a sort of sickening *pop*, but for some reason she can't get the safety pin through the other side of her lobe. It is stuck, the skin rubbery. "The ice is wearing off," she moans.

Pearl can't stop giggling. "Let me try."

"No way." Mouse tugs at the pin trying to get it out, but the skin has swollen around it, trapping it. "Man, it hurts!"

Pearl steps between Mouse's thighs and kneels down; her knees pin

Mouse's legs to the dock. She grabs the orange and Mouse lets go, terrified that if she doesn't submit Pearl will, in her determination, rip off her earlobe. Pearl's face is very close; Mouse closes her eyes, hears Pearl's breath. There is a sharp pain, and then, "There!" The pressure, the orange, are gone. Pearl fiddles, she is closing the safety pin. "There."

Mouse opens her eyes. Pearl's face is right there, right in front of her. Joy surges through her, euphoria from the pain, the intoxicating feeling of Pearl's weight pinning her to the dock.

Pearl feels it too – they stare into each other – and then Pearl kisses her. She kisses her, unfolds her legs and sits right on Mouse's lap with her thighs encircling Mouse's body, kisses some more. Her mouth tastes smoky sweet. Waves of pleasure and pain wash through Mouse. Pearl pushes her over so she is lying on her back, pins her wrists above her head, bites gently at her lips. Pearl's long blonde hair falls around their faces like a tent.

She sits up. Mouse tries to lift her head to kiss some more, but Pearl hasn't let go of her wrists. Pearl smiles down at her.

"Why do you always wear your hair in that braid?"

"What?" Mouse's mind spirals.

"Why bother having long hair at all if you just keep it in that braid all the time?"

Mouse takes a deep, shaky breath.

"I detect," she says, trying to sound mock weary, "that you have an opinion about my hair. I suspect that you are going to share that opinion with me oh, say, right about... now."

"I think you should cut it off."

"I think you should kiss me some more."

Silence. Mouse's heart hammers. This is the first time she has ever said anything like this out loud. All of the groping, kissing, hopes and fantasies have happened under cover of silence.

"Kiss me, Pearl."

"I'm going to cut your hair."

Pearl springs off Mouse and sprints up the path to the cottage.

"Don't move, I'm getting scissors!"

Mouse has an impulse to obey completely, to remain lying on the dock with the imprint of Pearl's knees on her thighs, Pearl's hands on her wrists. But she resists, shifts, sits up.

The water is calm, the day is coming to an end behind grey clouds. She reaches around and pulls her honey brown braid over her shoulder. It is thick, heavy and smooth, it's like an old friend. She's had it a long time.

She isn't sure she wants to cut it off. Her lips are hot where Pearl kissed her. Short hair will make her look like a boy; she always insisted on short hair as a kid and her mother hated it when inevitably she was mistaken for a son. In junior high school she started getting called "lezzie" too often, so she grew it out. Her thighs burn with longing. If she cuts her hair off now, everyone will know.

Everyone already knows.

Pearl hits the dock, running and brandishing a pair of sewing shears.

"You're not supposed to run with scissors. Didn't your mother teach you anything?"

"Not a thing." Pearl plops herself down breathlessly. She grabs the braid, pulls it behind Mouse and up; she considers, head tilted. "It'll bring out your cheekbones, your eyes."

Mouse thinks she is going to kiss her again, but Pearl rises and darts behind, still hanging onto the braid.

"Okay. Okay." She holds Mouse's braid like a leash. "Can I?"

"Are you actually asking me?"

"Well, yeah."

Mouse looks out at the water, the great grey flowing river. "Oh, what the hell."

It takes quite a long time for the dull scissors to shear off the braid. When it is done, Mouse and Pearl contemplate the rope of hair. Pearl arranges it in a spiral on the dock; it looks quite beautiful. Mouse laughs, an explosion of breath. Her ear throbs.

"Well, you better get on with it."

Pearl seems to know how to cut hair, Mouse notes with some relief. She works away for quite some time, singing under her breath and swearing at the scissors.

"Ah dun like Mundays..." Hair flies out like dandelion down. Mouse feels the pleasure of Pearl's hands on her head, the pleasure of her scrutiny, her detached regard.

"Is it Monday?"

"Search me. Damn. These aren't very sharp, my stupid mother. There." Pearl sits back on her heels. "I think you are done." She fluffs Mouse's hair with her hand.

"How do I look?"

"Like a dyke."

It hurts like a swear word. "Anyone ever called you that?"

"No." Pearl doesn't seem to care. "Of course not."

"I want to see."

Mouse stomps up into the cottage to find a mirror. There's one in the kitchen, over the wash basin.

It's great, what looks back at her. A tall girl still tanned from summer, bright eyes, the hair brown but sunstreaks through it, fluffed up into a longish buzz cut. It looks cool, a bit punk, especially with the safety pin in the ear. It looks good.

She touches her hair, spikes it some more; her head feels light. Pearl has followed her and stands on tiptoe to see herself in the mirror over Mouse's shoulder.

"It's good, eh?"

"It's good."

"You look way cooler than Samantha."

Samantha is the lesbian on the student union, third-year political science and women's studies. She stands up in meetings with the university administration and coolly points out the president's homophobia and sexism.

"She's a force," Pearl says, "but her hair's a bush."

"I heard she's a member of the Rhino Party," Mouse giggles, as if hair has anything to do with political affiliations.

Soon they are both sitting on the kitchen floor and laughing their heads off. They smoke more pot, and Mouse can't move. She is paralyzed. Her ear feels the size of a cauliflower, her head stretches up, up and up like a balloon.

She and Pearl argue. "The only problem with coming out is you," Pearl is saying, and Mouse wonders why she's fastening onto this. "No one would think anything of it, really."

"Shut up."

Mouse realizes that she has always had the idea that she would come out once she got a girlfriend. How can you come out when you've never even had a girlfriend? How could you come out, alone? Pearl isn't offering to come out with her. Pearl isn't her girlfriend.

But suddenly Pearl's on her, kissing, groping under her sweater and T-shirt, her hands move over Mouse's body like they can't find what they're looking for, desperate. She murmurs something; she licks at Mouse's pierced ear and pain shoots through, shocking Mouse into a cry. Pearl moans with pleasure; she licks Mouse's ear again.

Mouse is helpless in the face of this assault, this desire; a line from the play comes into her head, *well, I am standing water.* She says it, Sebastian's line when Antonio is exhorting him to kill his sleeping brother and seize the crown. "Well, I am standing water."

Pearl remembers, she speaks thickly into Mouse's ear. "I'll teach you how to flow."

Her tongue darts in, and the wetness of that sound sends Mouse into a puddle of desire.

There isn't a double bed in the cottage except for the room normally used by Pearl's parents. Pearl drags Mouse upstairs to it. Mouse wonders why they can't stay where they are (the kitchen floor is cold and hard, Pearl says) or fall onto the rumpled sleeping bags, the bearskin rug (there's no fire laid and the wind is whistling down the chimney). Pearl insists on pulling Mouse up to the bed and maybe it's better this way, maybe that's where real sex happens: in a bed, like real people.

"My parents' bed, my parents' bed," Pearl whispers as she shoves Mouse down onto it. It's almost dark now, Mouse can hardly see as she rolls over on top of Pearl. "This is where my parents have sex. Where my father fucks my mother."

"Shhhh…"

Pearl has gone limp. Pearl lies on her back as though unconscious, spread-eagled across the mattress.

Her eyes are closed. Mouse can see that in the dimming light. Pearl's eyes are closed and her limbs are dead weight. Her lips are slightly parted – Mouse can see teeth there, the sexiness of it catches in her throat. But Pearl's not moving.

"Pearl?" she says. "Pearl?"

Pearl's eyelids flutter, go still.

"Pearl."

Pearl lies as though dead.

"Pearl."

She's going to do this, Pearl is really going to do this – a game – she's going to drop it, leave Mouse cold. Mouse is so turned on, the teasing's unbearable.

"What do you want?" Irritation, an unspeakable rage, well up in Mouse.

Pearl lies there.

"What do you want?"

Mouse lays her hands on Pearl's shoulders, shakes her, a short, sharp shake. Pearl's mouth opens in a gasp; it could be pleasure or fear.

"What do you *want*?" Mouse shakes her again.

Finally Pearl speaks, she whispers. "Touch me."

Something goes cold in Mouse's belly. But she'll go through with it, she'll find out what Pearl wants her to do.

85

"Touch you where?" Pearl's eyes open, a brief, contemptuous glare, swiftly hooded.

So that's how it is. She has to find out for herself, do it right.

"Touch you... here?"

She slides her palms down from Pearl's shoulders, down the length of her torso, over the T-shirt to her sharp hip bones. She cups Pearl's hips in her hands, and Pearl rewards her with a brief widening of her eyes. Mouse licks her lips, her heart pounds. "Here?" She slides her hands across and down, over jeans to the top of Pearl's thighs. "Here?" She moves her hands to the insides of the thighs, pushes gently until Pearl's legs open. So much heat is coming from between Pearl's legs that even through jeans it feels like it could burn her hands. Mouse ventures up toward Pearl's sex, but it is too much, she is too scared. She stops. She takes her hands away. She kneels there on the bed in the strangers' room, smelling of cedar, of damp.

After a moment Pearl opens her eyes. "Have you ever slept with a guy?" Her voice is cold. Mouse feels like crying.

"Yes." She has. Once.

"Well, come on. Do it."

Do what? It's too much.

"I... I don't know what you want."

Pearl grabs Mouse's hand, pulls it with surprising strength up to her breast.

"Did he touch you here?"

Mouse doesn't like remembering sex with that guy, he was a loser, it was after high school graduation in a hotel room with a bunch of other couples. She'd been drunk out of her mind, and wearing a dress, it was awful.

"Did he?"

Pearl is insistent. Her grip on Mouse's wrist is strong enough to hurt. Mouse can feel Pearl's nipple hardening, nosing into her palm like a small, inquisitive animal.

"Yes," Mouse whispers.

"Here?" Pearl moves Mouse's hand to her other breast.

This isn't sex, Mouse thinks.

"Yes."

"Here?"

Pearl jams Mouse's fist between her legs, grinds the crotch of her jeans down against Mouse's knuckles. Mouse pulls her hand away and scrambles halfway down the bed, away from Pearl. The two of them glare at each other in the dying light, panting, afraid. Mouse realizes this. They are both afraid.

"Pearl, let's not do this. It's okay. I don't want it, not this."

"Well, I do." Pearl speaks authoritatively. "Here's what we're going to do."

She slides down the bed on her back, her T-shirt riding up over her ribs. She is irresistible, she will not be refused.

"I'm going to tell you where. You're going to do what I say. We're going to go through it, like that. And then you're going to remember it, and you're going to do it all again, the same way, without me telling you. I'll pretend that I'm asleep. That's what we're going to do." Her eyes, fierce, bore into Mouse.

Now here. Now there. Harder. Inside. Again.

It is the first time Mouse has ever touched a woman, really touched, there.

It's twisted, it hurts her. Pearl is wet, turned on, yet over and over she catches her breath as if terrified. Hot and scared at the same time. It isn't something Mouse can understand. It is her first time. She keeps words in her head to render it bearable. I don't like Mondays. I don't like Mondays.

$\mathcal{S}$ometimes at this time of year, a little early morning sunlight filters into the kitchen. It isn't much, but with the sun swung as far south as it can go, light creeps alongside the brick house next door and shines obliquely through the window: one of the compensations of winter. Stephen pulls his chair close and lifts his face to the pale warmth, holding his tea mug between his palms. He feels sort of sad and satisfied, and something else – it takes him a while to find it – peaceful.

He'd fallen asleep on Cheryl's couch, awaking at dawn with her leaning over him, murmuring sleepily, not unkindly, "Hey, you have to go now." So he'd retrieved his clothes from the floor – it was sort of exciting, in a tawdry way, to see the coffee table kicked over and couch cushions thrown across the floor – and let himself out.

Cheryl lives in a neighbourhood that is going to get "good" according to real-estate prescience, but at present, isn't. At that early hour no students or poverty-stricken locals were about and he'd walked alone, light growing behind bare black trees, streetlamps winking out.

It's a good thing he slept most of the night at Cheryl's, he thinks now, because on entering the apartment he'd tripped over a pair of purple Docs at the door. Well, at least it isn't a guy, unless it's a guy with freakishly small feet. Somehow it's worse when she picks up men.

He turns on the kitchen radio. Weather colder – a winter smog warning – then clear tonight and bloody cold. He'll have to remember to bring his toque to work; the owner of the bookstore won't turn the heat up. It is like working for Scrooge; he really does need fingerless gloves, and leaves his coat on most winter days. Only second-hand bookstores survive in this town, his boss is fond of pronouncing – people read books here, but not new ones. It is a musty, yellow-paged town, an English-course-list-novel-and-old-science-fiction town.

He looks up at the sound of someone creeping into the kitchen. What was Laura thinking? – God, she looks young. She freezes at the sight of him.

"Hey," he says. "I'm Stephen."

"Oh. Are you Laura's… roommate?"

"That's right," he answers. "Just a roommate." Why the hell is he lying? "Want some tea?"

"Oh… okay… is there coffee?"

An undergrad university student. Tentative, but used to being served. "No, sorry. Tea's there on the counter in the pot. Help yourself." The girl opens every wrong cupboard to find a mug, and eventually Stephen gets up to help her, and to find her some milk, and some honey, and to pour the tea. Always pleasant, he is, to the guests. She smells sweet, and a little bit like Laura, or maybe that's his imagination.

He hopes she'll drink her tea and leave him in peace, but she sits there at the table and wants paper. "To write on." He scrabbles around in the living room and finds paper and a pen.

"Will this do?"

"Oh… okay… thanks."

She settles down, sucking on the pen, and Stephen sits back in his chair with his now not-so-hot tea and stares out the window at the brick wall. The fight with his mother at the hospital echoes in his head. Why had he lied? He'd wanted to hurt her, to shut her up he supposes; he couldn't take any more of the barrage. Still, lying has always been abhorrent to him; it's unlike him to do something like that.

He'd wanted her to see him.

He'll have to pay the piper now; Pearl won't let this go by without punishment. She never lets anything go. He remembers the powerful feeling of the lie, how it felt to manipulate reality. But he pushes this down. He wonders if he can stay away from the hospital, just for one day, and feels his heart leap at the thought. He pictures himself finishing work and then going out, finding a chess game or a drink or maybe Laura would… or Cheryl…

He can't leave her there, alone.

The girl rustles around, sighing and playing with her long hair. She's written a few words, Stephen can read them upside-down: *Dear Laura… Last night was something I've wanted ever since I saw you at the Rainbow Dance…* He looks away.

"Oh… um… what did you say your name was, sorry?"

"Stephen."

"Stephen, how, um, do you spell *anguish*?" She twirls her hair.

After work Stephen walks the long way around, crossing the river into the east side of town to meet Laura. She'd texted him in the middle of a protracted negotiation with an old man over some soft, dusty Heinlein paperbacks: *Footbridge 4pm for pix. Please? xoL.* Stephen had cut twenty-five percent from the sticker price just to get the old man out of the store, shut the place down early and left.

Gold gleams through clouds where the sky has forgotten to close up. It's almost dusk by the time he comes to the paved trail where the railway tracks used to be, rutted with frozen footprints. He wishes it weren't winter. If it weren't winter he'd be able to walk down by the water, hidden under willow trees, ears filling with the great tumbling roar of the river. Even up here, the boom of water running through the dam pushes through his skull, obliterating thought – he loves this, the squeeze of all that water through massive concrete barriers, spray in the air, willows falling every which way, uprooted by surges and time. The sound fills his ears, blasting out the day: the bookstore, the girl in the apartment, his mother dying in hospital.

But he has to keep walking, walking past, and as soon as the dam is behind him the noise cuts out. Nothing but a dull roar now, and a memory of wet in the air, a colder face.

He sees Laura in the middle of the footbridge leaning on the rail, gazing into gold, the sun sinking through shreds of cloud like fish scales. There's something theatrical about her posture; she wears a long black wool coat belted at the waist, her dreads are tucked up under a beret. With her slender body, her scarf and hat, she looks something like an old-time movie star, he thinks, maybe that girl from *Breakfast at Tiffany's*, what's her name? Or someone French.

"Bonjour, mademoiselle, ça va?" Stephen hails her.

Laura turns at his voice. "Is it too much, do you think?"

"Yes. Well, I guess that depends what it's for."

"Laura Leonard, International Traveler."

Stephen eyes her. "My God," he realizes, "you're wearing lipstick."

"Yeah, and that's not all." She sweeps off the beret and her hair springs out in blonde waves, curling prettily around her face.

"My God," he says again. "You cut off your dreads." Something about the change makes him nervous.

"I've gotten all butchy since I started sleeping with you. I'm trying to get back to my femme roots."

"Since you started sleeping with me?" He wants to run his fingers through the curls. He joins her at the bridge's rail, touching his shoulder to hers.

She leans into him. "When I was seeing mostly women, I tended to go for the boy-girls, playing up to their masculinity by being femme. Around you I sort of want to swagger around. To compensate."

He remembers the girl from this morning. "For committing the crime of screwing a man?" He sounds bitter; he doesn't care.

"Oh, come off it." She smiles at him. "I really like sleeping with you, Stephen. You're a wonderful lover."

"I like sleeping with you too."

He reaches for her hand on the railing, but she doesn't see the gesture and moves her hand, waves in the air. "I like how it's affected my identity," she continues. "It's been interesting."

She is so matter-of-fact about it, so oblivious; the familiar pain and rage surge up, a hard thing. It's true, then – there it is, the terrible precariousness, the imbalance – she doesn't care for him as much as he cares for her. "I'm glad it's been so interesting."

"Stephen, I didn't – "

He cuts her off, not wanting to hear whatever she thinks she should say next to keep him in thrall. "That girl this morning – she wasn't exactly what I'd call a boy."

"Oh. She told me she met you. She said – "

"I don't care."

"...she said you were nice."

Nice, he wants to be nice, he spends his whole goddamn life being nice. "Was picking her up part of exploring your butchy side?"

"Look." Laura glares at him. "I thought we were okay. Are we okay?" As soon as her anger pushes out, his own evaporates. It goes into the numbness that hovers, always there, a mist around his edges. The lipstick suits her, he thinks. It brings out the creamy whiteness of her face, makes her glamourous, even if the beret is a bit silly. "Audrey Hepburn."

"What?"

"You look like Audrey Hepburn."

She looks away. "I don't get you," she says. The numbness stays with him, is a kind of levity. "Do we or do we not have an agreement about being able to sleep with other people?" she demands.

He won't answer the question; almost feels like laughing. "You're a traveler, you said. So, where have you been?"

"I'm serious, Stephen."

"I can see that." She's getting angrier and angrier. It breaks over him like a wave, like the water over the dam. "Go ahead. Be serious."

"Because if you're going to start having a problem with..." She stops, walks a few paces away, slapping her beret against her leg. She swings back. "Besides, it's not like you were home last night anyway."

The numbness stirs, goes cold in his belly. "Are you actually trying to be jealous?"

"Stephen!"

"Laura!" he imitates her.

"Fuck you. I mean… fuck you." She turns and marches away down the bridge.

He's being like his mother, he realizes, like Pearl, seizing on fragments, changing the conversation until the other person doesn't know where they are. He can't let her go like that. Anxiety stirs, swims up his throat.

"Hey, Laura, wait!" he calls. "I… I brought my phone. For pictures." It sounds like when he'd told Pearl he'd picked up the car. Pathetic. But she stops walking, turns slowly back to him.

"What's gotten into you?"

He feels suddenly tired. "Oh, nothing. Never mind. Let's take some pictures before we lose the light."

"You sure?"

"Yeah. Sure. So, where are you going, International Traveler?"

She stares at him a moment before replying, the way you assess a strange dog before holding out your hand. "Okay. Fine." She looks out at the pewter river. "It's about showing where I've been." Stephen remembers the sunsets in the other life-coach websites she's shown him, mentally compares those pictures with the leaning willows here, almost falling into the half-frozen, rushing water. "It looks pretty good here, don't you think?" Laura continues. "It could be somewhere in the British Isles, or… And over there…" she points to the opposite bank, "there's nothing but trees, and downriver, that church tower is pretty convincing. We could be in Ireland?"

"Laura," says Stephen, and stops.

"I started my travel blog today and it's pretty good if I do say so myself."

"Are you saying you want to create a false history for yourself and post it on the website?"

"Yes. I want to create a false history for my I-can-help-you identity and post it on the website. I've been to Ireland for sure. And somewhere else spiritual. Tibet?"

"Tibet might be hard. Don't they have mountains?"

"We can photoshop. Well, I guess we should wait for summer to shoot those, so I'm appropriately attired. Oh, and I was hoping for some standing stones."

Stephen stares down at the water. The surface here is smooth, but if you throw something down it gets sucked under, disappears with thrilling swiftness. The dam, downriver, makes sure of that. He fishes around in his pocket and comes up with some pennies, a ball of tinfoil, and a glob of the mysterious lint that always forms in the pockets of coats. He tosses each bit into the river: the coins and foil gleam like small shiny bodies going over; the lint gets caught in the wind, floating above the surface for a moment before touching down and getting sucked away. An image of his mother in hospital, sitting up in her bed, flashes through him like electricity. He turns back to Laura. "I wish you'd planned this with me a little more in advance."

"Oh. Sorry. You're right. We should have set a date... I just assumed... because we sort of talked about this the other day..."

"I mean, I have to visit my mother, and maybe I had plans for this evening..."

"Do you?" she says earnestly. She's always earnest and accommodating after bedding someone else. She reaches out and puts her gloved hand over Stephen's. He pulls away, feels rage again like a cold stone in his stomach.

"Well, no, but that's not the point," he says, "and by the way, that girl, that girl this morning, what's her name?" The image of the girl, self-absorbed and cute, writing that note, *anguish*, fills Stephen like anger.

"What does she have to do with taking pictures of me for the website? What does she have to do with *us*?" Laura demands.

Stephen feels it swelling inside him, almost desperate: it is this, the certainty that he's onto something important, that he has to hang onto. "You just don't get people sometimes, Laura. You have to tell the truth about things sometimes!" To hang onto the truth – what is it – that Laura is a liar and her lies hurt people – it's roaring in his ears. He hears his voice rising and doesn't care. "You hurt that girl's feelings." Idiotic, but it spills out anyway. "She's, like, in love with you, Laura!"

"No, she's not! That's ridiculous."

"How would you know? You didn't even get up to see her out."

Laura stares at him. "Well, like I said, and I can't believe we're talking about this *again*, it's not like you were home last night."

"I was home by six." It's a silly defense; why isn't he letting go of this fight? And then the cold hard thing pushes again into his stomach, a desire to crush Laura, to make her cry. To win. "Like you'd care."

Laura backs away from him a few steps, hands waving in an *I surrender* kind of way. "I've never seen you like this."

"I guess you don't know me very well."

"Look, if me bringing some silly girl home is going to upset you this much, I won't do it. I just won't."

"Yeah, right."

"Because if you want a break from the whole open relationship thing, if you need more certainty, that's fine." Her voice breaks, theatrically he thinks. "That's fine."

93

"Are you fucking serious?" All theatrics. "Are you acting like you think you owe me anything, any kind of loyalty? You'll do whatever you want. Like always." He can see it. "You'll sneak around."

Her eyes widen. "I don't do that, I'm *honest*... Look," and she gulps, wipes her nose on her coat sleeve, "it's just, with all you're dealing with right now, I'm, I don't know... Whatever you want."

"What are you saying?"

"With your mother and... I care about... I want to help."

"And what the hell does traveling to Ireland have to do with being a life coach?" he yells.

She stares at him, she looks scared. Stephen feels his body, the tension in it, his clenched jaw, stomach hurting, head thrust forward. His face feels distorted by cold, by anger.

Laura swallows. When she speaks her voice is quiet, almost pleading. "Because that's what they want. They don't want me, the Laura me. They want a guru. They want mountains and rock circles and fucking oceans."

"Everything's just a costume for you, isn't it?" Stephen puts all his bitterness into his voice. "It's all an act."

Laura turns her back, shoves her hands down into her coat pockets. "Life is a series of performances, Stephen. Once you get over being a kid. It's just that."

With a shock he realizes she's crying. He's never seen her cry before. She does it softly, her head turned away from him; only a little sniff, and her hand momentarily taken out of her pocket to swipe at some tears, give it away. Remorse sweeps through; his mind races to remember what he's been saying. What she's said. Had she suggested they could be, well, a couple?

"Laura?"

"Fuck off."

"Laura, I'm... I'm sorry." He reaches out, puts a hand on her shoulder. It's a relief when she doesn't pull away. "I didn't mean those things. I don't know what's gotten into me. You didn't do anything wrong." Shit, she's really crying; what an asshole he is. "It's me, it's my fault."

Suddenly she flings herself into him, burying her face in his coat, her body shaking. The force of this grief doesn't seem to have anything to do with him; he almost staggers, then recovers and puts his arms around her. "It's okay, it's okay," he says, while she gasps, "I'm sorry, I'm sorry," over and over. After a time she stops crying. He takes her face gently between his gloved hands, wipes tears from her cheeks with his thumbs. He kisses her. "You've got nothing to be sorry about," he says.

"I... don't leave, okay?"

Confusion swirls around him. "But I... you didn't ever want..."

Her eyes are dark, her lips tremble. "I... I want you though, don't be mad any more, okay?"

"Laura. Is this your way of asking me to go steady?" His heart beats fast.

"Just don't be mad any more."

He kisses her. And finally, he gets to run his fingers through her hair, her new, soft hair.

They wander through the riverside park. The bruise of the fight sinks down, fades. Laura leaps up onto rises and even into trees, striking heroic poses for Stephen to photograph, then dissolving into giggles. She starts talking in an Irish accent, deepening her voice to sound like a great man – Yeats or someone – setting down his thoughts for posterity. Her accent is good. "Several years ago it was nearing dusk as I crossed the arched wrought-iron bridge over the River Liffey at the centre of Dublin... No, wait... It was autumn when I was hiking in Tibet, and a young boy asked me the question that forever changed me. I was standing at the start of a well-used cart road – no, make that an *old rutted path* – at the foot of a mountain..."

As the light fades they walk along the trail, arm in arm. There's no one else this late on a winter's day; they have the park to themselves. They come to a small island connected by a short wooden bridge; Laura dances ahead of Stephen, twirling, arms outstretched. He takes a couple of shots, her silhouette against the last remaining bar of pale gold at the very rim of the horizon. She stops dancing, laughs, breath puffing out like smoke.

Stephen moves upstream. A massive willow overarches the river, almost falling in but still solid. He remembers this place; his mother sometimes took him here. There was a tree he used to like, probably long fallen into the water, this can't be the same one. He climbs onto the willow and, balancing, makes his way out over the water upon its thick, rough trunk. Branches encircle him. Stephen sits on the trunk and lets his feet dangle over the half-frozen water. The deep river flows by, always the same, always changing.

He remembers a night years ago, a place like this, somewhere along this stretch of river. He was a kid, maybe seven? It was summer, the sky arched overhead. His mother was on the little island with some other people, they were all smoking and playing hand drums. The drumming soared up into the night with the smoke, some people danced. Hot summer night with music and dancing; he sat and watched the people, idly playing spot-my-mother in the crowd. He lay down on the trunk and looked up into the sky through the branches. The stars overhead were so close, and he fancied he could see the different colours – he'd seen on TV that some stars are blue, some white, that there are even green and red stars – that night he swore he could see all the colours twinkling above. The tree embraced him, held him, branches like arms with twiggy fingers. Something moved in his chest and he felt his heart open and open and open, busting out, beating in his little ribcage. He was part of the tree and the water, the stars and the music. They all swept together in a whirl of tumbled-up love.

"Hey, Stephen?" Laura calls softly.

"Here." He hears footsteps crunching on snow, and she emerges from shadows under the trees.

They sit together on his tree. Laura fishes in her coat pocket and hands him a mickey of whiskey; he takes a swig, passes it back. The warmth feels good in his throat, his gut. Laura drinks, speaks in a soft voice. "As my Grandpa Smith used to say, there is no passion to be found in playing small." Her pale face gleams in the twilight. "I'll never forget how he put his arm around me and said, Laura, he said, never settle for a life that is less than the one you are capable of living. No, I've never forgotten Grandfather Gallagher's words…"

"Wasn't it Nelson Mandela who said that?" Stephen interrupts. "Something like that, anyway."

Laura waves her hand. "Details, details."

"It'll take more than a little photoshop to convince people you're Nelson Mandela's granddaughter." Stephen reaches for the mickey.

"Well, I need some kind of grandfather to lend me credibility. You inspired me."

"What are you talking about?" He hands the flask back.

"Somehow it changed the way I see you when I found out you have a grandfather. Made you more solid, somehow. Substantial."

It's cold now, icy wind reaches for them across the water.

"I'd better get going to the hospital."

They head back along the trail, barely visible now in the twilight. She puts a hand on his coat sleeve. "Hey, you okay?"

"Hmm?"

"You got quiet all of a sudden."

"I'm fine. Just tired."

"Did it bother you, what I said?"

"What?"

96

"The grandfather thing."

He remembers. "Oh, that I was an insubstantial ghost until you found out I have a rich grandfather? Why would that bother me?" He hugs her with one arm to make it a joking thing.

"That's not what I meant. Or thought. I just…" They cross the footbridge toward the downtown. "I thought I'd invent a grandfather and use his utterances – words of wisdom for the website, the book. You know."

Something uneasy stirs in him but he can't really tell why, and doesn't feel like taking it up. It's probably just being tired, that's all.

She lifts up her face to be kissed, and she murmurs under his lips, "I'm the same. I haven't changed."

Why is she saying that? He pulls back, looks questioning down at her.

Her crooked smile lights her face, but under that brims the sadness she always has, her deep sadness. "I've always invented myself."

His mother won't talk to him. It's ridiculous, something out of high school. He sits for almost an hour making occasional forays into small talk, while she just lies there, staring at the blank screen of the TV she's refused to get hooked up because it costs too much money. The plastic bag containing things he's brought her – fresh pack of gum, packs of cigarettes, two new murder mysteries, clean underwear – sits on the bed, sagging over to one side. At one point she sits up and thrashes around with the blankets, swinging her feet around to go to the bathroom; the bag slides onto the floor with a slithery thud and she steps over it like it's not even there. At least the hospital roommate is gone; it's a small consolation.

Finally Stephen pulls his current book out of his pocket – Philip Wylie's *The End of the Dream (special 1984 edition with Introduction by John Brunner!* printed in 1973) and reads about the world's ending. Pearl picks a book from her bedside table and they both read. Time passes. She stirs, gets out of bed again and grabs her coat.

"I'll come with you," he says and heaves himself to his feet.

They walk down the hall, Stephen hoping it doesn't look to the nurses like what it is: the unwanted son scurrying behind his mother like Prince Philip at a public engagement. When they emerge into the cold air at the north entrance it is fully dark, and he is relieved that there are no other smokers there. He waits until Pearl lights up and has had a couple of drags before speaking.

"I'm sorry about yesterday," he says. "I was way out of line."

Pearl takes another drag, looks sideways at him.

He speaks the rehearsed words. "I hope you can forgive me."

Her jaw clenches. The wind picks up, and she flicks a strand of hair away from her face with one finger. Then, "Oh, what the hell," she says.

They stand there, shivering. Stephen can barely remember seeing sunlight, real sunlight full in the sky. Funny how winter comes on; one is always surprised and bitter, and then comes a time you can't remember it being any other way. Pearl takes another drag. At times like this, Stephen wishes he smoked.

"What the hell," she says again.

"What does that mean?" Stephen keeps his voice light.

"It means, what the hell. I'm a goner. You're you. What's the point in fighting? That's what it means."

Stephen's words come tumbling like falling ice. "So you're not mad any more? I called that lawyer you know. David Pleasant. I called him. But I didn't try calling the… my… your father. I lied when I told you I had. I don't know why." Laura's voice, saying how finding out he had a grandfather made him seem more substantial, flickers through him. Had he lied to his mother out of some longing to be taken seriously?

"Listen," Pearl says, folding her arms around herself and shivering a little, "listen. I've been thinking. I'm it for you, you see. I'm the only family you've got. And that's too hard, right now. I realize that."

Stephen feels the ground tilt. He staggers back and comes up against the doors, cold metal seeping through his coat. I'm not used to it, he thinks. I'm unused to my mother attempting to think the world through from any perspective but her own. To think of me. He is almost afraid to breathe, lest he jar something.

"There's no one else," she says.

"Yeah." The syllable is so poor a response that he winces, but he lets it stand. That's all there is, *yeah*, an amputated yes, vowels fading out in the cold.

"I mean, I know who my bastard family is. But you don't. And I've always known it is better this way." Her voice shakes and she throws her spent cigarette away. "My mother's dead. So you won't know her. I went to the funeral. You were about three then. God."

She's tiny; he notices this as he sometimes does and it is always a surprise, how someone so huge could be so physically small.

"She was younger than I am now when she died," Pearl says. "Seemed old at the time. Not very fucking old now, I can tell you." She lights another cigarette, the flame a brief warmth illuminating her face, eyes dark shadows, downturned mouth to hold the cigarette. She takes three deep drags then tosses the thing into the night sky, a tiny flare. "Let's go inside. It's cold."

Pearl leads the way back in, the hall bright after the night outside. They get to the elevator without another word, and when the doors swish closed his mother turns to him. In the fluorescent light her face sags in a way he's never seen before, dark circles under the eyes, hollows under the cheeks, at her temples. She's so fragile there's something almost childlike about her, something pleading, but she holds herself upright, defying anyone to pity her, rigid.

"So here's the thing," she says, and the warmer air triggers a coughing fit. It's a bad one and as usual she keeps talking through it, broken words hacked out between spasms of dying, like a rehearsal. "I don't want you. Talking to. My bastard father. But I'll tell you." He wishes he could help; his arm reaches out but he can't, she wouldn't want it. They'd only ever hugged when she was drunk. "About your. Father, isn't much. Have to do. Maybe you can. Find him. I don't. He doesn't. Know you exist."

The coughing works itself out, she breathes again. It is his turn to support himself against the elevator wall.

"And then." She straightens up, forces words through her throat. "I want to get the fuck out of here." She puts one small hand on his sleeve. "I want to die at home. Not here, Stephen."

Pearl's oncologist is small and quiet, with a large head and thick, over-sized glasses; Stephen likes him. His voice sits in his throat in a way Stephen finds familiar and comforting; after a while, with a start of embarrassment, he realizes that the doctor reminds him of that character from Bugs Bunny, Marvin the Martian. He keeps hoping the doctor will say, *I wouldn't do that if I were you. I might get very, very angry.* But of course he doesn't. He talks about broccoli.

"Diet can be very important for cancer. Broccoli is good. Also garlic. Vegetables." He looks at Stephen through his giant glasses – a sad, not-very-hopeful look. "Does she eat vegetables?"

"She doesn't really eat much of anything," Stephen says slowly; he's reluctant to disappoint this earnest man. "She likes liquids… tea, coffee. Dewar's, mostly." The doctor nods and makes a note. "Well, she eats white bread and cheese sandwiches. Um, and I suppose you've talked to her about the smoking."

"Yes." A smile flickers. "She resists the possibility of quitting. She expressed this opinion in rather forceful terms."

Stephen smiles back. It's nice to sit here with this man, a man who has experienced Pearl. "Yes. Well, but I suppose, at this stage…"

"Yes. But there is always hope. I have seen some very strange things."

Stephen isn't sure he wants to hear this. It feels too hard. It's too hard to turn it all around, all the feeling and the thinking, this new central fact of his life, his mother's dying. He is horrified to find this refusal rising in him. He pushes it down.

"Do I need to look into home care for her?"

"Well..." the doctor rifles through his notes. "Mmmmm, discharged by the end of the week, after the last radiation treatment. Are you able to be at home with her?"

"Um, yes. I mean, I have a job, I work, but I can be there, spend nights and cook, well, make the cheese sandwiches..."

He's babbling. He's tried to think this through, about living with Pearl at the house. Setting up a bed in the living room so she doesn't have to take stairs to get to the kitchen; except the bathroom is on the second floor – maybe she'd be better off up there...

"The Red Cross has options, and Saint Elizabeth, a certain number of hours a week is covered. Someone to visit when you can't be there. I'd recommend this."

"Sure. That would be nice..."

"For you, not only for your mother. For your peace of mind."

"Yes, peace of mind..."

Stephen stops himself from saying, *peace of mind, that would be nice.* Four days. Then she'd be home.

"I could help." Laura stares at her computer screen with a frown of concentration. "I could go over during the day sometimes."

"That's okay. I'm going to arrange for home care."

"But it might be good to have backup. And it's only, what – fourteen hours a week that's covered? – so I can fill in." She pauses, scanning his face. "That is, if you want me to."

He sits next to her on the couch. "I just don't think it's necessary."

She speaks earnestly. "I used to volunteer for the AIDS Resource Network. I've done this kind of thing before. I'm comfortable with it."

Comfortable with it? Jesus. "No, no, it's not about that, it's..."

He can't picture it, can't see Laura sitting by Pearl's bedside and fetching her drinks or whatever. He doesn't want to see it. He wants to take care of his mother himself; he can do it.

"I'll be fine." She's looking at him with her big eyes. "Look, thanks, that's really generous of you. I will definitely keep it in mind." Her body sinks back a little; he changes the subject. "What are you working on?"

"Drafting some text for the site. Thanks for setting it up for me; you're sweet."

He leans over and looks at the screen. Her headline, in bold, is a quotation from Goethe: *Whatever you can do, or dream you can do, begin it. Boldness has genius, power, and magic in it.* Pretentious, he thinks.

"Do you really think most people have heard of Goethe?"

"But it doesn't matter whether they've heard of him – it's the spirit behind the words that matters."

"Most of those sites you showed me are pretty lowbrow." She's doing it again, setting herself up as something she's not.

She chews on her knuckle. "I know what you mean, but… I don't want to misrepresent who I am."

Laughter bursts out of him in a single gust. "What?"

She looks at him. "The spirit of who I am," she amends.

"Okay then. For a moment I thought you'd abandoned your travels to Tibet and all that. Whew, that's a relief." There's a wary look in her eyes; he'd better shut up. "What else you got?"

She scrolls down. "What do you think of this? It's not quite right yet… *Don't let your beginnings dictate your destination.*"

"Pretty good," he says.

"And a bit about my background. Because I don't have official training as a Life Coach, so…"

"There's official training?"

"Sure. Bogus colleges in the States and stuff. I'm pumping up my psych degree, my work as a yoga instructor, the time I spent teaching at the youth emergency shelter…"

"You should add the volunteering at the Aids Resource place," he says, swinging around to lie on the couch with his legs across her knees.

"Yeah, that too. That's in the list of personal challenges I've met. Like the yoga practice, and the hospice work – "

"You're listing personal challenges?" He can't keep the incredulity from his voice.

She throws him another look. "Yes, I'm listing personal challenges. My approach is that we are all heroic beings, with our own happiness as the moral purpose of our lives."

So that's why she offered to take care of Pearl. He sits up again. He doesn't care to make his dying mother part of Laura's spiritual journey. "Sounds like Ayn Rand."

"Yeah, I guess so, a little. But – "

"You've read Rand?"

"Sure. She's *so* problematic, but I like her message of self-invention…"

"I didn't know you read Rand. I didn't know you read books."

She stares at him. "Of course I read books."

He tries to lighten his tone, make it a joke. "Isn't that what you told me once?"

"I don't know what – "

"You said you could never get through a whole book because as soon as you start reading you get horny and masturbate."

"I never said that!"

Her eyes get so bright when she's angry.

"Well, you did joke about it… Look, I'm not saying you aren't literary – "

"Stephen, I know you're going through a very difficult time, but please try not to pick on me."

A very difficult time. That describes his dying mother?

The anger in him feels good, cleansing, like arousal. Her cheeks are flushed, her hair moves as if full of electricity. He can see her breasts through her thin shirt; he wants to stop fighting, forget everything. Can't he just forget everything? He reaches for her, wanting to kiss her. She jerks away.

"What are you doing?"

He'll keep joking, that's what he'll do. "Look, we haven't had sex since we said we were going steady, and I have to say I'm concerned about the state of our relationship – "

"You can't just grab me whenever you feel like it! I'm really hurt here, Stephen!"

"Oh, you're hurt." It comes out before he can stop it.

"Yes. You're being very hostile. You accused me of stupidity, you rejected my offer to help with your mother – "

"So that's about you now?"

"What?"

"My dying mother is an opportunity to expand your list of personal challenges?"

An awful silence falls between them. He thinks she's about to get up and leave the room, but she snaps the laptop closed and rounds on him instead. "I can't believe you just said that."

"Said what?"

"You heard me." She speaks emphatically.

"Heard what?" He'll stay slippery, he won't engage.

"Don't feign deafness. I'm not sitting on your bad side."

Her eyes are hard points of light; the blades are out now, he thinks, the blades are drawn.

"Look, my mother is coming home in four days. That's all I can deal with right now."

"And I offered to help with that and you just ignored me!"

Stephen feels the smile on his lips. He knows this happens – idiotically, when he is angry, he starts smiling – he hates it about himself. It happens whenever he fights with Pearl, and she twits him about it, idiotic smile, crazy to smile at someone when you want to kill them. *Go ahead, psycho smiler,* she used to say. *Go ahead, make my day.* He wants to hurt Laura, break through her professional restraint. He wants a fight.

"Is this about my grandfather?" he says through his teeth.

"What?"

"Is this about getting money from me, from my grandfather?"

"I never asked for that!" She's thrown her head back; two spots of red colour her cheeks.

"Are you sleeping with me," he says softly, "to get money for your phony life?"

She dives for him, slapping his face, his head, sending his glasses flying. It's such a relief that he almost laughs. He grabs her wrists, as gently as he can. She's fighting, twisting and keening – gets on top of him – rips one hand free, slaps his face. Slaps him again. He manages to flip over, pinning her, but she wriggles off the couch. He hangs onto her wrist and she twists her head to bite him, hard. Stephen grunts and lets go; she springs to her feet, panting. He crouches, ready for her to fly at him again. But she just stares at him. Her face crumples. She runs into her bedroom and slams the door.

He's filled with energy, the adrenaline of the fight. His hand is bleeding, he finds his glasses halfway across the floor. No sound from her room.

He has to get out of this place, the close air, the tumbled laptop. He swings his coat over his shoulders and goes outside, slamming the door.

The cold air feels good. It's cleansing, this feeling. His feet pound, he could run. His hand throbs – he sucks at it, the blood. Fragments of the fight come back. *You rejected me,* Laura'd said of her phony offer to help with his mother. As if that was the point – making sure she got attention. She was so self-absorbed she couldn't even understand what he was going through.

So many fights with his mother ended like this: him leaving, playing over the words again and again in his mind. Improving on things he could have said, getting angry all over again at her accusations. He'd walk around and when he got back home, the air would have cleared. He and Pearl never talked of their fights. They happened, they were over. That's all. Sometimes he saw a pattern in it, unrelated to any real reason for fighting; periodically his mother would push him until he lost it. She needed the fights somehow.

He knows from experience, though, that most other people want to work things out after a fight. Girlfriends especially. When he gets home he'll have to "work things out" with Laura. Apologize, probably. Like for that crack about the money and her phony life. He's never been in a physical fight with a girl before; it's sort of exciting that she flew at him. But really, he started it.

He started it.

The euphoria sinks away as if someone pulled a plug. An image of returning to the apartment to find her dead, having killed herself, flashes through him. She'd had a horrible childhood. Maybe she can't handle this.

It would be as if he'd killed her.

He's come to the foot of the courthouse hill, climbs the steep sweep of park to the top. Some kids pant up and down the slope, sliding, screaming, slipping between tree trunks. Stephen pauses, the city spread out before him, lights cold in the night. Trees rise like black columns between him and the light.

All that self-help stuff is Laura's survival. He'd attacked that, her life raft, the thing she'd built to stay alive.

He flings himself down onto the snow. It's packed almost to ice and he skids headfirst, gaining momentum; he slides and tumbles, half laughing, his breath plunged from his lungs in rhythm with his falling. The world is upside down, then the sky spreads above him; it's fast, it wheels and jolts until with a burst he comes up against a tree trunk, protected with old car tires. He lies there, exhilarated, looking for stars, but he can't see through the branches, the clouds. Snow has made its way up his back, under his coat. A crazy carpet careens toward him with two squealing kids. He walks back to the apartment.

Laura's door is still closed. He taps softly.

"Go away."

Her voice is choked. The last shreds of exhilaration leave him, remorse kicks him in the gut. "Laura, I'm sorry."

Nothing.

"Are you okay?"

"Leave me alone."

He clears his throat. "Okay. I'll go for a walk." Maybe she's afraid of him now; yes, she probably is. Good work, Stephen, he tells himself. Good fucking job. "I'm, look, I'm sorry, okay? I'll come back later. Maybe we can talk then?" No answer. "Okay then. See you in a bit." He pauses. "I'm really sorry."

He heads downtown. Street lights flood the sidewalk, people reel in and out of bars. It's Friday night, he realizes, getting late, he's lost track. His feet take him to the East Wind Café. He'll see if Dieter's there and has time for a game of chess; that'll clear his head.

The place is crowded, a band just getting started, some kind of emo thing. Dieter looms behind the bar. He waves Stephen in. "Hey, man. Want a drink?"

"Sure." Dieter gets a Tiger for Stephen. "Too bad it's so busy. I was hoping for a game."

"Well, thanks for wishing prosperity on my business." Dieter grins as he hands Stephen a pint glass. Stephen moves to a table in the corner, the table that has the chess board painted on it.

He likes this about the East Wind – you can just come in here and sit, it doesn't matter. There's almost always live music. It's where a lot of the beautiful young things hang out, but old guys come in too, like Spider who passed away last year, the world's oldest punk; or that recovering heroin musician guy. Lots of self-styled intellectuals, lots of pretty girls. You can always find someone to talk to if you don't want to be alone. He wishes again that Dieter weren't working, gulps at his beer, trying to drown the coldness inside himself. His hand hurts where Laura bit it, but it's stopped bleeding. He hopes it gets infected. He deserves it.

After another swig, he pulls up the little box from its place on the floor and begins to lay out the pieces. Someone will play him; it usually happens this way. He's almost done when a young guy, whippet-thin, starts setting up an easel with a half-finished canvas on it.

"You don't mind?" he asks. "Light's good in this corner."

"That's fine." Stephen's seen the painter before; he likes to work to live music, often breaking into wild movement, loaded paintbrush arcing dangerously through the dancers. Stephen finishes lining up the pieces and sits back, nursing his beer, waiting. Yeah, he's pretty much the oldest guy here tonight, excepting Dieter. Guys with metal in their faces and hemp chokers around their necks. Only two girls so far, dressed in the inevitable black and dancing with each other while the boys sway on the edges, worshipping the all-guy band hunched over their instruments; the lead singer screams into the mic.

Stephen is halfway through his beer when a man walks through the door, a middle-aged guy in a trench. Broad shoulders, clean cut. He hesitates at the entrance, scanning the crowd, makes his way to the bar. He and Dieter talk close against the noise. Stephen sees Dieter shake his head, say something, but the man is already walking away, wading through the boys, skirting the dancing girls but throwing them a quick, searching glance. Stephen hopes he's not a cop – they're way over capacity and pot smokers throng the patio. But then the man sees Stephen in the corner. He heads toward him, sitting uninvited at the table.

"I'm looking for my daughter," he yells over the throb of the music. "Her name's Amy."

"Are you a cop?" Stephen asks.

The man looks at him with disgust. "I'm her father. She comes here; do you know her?"

The man drums his fingers on the table, but under his authority and arrogance lurk hurt and fear. Stephen's pretty sure he knows the girl. "Long black hair?" he asks. "Combat boots? She's kinda small?"

"That's the one."

Yes, Stephen knows her. Smart girl, younger than she looks but tough. He eyes the man. "Yeah, she comes in here all the time. Why?"

"Do you think she'll come here tonight?"

Stephen shrugs. "Probably." The man's eyes stray to the painter, to the swirls of stars spiraling over the canvas, a tree reaching abstract arms to a pale moon. "You play chess?"

The man rakes his eyes back to Stephen, contempt ringing in the air. "Yes." His cheeks are pink with cold and faintly stubbled grey.

Stephen feels pleasure seeping through his bones: an opponent, someone he hasn't played before. He gestures at the board. The man's eyes pull down to the pieces, the pristine, irresistible black-and-white rows.

"She comes in here most nights," Stephen says. "Could play while you wait."

The man takes off his hat; he's balding. "She's run away from home." Stephen starts to feel sorry for him, but then he goes on, "Ungrateful little prick. Sure."

The man moves his chair so he has a clear view of the entrance to the café, and shrugs off his coat. Then he actually rolls up his sleeves, and Stephen sits up straighter. A game. It will cleanse him, cleanse everything, take this heavy anger and guilt off his shoulders and replace it with purity, strategy, calculation, the perfection of a game of chess.

"White?" Stephen offers.

106

"Black. I play retaliation best."

Stephen opens by sending out his king's pawn. The man meets him. Stephen plays his king's bishop's pawn in the classic nineteenth-century move. It's a swashbuckling, brazen strategy, offering black a "free" piece in exchange for the position.

"King's gambit," the man says dismissively, and knocks Stephen's bishop's pawn off the board.

Stephen sends out his knight. The man places his bishop in front of his king, moving decisively, placing his pieces with a bang. Stephen knows that the man underestimates him, believes that he will protect his white king with his pawn, take the bishop with his knight, thus leaving his own king open to an attack by the black queen. So he sends out his king's rook's pawn. It's a cocky move, weakening his own king's side in order to stymie black's offensive potential.

The man plays his knight, Stephen answers with his queen's pawn; he loves playing these wild, open positions. The man sends out his queen's pawn and Stephen, wondering if he's being a bit dense, takes the black pawn with his dark-squared bishop.

The man sits up, glancing at Stephen through dim light, the screaming guitars. He considers a moment, recognizing that his opponent has seen through his initial strategy, is perhaps better than he had thought. Good, Stephen thinks. He takes Stephen's king's pawn with his queen's, threatening Stephen's knight. So Stephen sends his knight over the man's pawn, leaping toward the black king.

The man counters with his own knight. They are side-by-side now, face to face on the board, both in weak positions. The music pounds, the girls dance, arms windmilling like they're weaving themselves something out of air. The painter works a sun across the sky. Stephen takes the bishop's pawn, but the man ignores the threat on his queen and rook, and instead takes a pawn and checks Stephen's king.

Stephen considers his next move. When he looks up the man is staring at the door, then his eyes roam across the dancers, the swaying shoreline of slender, androgynous boys, the painter. "Something wrong with you guys," he says, his pale eyes coming back to Stephen.

"*You* guys?"

"It's not that you're feminine," the man goes on. "It's more like... you constantly apologize for being men."

Always cultivate contempt for your opponent, Stephen thinks; that Bobby Fischer maxim. "I'm not them," he says, but the man isn't listening, he's scanning the crowd. Miserably, Stephen takes the black bishop with his

107

rook. He's playing badly, he knows that. The man now has three free pieces and a checking move at his disposal; he should win this game, now. Anguish rocks through Stephen's body. He wishes everything were different, everything: this game, Laura's hurt, his mother's disease, he himself especially; everything, all of it. But you have to keep going, keep playing, don't you? Maybe the man will overlook something. He's arrogant enough.

The man takes Stephen's rook with his queen, of course, and Stephen blocks with his pawn. The man takes Stephen's bishop with a knight.

"They're not even my generation," Stephen says.

"What? How old are you?"

"Thirty."

The man stares. "Really? Thirty?"

"People generally say I read younger." It's true and it drives Stephen nuts. He can't retaliate with his pawn; it's pinned, protecting his king, so he takes the black king's pawn with his queen's pawn. At least that will secure any offensive advantage he had left. "I fought in the Iraq war," he adds.

"You what?" the man yells over a sudden surge in sound. He takes a pawn with his queen, says, "Check!"

"I said, I fought in the war in Iraq. In 2003." The man thinks he's going to force Stephen into a king's walk. "Got discharged for insubordination." Stephen moves his king in front of his queen.

The man stares at him. "Canada didn't fight in Iraq," he says. Stephen knows he thinks the game is over, thinks he's moving in for the kill. The man sends his queen to king's bishop seven. "Check," he says again.

"I was with the forces in Afghanistan; we got transferred." Why is he lying? Who cares if this guy doesn't think he's a man? Instead of hiding his king in the corner – among his queen, pawns, the knight and castle – he takes his king out onto the board.

The man moves his queen diagonally to block Stephen. "Check!"

"Yeah, okay. I lied about Iraq," Stephen says, but at that moment the man's head snaps to the doorway. Stephen twists to look – the Amy girl is walking in. She sees the man and pauses a split second, but instead of running away she strides across the room to the chess game.

"Are you following me?"

"Sweetheart..." The man's voice is different, almost tender.

"I said, are you following me?"

"I got here first," the man points out.

"Well, get away from me. I'm sixteen, I can live where I want."

His voice rises. "And I'm your father and I might have something to say about that."

Stephen eases his chair back from the table, trying to get out from under the private venom. He hopes they finish the game, though. He'd dearly love to beat this guy, this confident father, this prick.

"Bryce is a nice guy!"

"If you call *nice* dropping out of high school to deal pot." The man stands up and tries to take the girl's arm. "Look, just come home, okay, sweetie?"

"Fuck you!" She snatches her arm away; Stephen thinks she might spit. "Mom says it's okay to move in with Bryce."

The man grabs at the air in a bizarre, almost comical gesture of frustration. "She's just playing good cop!"

"Not much of a stretch, with you as a dad!"

"We'll see about that."

Stephen wonders what it would be like to have two parents fighting over you. He'd moved out when he was sixteen, too. Pearl hadn't minded; they'd actually gotten along better after that.

"You don't even pay your fucking child support," the girl is screaming. Oh. Divorced.

The girl turns and flees the café, and the man scrambles for his coat and hat. He catches up with her on the sidewalk; Stephen can see them through the window gesticulating at each other. He looks back down at the game. He can see where it's going; the man is snatching defeat from the jaws of victory, playing too arrogantly, underestimating his opponent. Too bad. He finishes his beer and is about to sweep the pieces back into their box when the man suddenly appears back at the table. "Let's finish."

"What?"

"She took off." The man sits down, wiping his brow. "Her mom says she can move in with the scum, she can move in with the scum. Let's finish the game."

Stephen stares at him. "You're kidding."

"She's sixteen, she can do what she wants to, right? Just like her Mom says. I'm just her father." He turns and looks at the door with what might be longing, Stephen isn't sure; but the girl is gone. The man rubs his hand over his head. "Well, she'll come crying to me when that piece of shit dumps her. Your move."

Stephen's sure the man will see it now, how he's going to be beaten – it's obvious. But the man goes on talking. "*Bryce.*" He spits the name, gives it a lisp. "He's just like all the rest of you in this goddamn place. Drug-addled conformist individualists."

"Conformist individualists," Stephen repeats. "I like that."

"I'm a high school teacher; I'm familiar with the type."

That explains his know-all attitude. "Where?" Stephen asks curiously. The man names a south-end school. "Tough place."

"You're telling me. Your move, let's go."

"They got a chess club at your school?" Stephen asks.

"You kidding?"

There's something about the man Stephen almost likes, now that victory is certain. He's almost sad to finish him, almost regretful when he moves his bishop out to stand between the man's queen and his own king. The man moves his queen's knight's pawn up to threaten Stephen's pinned bishop; incredibly, he still doesn't see it, the open road. Stephen would have hated the man if he himself were the one being beaten. He sends his queen all the way to the other side of the board, face-to-face with the man's king.

"Checkmate."

He reads the dawning realization in the man's eyes as he sees how Stephen has been playing him. It has been, Stephen thinks, an ugly game. "Good game," he says, holding out his hand, but the man won't shake, leaves the café practically blindsiding the dancers. That's poor form, Stephen thinks. Even when you get slaughtered, you still shake hands.

Laura's in the kitchen when he gets home. He hangs by the door. "Hello?"

A pause, then, "Hello."

He kicks off his boots and walks into the kitchen with his coat.

"Laura, I'm sorry."

"I'm sorry too."

He feels appalled. "No! It was me, it was my fault."

She sits, head bent, staring at the table. "You hate that I'm inventing things for the website."

Check. His mind races, wondering what to say, how to be honest. "Look, it's none of my business. I think..." He sits. He'll try to work this out, he owes Laura that much. "Okay. Something about lying..." Shit, that sounds accusatory. "Not that you're lying..."

"Well, I am." She looks up at him.

"Okay, but, well, it's understandable..." This is ridiculous. "Look, I guess I just don't understand why you're doing it."

"I understand why you don't like it."

"You do?"

"It's like your mother. The way she always lied to you." He stares at her blankly. "About your father."

He sits back in his chair so suddenly it almost tips over backwards. "What the fuck."

"It's true, isn't it? You told me about that. The lists that never went anywhere."

He can't remember telling her that. It's none of her business. "Don't..." he begins. He stops, tries to soften. "I don't really want to be psychoanalyzed right now," he says. Check.

They sit there at the kitchen table. The room fills with silence, like drowning in a flood. Stephen can't move, his tipped chair wavers on two legs, adrift. Humming builds in his ears, he can't breathe.

It's Laura who speaks first, she's the brave one, she brings the air back. "Why do you think we keep fighting like this?"

"I don't know." It comes out as he releases his breath, a groan. He tips his chair back to the level and buries his face in his hands. "I don't know."

"Maybe it's what we know how to do best."

"Well, I don't like it." That's a bit of a lie, isn't it? He sort of likes it; when they fight he feels clear, strong, reckless. But he doesn't want to like it. That's true. He sits and sweats inside his coat; Laura's face grows still.

"When I was little..." she begins, then stops. "Maybe if I tell you... you'll see why I build things. Fabricate. My mother was not all there, you know?"

Stephen nods, miserable. "I know." *I'm a total asshole,* he thinks. *I don't deserve to be happy ever again.*

"Anyway. She wasn't very... compassionate. And I remember the first time I got outside myself, realized that this wasn't how things had to be." She's looking at the table again and with one hand traces a pattern on the surface, over and over. "We were taking a bus to Toronto and I was maybe seven. In the lineup my mother did what she always did, called attention to herself and to me. Coughing loudly, yelling at me, telling me not to sit down because it's dirty, *You're so stupid!* I knew people were looking at us and I felt ashamed. I remember feeling really floaty. And then we got on the bus, and I threw up on myself. She started yelling, *What'd you do that for? What'd you do that for? You didn't eat nothing today – what'd you do that for?* I reached for her but she said *Don't touch me, look at you! Get some wipes from the bathroom, clean yourself up!* I got up and had to hold my T-shirt so it wouldn't dribble, and I walked all the way up the aisle and people were looking at me. I figured they thought I was a retard, just like my mother. I tried to clean my shirt in the bathroom but there was no water, only toilet paper, and it smelled bad. When I got back my mother said *I'm not sitting with you now, you stink! Stop crying, you're not a baby.*

111

No, sit over there. I got up, and then this woman across the aisle said, *Hey, you can sit with me.* I looked at my mother because she said I shouldn't talk to strangers or they'd rape me."

Laura stops. Stephen wonders if she's crying; the story's unbearable. But she continues.

"The woman looks nice and my mother's there, so it's okay, right? I sit with her and she starts talking to my mother over my head, saying, *You've got a really pretty girl, you know that? And what a nice kid.* My mother says, *Yeah, she's okay* but I can see she's pleased. And then this woman, I can't believe it, she gives me some trail mix to eat, and some water, and then she actually gets a T-shirt out of her bag and gives it to me. My mother tells me not to take it, but the woman insists. I sit with her for the rest of the trip and she talks to me like I'm a person. I tell her I like horses, and about TV shows, and reading, stuff like that. And when we get off the bus, she whispers to me, *Don't forget, you are a wonderful little girl.*" Laura's voice breaks. "*You really are. No matter what anyone says.*"

"You are, you are wonderful," Stephen says. He hates himself so much he can barely contain it. "You are."

Laura and Stephen sit and the imagined stench of bus and vomit slowly drains out of the room. Stephen stirs, shrugs off his heavy coat. Laura's eyelids flicker, she looks so tired.

He reaches out and takes her hand.

"People couldn't handle that," she says so quietly that he leans in to hear. "That little girl, that person. Meeting that woman gave me... a key, or a bit of light. And later, I found the support groups I needed, and, you know. The strength to invent myself." Stephen curls his fingers between hers. "That's what I'm giving people. The chance to invent themselves."

He casts around for something to say. "I don't know how you survived that."

"A person with a strong enough why can bear almost any how."

"That's good."

"Oh," Laura shrugs, "it's Nietzsche."

"Well, it's still good."

"They print it on Celestial Seasoning herbal tea boxes."

"Oh. Well, still..."

"It's good." She begins to smile.

It's weird, going to the hospital with Laura. He's so used to going on his own. Stephen's driving, even though he has a momentary impulse to ask Laura to take the wheel. They stop at Burger King for fast food, drive-through, and the line is slow. As they wait, jerking forward by intervals, he takes a sidelong look at her face. Her profile, with its firm little chin and cute nose, is sculpted, shadowed, still.

This will be the first time Laura meets Pearl. This is also supposed to be the time Pearl tells Stephen about his father. The whole thing is probably a really bad idea.

"So Saint Elizabeth Health Care has arranged for a home care person," he says.

"Hmm?" She turns to him slowly, a trifle dreamily, then, "Yes. Saint Elizabeth."

"So she's got someone there while I'm at work, during the days, for a few hours anyway."

"And on weekends."

She's being patient with him. "I've already said all this, haven't I?"

"Yes, but that's okay. Go over it as often as you need to. Probably makes you feel better."

They finally make it to the window, place their order, and park to eat. Laura knows of his dislike of going into fast food restaurants. He hates sitting in those places – too much like too many times when he was a kid. Pearl had loved going to fast food joints; he'd grown up on Burger King, McDonald's, Wendy's, the names and menus blur together.

Knowing now that his mother was born a rich kid, he wonders how much of this was her rebellion, a deliberate trashiness. How much of his life has been circumscribed by her need to escape the life she'd been born into?

He rolls down the window and pleases himself by a perfect toss of the wrappings into the garbage can.

"I still worry it'll be too much," Laura says as they head to the hospital. "Too much for you."

"I'll be fine."

She puts her hand on his knee. "Of course you'll be *fine*. But maybe you don't have to do all of it. Doesn't she have any friends?"

"Yeah, she has friends." Stephen thinks of them: a couple of the staff at the seniors' facility; a guy who is a regular at Pearl's favourite bar; the boyfriends who've come and gone. Who was the last one? Stephen can't remember his name; it'd been a while, a couple of years anyway since anyone serious. That woman he's pretty sure his mother had been seeing, three or four years ago – a carpenter – he'd never known her name. Come to think of it, she kind of reminds him of Cheryl. He shudders.

"Cold?"

"No. Just thinking of Mom's friends."

She sighs. "I wish you'd let me help."

"We've been through this." He steels himself for an argument.

"I know. But still… I could help, Stephen."

"Wait until you meet her. Your enthusiasm may flag."

When they get to the hospital Pearl is out of her room, and Stephen leads the way down the chilly halls to the illicit smoking area. There's Pearl and a few others, including Mary, the tracheotomy patient, smoking through her wrinkled yellow throat.

"Hey Mom. Mary." Stephen doesn't know the names of the others. "Mom, this is Laura." This is going to go badly, he knows it; really, really badly.

"Hi, Pearl," Laura says. Oh God, she's going to call his mother *Pearl*.

Pearl draws a deep lungful of smoke and exhales, squinting at Laura through the cloud. "Hello," she says. "Laura."

"Mom's fallen in with a hard crowd," Stephen says to Laura, gesturing at the assembled wrecks of humanity. "The tough kids." An old man in a bathrobe with skinny sticks for legs hacks out a laugh.

"They're busting me out of here," Pearl says to the smokers. "Next week."

"Next week?" wheezes an enormous lady sitting on a plastic chair. "That's soon."

"Yes, that's soon," murmur a couple of the others. In the sick dim glare of the parking lot lights, in the scudding snow, they look medieval, wrapped in bandages and robes, some leaning on crutches.

"Yes, Tuesday. On Tuesday I shall go home, where every third thought shall be my grave." Pearl draws heavily on her smoke, the ember lighting her face.

"Um, hey," Laura says softly to Pearl, "do you think I could bum a smoke?" Pearl looks at her. "I'll bring you a pack next time I come," Laura smiles, "if you like."

"A smoke? Sure. Sure, you can have a smoke." Pearl takes a pack out of her bathrobe pocket and flips the lid open; she fishes a lighter from her pocket and lights Laura's cigarette, a curiously chivalrous gesture. Stephen watches the two women in the glare of the flame, their eyes meeting, crinkling in smiles at each other. He didn't know Laura smoked.

"Thanks," Laura says, flipping her hair.

"What was that supposed to mean?" Stephen asks.

"What?" his mother snaps.

He shifts from foot to foot. "Where every third thought shall be my grave." He senses Laura looking at him, knows she's thinking *be nice to your dying mother.* He has no patience for it. "What's that supposed to mean?"

The old man shuffles toward the door. "Good night, ladies. Gent," he says with a cheery wave, and Stephen lunges to hold the heavy door open for him.

"Well, Stephen," Pearl says, gesturing with her cigarette, "other than the obvious fact that I am going home to die, I was quoting Shakespeare. *The Tempest.* Someone says that, I forget who. Prospero?"

"Yeah. Prospero," Stephen says.

Laura jumps in. "I think you're right, he says that near the end."

I'm spoiling for a fight again, Stephen realizes. He keeps his grip on the cold metal of the door handle, willing himself to silence, to patience. He hates this, hates that his mother knows she's dying and insists on the fact of it, casting herself as the noble martyr. And yet would he want it any other way, some Hollywood version of reconciliation and sweetness? Be quiet, he tells himself. Be quiet.

"Have you read that book on Shakespeare everyone's talking about?" Laura's saying to Pearl. "It's on the bestseller list – "

"Oh, I know the one you mean. I read a review."

"Just what the world needs," Stephen hears himself saying. "Another book on Shakespeare."

"I thought it was interesting, though," says Laura. "They're speculating that the plays were actually written by the troupe, and Shakespeare was the front man, a brilliant poet and all that, good for impromptu verse at the pub – "

"*The Shakespeare Conspiracy,*" Stephen remembers.

"Is that by the *Da Vinci Code* guy?" the fat woman wonders, kicking her feet like a little girl in her chair.

"No, I wouldn't think so," Stephen answers.

Pearl snorts.

"I think it is. *The Shakespeare Conspiracy,*" the woman insists. "I think it's by the *Da Vinci Code* guy."

"Sure." Pearl rolls her eyes and Laura stifles a laugh. The tracheotomy lady lets out a terrifying rattling wheeze and starts fiddling with her wheelchair. Stephen opens the door for her and she wheels past him into the hospital, clipping the toes of his boots. When he turns back into the gusting wind, Pearl's reaching out and tucking a piece of Laura's hair behind her ear. "If you ask me," she says, "it's pretty obvious. A collection of drunks wrote most of those plays. I mean, look at Falstaff."

"But what about *The Tempest* being Shakespeare's swan song and all that?" Stephen puts in. He thinks of *The Tempest* as his play. His mother used to read it to him when he was a kid. She made it fun, especially the Caliban scenes; she did all the voices. He likes the idea of Shakespeare writing it. It seems important that he had, that he'd said farewell.

"Stephen wants to believe in Shakespeare," Pearl says, "like some people want to believe in God."

Stephen keeps his mouth shut.

The women finish their cigarettes and they all troop inside; Pearl takes the lead, followed by Laura, Stephen in the rear. Pearl's walk is painfully slow; her shoulder blades show through her dressing gown, she's so thin now.

"Your girlfriend's cute," she says, looking back at Stephen with a dirty laugh, then goes on to Laura, "I named him after a character in *The Tempest*, you know. Stephano, the drunken butler." She mimes drinking, slurring the words, "This is a very scurvy tune to sing at a man's funeral." She raises her invisible bottle in a toast to Stephen. Their eyes meet, she spits the words. "Well, here's my comfort!" With another laugh she turns the corner into her room, pretending to be drunk.

By God, if she wasn't dying, he'd kill her.

He and Laura get Pearl settled in the bed; she needs more help now, getting up, pulling at the blankets. Laura keeps trying to meet his eyes, but he can't look at her, and finally she retreats to perch on the windowsill.

"I thought Stephen was my father's name," he mutters once his mother is settled. Still no roommate – he wonders if she's died. He sits in a chair, grateful for the little wheeled table separating him from Pearl. "Didn't you tell me that once?" He glares at her. "That my father's name was Stephen?"

Pearl throws her head back. "What are you sitting there for?" she snaps. "Come around to this side so you can give me a foot rub."

There's a strained silence. Then Laura says, "I'd be happy to do that, Pearl. If you don't mind me. I give pretty good foot rubs."

Stephen finally looks at her, and to his astonishment she isn't looking at him with disgust. Her eyes are full of sorrow. She knows that Pearl is baiting Stephen, and she knows that if he moves to the other side of the bed his deaf ear will be towards his mother. She knows that Stephen is being a shit and that he is ashamed. Laura sees it all. Gratitude floods him.

"It's okay," he says. "It's okay. She likes how I do it."

He drags the chair around and rubs his mother's feet. Pearl and Laura keep talking and he has to keep saying **pardon** and **what** and sometimes just pretend that he's understood what they were saying. Pearl's telling Laura how fat he'd been as a boy. "He was fat," she says. "My God, that boy was fat. And he needed glasses from Grade Two on. So there he is, this fat kid with glasses, oh boy."

"Yeah, I was a real winner," Stephen plays along. His mother's feet are puffy, the skin distended with fluid. He works at them with his thumbs, trying to send the puffiness back up the legs, back into the lymph system where it belongs. He wonders if it's the radiation that has done this, or just the fact of her being in bed much of the time.

Suddenly he's aware that Pearl knows he's thinking of her feet, that she feels embarrassed. She says something he can't hear, he says *pardon*, and she snaps, "Real beauts, aren't they?" She's gazing at the swollen things with sadness, disgust, a tension around her eyes and mouth.

"They're fine," he says, trying to smile. "They're fine."

"Anyway," Pearl continues more loudly, "when he was oh, I don't know, seventeen, he got contact lenses – "

"And I lost some weight," Stephen puts in, knowing what comes next.

"... and he finally lost weight. Stopped eating chips or whatever. The no-chip diet. Went to Toronto to university."

He remembers the feelings of leaving: excited, determined, epically tragic. Because he'd thought this was it, he was going to make the break from that small town and his mother, go to the city and find out who he could be, on his own. He remembers taking the bus down, finding his residence room, realizing that no one knew him from before. He wrote poems, got two published in a student paper. People thought he was cool. He was going to stay in the city for the rest of his life.

"And there he was," Pearl goes on. "Suddenly he was quite the thing."

"He still is," Laura says. Stephen looks at her with surprise. She smiles and winks at him.

"Oh, that's nice," Pearl sneers, and Laura laughs.

It's like she gets it, Stephen thinks. It's like she gets the fluctuation of it, how Pearl is with him, meanness and tenderness, the see-saw. She's so tiny sitting there, her blonde curly hair and her little gossamer-thread emerald-coloured sweater, her stripey tights, her cut-off skirt and boots, but her eyes are older, she isn't new at this. *Where did you come from?* he wants to ask suddenly. But he just ducks his head and works at his mother's feet.

"Is that too hard?"

"No, that's great, that's great. You're good at that. He's good at that, Laura, that's one thing." She turns back to Stephen. "Maybe that's how you got those girls in Toronto."

Stephen's first year away had been a confusion, a bewilderment of girls.

"They liked my eyes." He'd discovered at eighteen that he had deep blue, almost violet eyes ringed with black lashes, discovered that girls were drawn almost irresistibly to these eyes.

"Which is why it's beyond me that you insist on wearing those awful goddamn glasses," Pearl says.

One night, in his second year at university, his mother called him. It was late. She was crying. She missed him, she wanted to die. He felt angry and guilty, so guilty, and he hung up the phone. But it was as if that call made all the light change. It took another year for his momentum to totally run out; that, and getting busted for writing essays for other students. Some dimwit handed in the envelope containing not only the paid-for essay, but also Stephen's cover letter and invoice.

He'd gotten on the bus and gone back north to town, to figure out where to go next. And stayed. Nine years, now.

"I've told you. Contacts hurt – my eyeballs get all dried out or something."

"Then use drops. Not *that* hard, Jesus, leave my toes on my foot for the love of God."

"Sorry."

"You've got my eyes."

"It's true," Laura puts in. "He does have your eyes."

"A real hit with the ladies," Pearl says.

Stephen can feel the craving in his mother's body, practically see the cigarette materialize in her hand. She gestures into the air, fingers curled. Something sparks in the air between the two women. Stephen speaks quickly. "Also, I didn't talk much."

Laura and Pearl look steadily into each other's eyes. Stephen works at his mother's feet. After a moment Laura looks at him across the bed, says something and he has to say *pardon* again. She repeats, "You didn't talk?"

"Not much."

"That must have been a refreshing change," Pearl says.

"I think they interpreted my silence as depth, instead of terrified incomprehension." He laughs, a dry sound. Laura laughs with him.

"Do you mind not doing that?" Pearl snaps.

"Sorry, what?"

"You're just going over the same place over and over." Pearl pulls her feet back, hides them under the covers. "You're not paying attention."

"Sorry. I'm making him talk to me." Laura stands.

"You headed out?" Stephen says.

"Yes – sorry – I didn't tell you. I have a counseling session."

"I'll drive you and come back here – " He begins to rise.

"No, it's okay. I'll walk. I'd like to."

He doesn't want her to leave. "Don't be silly."

Pearl says nothing, just looks from one to the other, a tight smile on her face.

"I'm not being silly. Really, I'd like to walk home. It's a nice night."

Stephen looks pointedly out the window at the blowing snow. "I'd feel better if you took the car."

"It's okay."

"I'm serious! You take the car, it's a deal. I'll see you later."

"Yeah," Pearl says loudly. "Take my car."

Silence. Laura hesitates, then nods, first at Pearl, then Stephen. "I'll be at the apartment." She comes around the bed to him. There's an awkward moment where she leans in to kiss him and he doesn't expect it; he flinches, and feeling the mean laugh inside Pearl, he flushes like a teenager. Laura whispers into his good ear, "I'll see you at home," takes the proffered car keys, tells Pearl how nice it's been meeting her, and is gone.

Stephen stands unseeing in front of the cold glass of the window.

"She seems nice." Pearl's voice is dangerously pleasant.

"She is." He doesn't turn around.

"A little young for you."

"She's twenty-four."

"And you're thirty."

Stephen glares over his shoulder. "Well, she's smart."

"And cute."

"So she's cute. So what."

"It won't last," Pearl says.

He blows air out his nose, stares at her for a strangled moment. Then he takes his glasses off and reflexively cleans them on his shirt. His mother is right. It probably won't last. God, he hates her sometimes.

"It's nice," he says, "for now."

There's a silence, then Pearl says, "I got a card from work today."

"Really?"

She hands him a card with a lavender heart on the cover, lace and dried flowers glued around it. "They all signed it. Staff, geezers and all. Look."

Signatures fill the inside – firm ones from the staff, and then a variety of copperplate old-people's signatures, some shaky beyond reading. Lots of little notes. *We miss you,* and *It's not the same without you.* One signed Mrs. Henderson: *See you soon in the place where there is no more parting.* And a Mr. Mulligan wrote in tiny, careful letters, *It's not fair. I'm ninety-four.*

119

I wish I could give you all my years, my dear dear girl. Remember the Trilliums.

"What are the trilliums?" Stephen asks. He must keep down the lump in his throat.

"Mr. Mulligan? I took him for a drive last spring. The woods were white with them."

That was nice of his mother, he thinks, to take this old man out for a drive in spring. He wonders what other things there are, things he doesn't know about her. Another silence creeps in, until Pearl interrupts it. "I want a smoke."

"Want to go out again?"

"No. I'm too fucking tired." She takes a deep shuddering breath, lets it out. "Never thought I'd be too tired to smoke."

"You're not too tired to smoke. You're too tired to walk outside. Soon you'll be home and you can smoke your head off." He hopes this will cheer her, but instead she goes into him.

"Look at you! Thirty years old and going out with this little blonde cheerleader. It's supposed to be my fault, I suppose. If she really is your girlfriend. I wouldn't put it past you to hire some little missy thing to pretend, just to drive me nuts."

"I thought you liked her!" he protests.

"Sure, I like her. But not as your goddamn girlfriend."

"Oh, come on."

"She'll dump you in three seconds flat. She's probably enamoured with the tragedy of it all – you with the dying mother and all that."

"Look, I'd appreciate it if you... Just try to be nice, or polite, or something."

"So now you're calling me impolite."

"Well, you are."

"Lessons from the master."

He jumps up, starts pacing. "It's just... you never let it go."

"Let what go?"

"Anything!"

He's almost shouting, but she doesn't raise her voice. She sits there, a queen on her bed. "I can't think about everything that comes out of my mouth. That's not how people work. You're too sensitive. I can't think about every goddamn word before saying it – no one can – except maybe you, Saint Stephen."

"Let's not descend to name-calling, okay?"

Pearl folds her arms across her chest, blue eyes burning into him.

120

"Stephano, my drunken butler. I love it when you try to tell me how to be a human being."

He thinks how strange it is that she isn't coughing. Maybe it's the steroids they're giving her. His whole life their conversations have been punctuated by coughing fits: wheezing, red-faced, shaking, nearly puking, terrible, lung-spastic fits. But tonight she just talks, glares and talks. No coughing, no break.

He needs to apologize and sweep the whole thing under. He takes a deep breath.

"I think you should just go home," Pearl says.

He lets the breath out. She's forgotten. She's forgotten her promise.

"You were going to tell me about my father."

Her eyes narrow, and a gleam of something – pleasure, cruelty, fear, he can't tell what – goes through the blueness.

"All right, then." She spends a bit of time arranging the sheets. "All right."

She asks him to find a comb so she can fix her hair. She fusses with her dressing gown, taking it off and draping it over the head of the bed. Finally, she starts talking.

It was 1979. She was eighteen. She'd gone to the island with a friend. "You remember the island, don't you?" she says. He does, a little. They'd gone there when he was small.

"Wasn't that where I almost drowned?"

"What? Oh, you didn't *drown*. So anyway, Mouse and I – "

"Mouse." What a weird name.

"Well, Mandy, but I called her Mouse. We were working on a play, a play together... *The Tempest*. You remember me reading that to you when you were a kid?"

"Yes. I sure do."

Pearl's head jerks to one side. "Yeah. Anyway, I was young, you know, and I got drunk and went into town on the boat. Hooked up with this guy."

She's having trouble looking at him, he realizes; is she embarrassed?

His heart is hammering so fast he puts a hand up to his chest, thinking he'll feel the beating muscle jumping out between ribs.

"Yeah..." Pearl's head droops. "Look. I really need a damn smoke to do this. Can we grab a wheelchair or something? I don't think I can make it down that damn hallway again."

Stephen commandeers a folding wheelchair from the nurses' station, adrenaline running through him like wine, no matter how hard he tries to calm himself. Pearl is already sitting on the edge of the bed when he returns, her dressing gown tied tightly around her waist. He's never wheeled anyone in a chair before. One of the brakes is down, and they go in tight circles around the room before figuring it out. Stephen barks out a laugh. At last they get into the hallway and down to the doors. No one else is there, thank God. Pearl takes her time getting a smoke out and lit, and he shuffles from foot to foot.

"This is a little surreal," he says.

His mother looks at him through the smoke. "I suppose it is." She draws in a lungful, goes on. "The thing is, I can't remember his name."

"What?"

"Well, I'm sorry. I've been trying. I just don't remember it."

Stephen stares at her. "You don't know his name."

"Well..." she shifts in the chair. "Come on. Do you remember the name of everyone you've ever slept with?"

He thinks for a moment. "As a matter of fact I do."

"Oh, come on."

"I do! God, Mom – "

"The thing is, I used to give people nicknames all the time." She sucks back smoke, lets it pour out of her nose. "So I called him Randy. But that was a joke, see?"

"Oh, God. Whatever." He walks over to the wall, begins pounding his forehead gently against the brick.

"So I'd bet his real name began with an R," his mother's voice comes faintly behind him. "Robert, maybe. Or Richard. Except then I'd have called him Dick." She starts giggling, but stops when he turns and looks at her. "Sorry. I mean, though, I used to do that. Like, Mouse was really Mandy, and so on. But not always. So I don't really know – "

"A last name?"

Pearl stares at him. She smokes, squinting, he thinks, like Clint Eastwood. "Look, are you thinking you want to look this guy up?"

"I don't fucking know!" He loses it. "I don't know, okay? I don't know what I want to do! But it'd be nice to have the fucking option, you know?"

She stares him down. "Well, I'm sorry. Really. I am." Finally she looks away, looks down at the dirty snow. "I never knew his name."

He rubs his forehead. "Do you know – remember – where he was from?"

"Well, that's the thing too. We got together in this town near the Thousand Islands. Gananoque. But I know he wasn't from there. He'd come up to work at the gas station for the summer, from somewhere else, and stayed on through the fall. He, well, dealt pot on the side." She looks at the end of her cigarette like she's trying to remember something, and Stephen leans in to hear, but all that comes out is, "He was tall. And he had brown hair."

"I have brown hair."

"Yes." His mother looks at him, sad. "You have brown hair."

"I'm not very fucking goddamn tall, though, am I."

"Really," Pearl says, "you look a lot like me." She throws the butt of her cigarette into the darkness. "I never saw much of anything else in you."

On the way out of the hospital Stephen sees himself reflected in the glass of the sliding doors. He steps aside to let a couple entering pass him, the doors close with a faint scream, and there he is again. Thin. He slouches. Glasses, pursed lips, obsequious smile, ducking head.

Laura would leave him. All the girls who liked him, left him. Fluttering off like a host of fleeing Ariels.

He gets out to the parking lot, can't find car keys in his pocket, can't find the car where he recalls parking it, gets frantic, remembers that he'd made Laura take it.

Walking to the edge of the lot, he swerves around a snowbank, a tight little circle like the one the wheelchair made in the hospital room. He thinks he's looking for a low place in the snowbank to step over, but then he's on his knees, pounding and clawing at the snow, hurling fistfuls of it in crystalline arcs against the electric light.

He knows he looks ridiculous; the brain won't shut off.

His breath comes in great ragged bursts. He's shouting, pounding.

"I – just – wanted – once – to know – fuck – one fucking – thing…"

His glasses fly off into the dark. He falls on his face in the dirty snow, pounding his face, his head, scrabbling.

He's lost a glove and his rage runs out. He lies there spread under the lit-up night.

Stephen finds himself in a liquor store, buying a bottle of vodka. He heads for the river.

He feels small under the overarching darkness. "Here's neither bush nor shrub…" He'd loved that scene when his mother used to read it to him, remembers giggling with her, huddled together under his blanket in the dark room.

That seems strange now; why did they read under the blanket with a flashlight? It's not like there was some adult to come and tell them to go to sleep. Caliban and Trinculo lie together under a cloak, terrified of the storm, and the drunken Stephano comes upon them and thinks they are one monster with four legs. "He shall taste of my bottle: if he have never drunk wine afore, it will go near to remove his fit."

He crosses the railway bridge, stopping midway to drink. His left ear throbs; he'd pounded it against the snow back at the hospital.

On the other bank of the river he sees a flickering light. There's a big old tree with someone at the foot of it; someone with a flashlight. The light beams up into the tree in great arcs. It draws him, he crosses the river.

It's a girl, the girl he's seen before. She turns as he approaches, anxious, breathing heavily. She points into the tree with the flashlight; there's a bundle up there, rags or something. She's shorter than he is, the branches of the tree are above her head, but it's unmistakable what she wants.

He hands her the vodka and jumps, seizing the bundle between his bare palms. It's heavier than he thought it would be, and when eyes look out at him he almost drops it. He hands her the baby.

She takes the baby with one arm, drinks from the bottle with the other.

"You gotta figure out something about this baby," Stephen says.

The girl nods.

Stephen rubs his ear. The girl hands the bottle back, questioningly pointing at his ear.

"I got hit when I was a kid. On the school bus. Bullies, you know."

She joggles the baby; he drinks, passes the bottle.

"Blood came out of my ear. The pain was pretty bad, but after a few days it was so bad I told my mom. She took me to a doctor who said he wondered how no one had noticed the boy had an ear swollen to twice its size, red and oozing pus."

The girl hands him the vodka.

"Thanks. The eardrum broke. It's never bounced sound the right way since."

Vodka burns down his throat and makes him gasp.

"Hey, you talk or what?"

But she's pulled her hood up, is walking away over the snow with the baby.

"See you."

She waves her hand into the air.

"Don't let that baby climb any more trees."

She waves again, almost lost from view now in the darkness.

He finds a park bench and sweeps the snow off with his sleeve. He catches a scent on his bare hand: Pearl's feet. He drinks again. *He's good at that; that's one thing he's good at.* Something like that. During his "hot" phase when he'd first left home, a girl in his U of T residence down the hall had taken a shine to him. She'd been in the music department, he remembers: a jazz vocalist. She'd invited him into her room to listen to a CD, convinced him to give her a neck rub, had been surprised at how good he was. She'd started making all these hmm and mmm noises, sensual, and he started to get turned on. She writhed under his palms, turning a flushed cheek to the back of his hand, her lips parted, and suddenly he'd been violently repelled. Terrified, really, he thinks now. He'd pretended to the girl that he felt sick; he *had* felt sick. He'd fled, back up the hall to his room.

The river is frozen out from the banks, but in the middle the current runs strong, past small islands with toppled willow trees, home to herons and ducks in summer. He gets to his feet, walks through the stately houses, around and through a baseball park, ghostly like an abandoned movie set now in winter. The main bridge soars up over it. He loves bridges over water. He loves hanging over the rail, watching the everchanging current, loves throwing things in. He gets under the bridge, into the echo and that smell of urine and garbage and water that always lives under bridges. He's given his mother so many neck rubs, foot massages; she'd trained him young. *It's you and me, kid, we're in it together*, she used to say. He leans against the curved concrete of the bridge's underbelly, he drinks more. He's feeling it now, the burn in his gut, swagger and heat. He'll go up on the bridge, that's what he'll do, he'll throw something in. Throw a suicide note into the river – that strikes him as funny, so he fishes a little notepad out of his coat pocket and a chewed up pen, flips past some chess openings he'd scribbled down and an aborted grocery list, finds a blank sheet.

Dear, he begins, and hesitates. Who will he address it to? Not Laura, that's too weird. He drinks, the bottle is almost gone already. No, Pearl. It would have to be Pearl. Who else. *Dear Mom. Looks like I beat you to it. Surprise!* It's hard to write in the cold; the page keeps flapping in the wind. He'll write about that, the cold, a storm like in *The Tempest*. He writes: *There's no shelter here, nothing to keep off the wind.* He thinks for a moment, blows on his fingers to warm them. *There's no safety. Misery makes strange bedfellows; we're in it together, you and I. Here's to you and me.* He signs it. *Drunken Stepheno.*

He folds the paper, surprised to find that his hands shake. Teeth chatter. Up the bank he staggers, bottle in one hand and note in the other. Onto the bridge. He swerves onto the road and a car roars by, driver hanging on the horn, a real Doppler effect that one. Another one, a truck this time. He gets back up onto the sidewalk, the downriver side of the bridge, half falls against the balustrade.

The cap of the bottle is the first thing to go, down into the dark, into the coiling black muscles of the swollen winter river. Then his remaining glove – easy things. He drains the bottle, spits the final mouthful into the air, an offering to the river god. The bottle goes down, end over end, flashing in the streetlights until it falls out of sight. And then, where to put the note? It'd be nice if it were still on him when they find him. He opens his coat and puts the note in his shirt pocket, carefully buttoning the coat up again. Then he thinks, my boot would be better, so he reverses the whole procedure and unlaces his boot, puts the note in there and shoves his foot back in, laces up good and tight. A car going by unleashes some derisive yells, is gone.

He straightens up, puts his hands on the cold concrete of the balustrade. He leans there, only gradually becoming aware of a hard thing digging into his thigh. He takes his phone out of his pocket, flips it open. Its pale green light burns into his eyes.

Fingers numb, he accesses his phone book. He might as well, he thinks, why not? He dials the number of the man who is called his grandfather.

Misery makes strange bedfellows. There's no safety. Here's to you and me.

Pearl is drinking. Really drinking; it started after the incident on her parents' bed and Mouse hasn't done anything to stop it. She *can't* do anything; she's locked into herself, images from the sex they had flashing through her.

Pearl spent the rest of that night polishing off the last of the beer. By dawn she'd moved on to the sacred stashed mickeys of her father, and now, around noon, she's working her way through a half-full bottle of Crème de Menthe from the sideboard. It's so old there are greenish sugar crystals around the mouth of the bottle.

"Dear old Dad comes through for something," she says. "Old booze hound. That's a brave god, and bears celestial liquor. I will kneel to him."

Pearl slides down off the chintz-covered cushions; they bounce and settle on the floor like children's toys. She kneels and raises the bottle.

"I'll swear, upon that bottle, to be thy true subject."

She puts the neck of the bottle into her mouth and slides it in and out like she's giving it a blow job.

By now, Mouse has figured out that there is something very wrong with the way Pearl thinks of her father.

"Why the hell aren't you drinking?" Pearl sways on her knees. She fixes Mouse, sitting on the sofa, with a baleful gaze, walks on her knees toward her. "Here is that which will give language to you, cat: open your mouth." She grabs Mouse and tries to put the Crème de Menthe to her lips.

"Give it a rest, Pearl."

"This will shake your shaking, I can tell you."

"And yes, you're very smart, you remember everyone's lines, very good."

She is beginning to hate Pearl.

Pearl rolls onto her back on the floor and puts her feet into Mouse's lap.

"Rub my feet. Please. They hurt."

Mouse is incredulous. Pearl wiggles her toes and looks up slyly, beguilingly.

"Please? I'll... look, I'm stopping drinking. Look." Pearl tips the Crème de Menthe over onto its side and shoves it. It rolls away under the couch, a sticky trail dribbling from its mouth. "Rub my feet, please?"

Mouse takes one perfect foot in her hand and begins running her thumbs up and down it. Pearl makes happy noises, almost like purring. Maybe, Mouse thinks, she'll pass out and sleep this off. Then they can get the hell out of here. She is trapped, she can't drive the boat, she barely knows where they are.

"... for aye thy footlicker," Pearl murmurs. Her eyes are closed, she is rocking her head gently from side to side with pleasure. Suddenly her eyes fly open. "Come, swear to that; kiss the book."

She pulls her foot from Mouse's grasp and waves it in Mouse's face, nearly clocking her in the mouth.

"Aw, come on, Jesus!"

"Kiss it, kiss it!"

"Go fuck yourself."

Mouse stands. Pearl grabs her ankle.

"I will kiss thy foot: I prithee, be my god."

"Let go! Smarten up!"

Mouse strides away, leaving Pearl moaning on the living room floor; she has to get out of here, out, anywhere, she will go onto the dock.

"Here's neither bush nor shrub to bear off any weather at all, and another storm brewing, I hear it sing in the wind – "

Mouse lets the screen door slam behind her. Pearl raises her voice to be heard, slurring the words.

"If it should thunder as it did before, I know not where to hide my head!"

"Fuck off!" Mouse's feet tumble down to the dock.

It's a cloudy day, a bite to the wind. She sits on the dock and hugs her knees. The alien water clomps and gulps inside the boathouse, against the dock, the rocky edges of the island. The rock's different, the water smells of nothing salt, the trees are too big and too green. There's not even a goddamn tide in this water.

She wants, then, more than anything, to be home. Where things make sense, where she can see her dad and even her crazy mother, her indifferent and teenage-superior brother. She wants to see her father, to lay her head on his chest like she used to as a little girl; she remembers that so clearly, curling up in his lap as he watched TV in the evenings. *You're getting to be such a big girl! Soon I'll have to sit on you.* She always giggled – the comfort of the absurd joke, as if she could ever be as big as her father – and nestled her head on his chest, the warmth and musky smell of him. And the scent of alcohol, she realizes now, that astringency was part of the scent of comfort to her. Hearing the thumping, reassuring beat of his heart,

128

right under her ear; how safe she was with him. She wants to cry with her longing.

But Pearl staggers down the path behind her. Mouse won't look, she won't grant Pearl the satisfaction. Uneven footsteps hit the dock, a small hand falls on her shoulder. Pearl leans into her face, peering at her.

"Hey," she says, "what're you doing here?"

"Sitting."

Pearl considers this, then collapses next to her. Mouse moves away. Pearl looks out at the water, cocks her head to one side. "What's your name?" she asks brightly.

"What?" Pearl can't be serious.

"Yeah. What's your name? Can't, can't quite recall..."

"Oh. My. God." Mouse emphasizes every word.

"Thou debosh'd fish."

"That's nice. You remember every line of that goddamn play, but my goddamn name has somehow escaped you?"

"Monster, I do smell all horse piss..."

"Pearl, give it a rest. Pass out or something. Please?"

"... at which my nose is in great indignation."

Mouse considers striking Pearl across the head, maybe knocking her out. But Pearl heaves herself to her feet and makes her way into the boathouse. When the door opens it nearly swings her off her feet but she gamely clings onto the latch, stays upright. When she disappears inside Mouse strains to hear, expecting at any moment the splash of Pearl falling into the water, but it never comes. Pearl is rummaging away in there, amongst the fishing rods, water toys, canoes, life jackets, brooms, rope, funnels and gas cans, nets, old windows, and lawn chairs, for what Mouse can't imagine until Pearl emerges victorious, brandishing a mickey of scotch.

"Dear old Dad. I could, could've known I could count on him!" Pearl fumbles with the cap.

Mouse jumps up and rips the mickey from Pearl's hand, and with all her strength she hurls it into the river.

Everything goes still for a moment, everything except the bottle. It arcs through the air – amber liquid rippling out – lands in the water with barely a splash, and is gone. Neither girl moves.

Then it's like a truck that has been coming toward you and suddenly is next to you, rushing by, the overwhelming weight and speed of it. Pearl cries out and lunges toward the water. Mouse grabs her around the waist. Pearl struggles and screams, her lips peel back from her teeth and she screams like an animal. Mouse throws her down on the dock and sits on her. She is afraid Pearl will drown herself. After a short struggle, Pearl goes limp. She rocks her head back and forth, moaning a little.

"Oh, but to lose our bottles in the pool..."

"Will you stop it with the damn play!"

"... there is not only disgrace and dishonour in that, monster..." Pearl's voice is gaining in strength and clarity, "but an infinite loss!"

Mouse spits words into Pearl's face.

"Hell is empty, and all the devils are *here*."

She doesn't care any more. Pearl can drown herself. She doesn't care.

Mouse coils up on the dock. Pearl sings inside the boathouse, her sweet, high voice lurching from note to note. *Where the bee sucks, there suck I: in a cowslip's bell I lie...* An engine roars into life, drowning out the singing.

The boat emerges into open air. Pearl is still singing, her mouth moves but only the sound of the engine comes out. *Merrily, merrily...* She steers the boat out onto the vast river. Mouse doesn't care if Pearl drowns, doesn't care if she herself never gets off this island. She'll cope. Pearl's rich sick horrible family will find her there come spring, a corpse. She is surprised that tears are streaming down her face.

The whine and roar of the boat engine carry over the water even as the boat retreats, becoming smaller and smaller still. Wind picks up, carries the sound of the engine away.

Mouse can't hear the boat now.

The boat has disappeared.

It is terrible, sitting on the island alone.

Many hours pass. Mouse's bravado disappears and she no longer derives any vengeful thrills from the image of Pearl's family returning to find her rotting body. She has become preoccupied with the thought that Pearl is so drunk she will sink the boat and die. This is not unlikely and Mouse is a sensible sort.

Alone on the island there is no shelter from these images: Pearl passed out, the boat crashing on rocks, Pearl's pale body sinking slowly through green and black depths, her hair floating around her face, mouth open, the alien element rushing in, filling her lungs, filling her body from the inside out.

The sky has darkened and the wind gets stronger, a taste of arctic air in it, some great corridor of winter teasing down from expanses of ice.

She trudges into the cottage. She is alone. The phone is dead. She told no one where she was going. Looking back, this seems the ultimate folly – to go off with this girl she barely knows to a place she has no way of getting

130

back from. The feeling of connection she thought she had with Pearl now seems ridiculously juvenile. She never really knew this person. The connection was a dream.

She has no idea why Pearl wanted her here.

She fishes some bread out of the bags of groceries, makes herself a sandwich.

She supposes she did it because part of her hoped she and Pearl would fall in love. And this was so frightening, so dangerous, that she didn't want to speak it. It's all confused in her mind now, whether she was afraid it would happen or that it wouldn't; or was she fearful of some terrible hammer of hatred falling on their heads were their perversion to be discovered?

Secrecy around sex is a second skin for Mouse.

Her anxiety is so acute that she can't eat the sandwich.

It occurs to her that "the big house" might have a working phone. She walks up to the forbidding mansion. She tries every exterior door (there are six), her feet making a hollow, lonely sound on the porches; all locked. Every ground-floor window has big wooden shutters closed over them, fastened with padlocks; what was the caretaker's name? Pearl had spoken of him fondly, the only person from her past to be rewarded with fondness, Mouse realizes; Floyd, that was it, Floyd Lachambre.

Well, Floyd sure did a good job with those shutters. Mouse can't get in; it's no use.

The monument to the grandeur of Pearl's family past broods over formal gardens, vast lawns. They never use it, Pearl had said. Sometimes they'd put extended family in it if there was a big reunion, and guests might stay over; sometimes the adults would have cocktails on the porches. Three stories, gables, it should be pretty but it frightens Mouse. She considers trying to break into an upper-storey window and hurts herself trying to shimmy up a porch pillar, falling into a yew bush below.

Dark is nosing around now; it's cold. Mouse retreats to the cottage. She puts on every sweater she brought with her, and lays a fire. There isn't much firewood left, she'll have to find more tomorrow. She uses long matches from the mantelpiece to light the kindling.

She wonders how long she should wait for Pearl before beginning to try getting off the island alone. As she thinks this, she realizes how stupid it is – she should be trying now, immediately – Pearl may never come back. Princess Miranda, gone off to Milan while Mouse squats here on the hearth.

. She should make a signal fire, maybe? Set fire to the whole damn boathouse and dock. *What a thrice-double ass was I, to take this drunkard for a god.*

The flames catch, blossom up like wildflowers and she waits until they are strong enough before carefully laying a log across them. The birch bark crackles, the flames lick, scent of smoke and fire. A green flame leaps up and with it an image of her father fills her, a sense of him, as if he's present. Mouse feels terrible pressure in her chest, puts her hand there. A voice is grunting, crying out, hers, his. She falls forward on her knees, doubled over with it, the pain of it, it's so strange, like her heart is breaking within her.

The night passes slowly. Her sleep is filled with dreams of drowning; she feels her father standing behind her in the dreams but she can't turn around to face him. This sensation returns with the regularity of a nightmare funhouse, a roundabout of confusion and pain.

Finally morning light greys the big alien room.

Mouse pulls her blanket over her head, can't bear to get up. She lies like this until she hears the drone of a boat engine. She lies there wondering if this is real until it seems to be getting closer. She untangles herself from her blankets and goes out onto the screened porch.

There is a boat coming towards the island. It gets closer. It is *the* boat. Pearl has come back.

Relief sweeps through Mouse, then terror, such a quick flash she barely registers it, the way a man stabbed in a movie puts his hands to the wound and looks up at his assailant with mild surprise at the sight of blood coming out of him. But the knife-blade of terror is swiftly swamped by Mouse's rage. The rage makes her think coldly, clearly. She must force Pearl to take her off this island, now, today, she can't risk staying here another moment.

She walks slowly down to the dock. She feels grotesque in her layers of sweaters, a giant waddling creature.

The boat comes in, faster and faster. Pearl swerves at the last moment to make a loop back out into the river, to slow down.

Mouse sees at her feet her old braid, lying in a spiral, yesterday's hope and transformation. She picks it up. Pearl cutting her hair seems like months ago. She drops the braid into the water, watching it sink down and down; she thinks she can see it coiled creature-like on the rocks below.

Pearl brings the boat in, slowly now. The wake washes against the dock like applause.

"Mouse, Mouse, Mouse, Mouse, Mouse!"

Pearl eases the boat into the boathouse, disappearing; the engine cuts. Mouse hears Pearl banging around in there, wonders if Pearl is still drunk. Pearl emerges onto the dock, a crazy smile on her face, arms outstretched.

"Mouse!" Her voice is hearty and fake.

"If you fucking try to hug me, I swear I'll knock your teeth down your throat and out your arsehole."

Pearl puts on an expression of hurt. "What's the matter?"

"We're leaving. Now."

Mouse wheels and marches back up to the cottage. She will pack everything, put it in the boat, make Pearl take her away from here. Pearl trots behind her, tries to take her arm.

"Get the fuck away from me."

Pearl stops, expects Mouse to stop too, but Mouse keeps going and Pearl is forced to follow her. "What?"

They reach the porch and a scent hits Mouse. She grabs Pearl's wrist and drags her close, sniffs at her hair.

"You smell like aftershave." She shoves Pearl away. Mouse has never wanted to strike another person as badly as she wants to let loose on Pearl right now. She might yet; a good clean rage fills her. Pearl smells of men's aftershave. "You fucked some guy last night."

Pearl stares, then tosses her head. "So what?"

"You're sick. You know that? You're disgusting."

Mouse charges into the cottage, flings socks and underwear into her backpack. She yells over her shoulder, "We're leaving as soon as we're packed up. I'm not dealing with your stuff." She mutters to herself, "Deal with it yourself."

Pearl walks slowly to the doorway and leans there, watching; this makes Mouse feel trapped. She abandons her packing and muscles past Pearl into the kitchen, starts consolidating the food. Her stomach growls; she is hungry. It's all so crazy, it's surreal, this. She isn't the kind of person who ends up like this, ends up with these kinds of feelings.

Pearl has followed her into the kitchen and Mouse tries to ignore her.

"Don't worry," Pearl says. "You can be the daddy."

The can of tomatoes in Mouse's hand falls, rolls across the floor. Her body, she notes, is shaking. She turns to face Pearl. The look on Pearl's face is almost pleading; there's a strange light in her eyes.

Mouse thinks, *Pearl's pregnant.* She's pregnant.

"You don't make any sense." Mouse hates herself for the tears that come into her eyes now, the choke in her voice. "You don't make any sense."

Mouse's knees are weak and she sits down on the floor so she can hide her face from Pearl, bury her face in her hands.

Mouse never sees the production that she started stage managing. She quits. She quits everything: the play, university, Pearl. When she and Pearl

133

get back to school there are messages waiting for Mouse. Her father has had a heart attack.

It is sudden, complete, and he is dead.

She goes back to Newfoundland for the funeral. As they lower the coffin into the hole in the stony earth she embarrasses everyone by trying to throw herself on top of the box. Her brother has to hold her back. She feels her mouth gaping, tears and snot running down her face, spit coming out from between her teeth. Her brother's breath sobs in her ear as he restrains her.

Everyone says, afterwards, that this is so unlike Mandy Brown. She has always been such a contained child.

Her mother wants her to stay in Newfoundland after the funeral. Her brother is in the middle of his second year of high school, and every day he is cruel to Mouse in a tired sort of way that comes from the depths of his misery.

She knows this but it is still too much to bear; that, and her mother's brittle, tearless grief. Mouse cries. She cries everyone's tears for them, and they dislike her for it.

She feels her life getting lost inside loss.

She manages to apply to a university in British Columbia and they accept her to start the January term.

This is a different ocean. The land doesn't rise up to meet it, like it does at home, the ocean doesn't pound against it. The ocean, here, heaves in great deceptive rolls onto a pliant shore, a shore that bows its head and washes under. Here there are no divisions.

No winter, that is the next strange thing. Green things grow and Mouse can't shake the idea that she will stumble in the woods and fall; greenness will overtake her, growing over and into her until it comes out of her eyes, her ears, stops up her mouth with green snaking branches, until she is crucified with green. She is unable to study; some days she can't even get out of bed.

She slows down, and slows some more. She feels invisible to everyone around her.

She blames Pearl. She doesn't stop thinking of Pearl, can't. Pearl cast a spell on her that has made her this slow, shambling, invisible person. Pearl herself has taken the boat, she has roared off into high regions of speedy madness. Maybe, perversely, the slowing will allow her and Pearl to find each other again, on the other side of the spherical firmament. She, the efficient one, the reliable one, now moves so slowly that anyone else whizzes by her, blurs. Buildings rise and fall in the time it takes her to walk two strange blocks of city.

She likes to sit by the alien ocean. Here she can feel almost normal; the highest edge of tide laps at her like the waves used to do. She was normal, once. She remembers this.

One day she is sitting beneath one of this place's huge maple trees, each leaf a spreading wet giant; they cling to the tree, they throw yellow light.

The yellow light contracts, sucks back like a wave.

The tree turns flame red and hurls all its leaves down upon her.

She is back in Ontario and things have sped up again. She is back, on the island.

Four years later, and she has heard from Pearl. She gets a phone call and it stuns her for a moment. They talk. Pearl invites her out to the island again and Mouse accepts; there's a faculty strike, she takes some time off.

For the rest of her life it will seem like this: that after her father's death she lived submerged until this moment, now, on the island again. Four years. She knows this isn't exactly true. She accomplished things: she went to B.C., she dropped out of university, she worked in a restaurant, she went home for Christmases, it was awful every time. She hooked up with a woman named Marlys; they moved in together; they broke up. She went back to university and began a degree in economics and business management, she has a gift for it and is doing well. But it isn't until now, four years later, that the fog lifts at last, seemingly of its own free will: the grief of losing her father, the madness induced by Pearl. Indistinguishable, perhaps, in some ways.

"My life feels like my own again." Mouse stretches, looks out across the river. No tides, here, she remembers. She has a beer by her elbow, is wearing a stupid golf visor she found up in the cottage just to annoy Pearl. Pearl looks older, even though it's only been a few years. Her perm has grown out, her hair is straight, lovely. She still smokes. She doesn't drink as much; some people would call what she consumes acceptable.

Mouse looks over at Pearl, sees the way the bitterness has settled around her mouth. She feels detached, comfortable; it's hard to believe she was ever in love with Pearl. Pearl stands, gets another beer. She has stretch marks on her belly. She doesn't do handstands any more.

The little boy plays at the water's edge. During the week she spends here, Mouse catches Pearl looking at him, over and over again, an expression of terrible bewilderment in her blue blue eyes.

The old man's house is big. Really big. Stephen gets lost trying to find it.

He drives through the old-Toronto-money enclave – winding roads, one-way streets and speed bumps – acutely conscious of the shabbiness of the car. He extrapolates the address from an adjacent home that has been recently renovated and sports (among landscaping, flagstone driveways, and a garage that looks like an English garden cottage) large, clear numbers. The house, his grandfather's house, has none.

It's red brick and set back from the road, partially hidden behind trees. Stephen parks and approaches by foot up the driveway; he doesn't want the old man to see the car. As he gets closer the size of the house unfolds. There's a wing off to the left, a turret tower, an old-fashioned greenhouse or conservatory. Dense, trim yews gleam darkly on either side of the front door, catching the afternoon light like a crowd of hard green eyes.

He rings a bell, a woman answers the door. She gives an impression of tidiness; that's all Stephen can read through the white noise in his head. A small, neat woman, who is she – his step-grandmother, the old man's latest wife?

She takes his coat, then leads him through the entranceway, chilly pale grey, and into a kitchen. It's been redone; the shine on the floor-to-ceiling oak cabinets is almost blinding, the range hood is made of something like carved marble, the backsplash features tiles from Provence. There's no refrigerator; Stephen guesses it's camouflaged behind one of the oak panels. Somehow, despite the attempt with all the yellow, it feels cold. He expects to sit in the kitchen and pauses by a row of leather bar stools, a massive marble-topped island. But the woman leads him on, down a hall, to a masculine sort of den.

"Your guest is here," she says and slips away, and it's only then that Stephen realizes the woman is a servant.

The old man sits behind a desk. There's a drink at his elbow, he wears reading glasses. He looks up, and Stephen thinks, he's handsome. Blue eyes look over the half-glasses at him. They stare.

"Stephen."

The old man rises. He takes off his glasses and puts them on the desk, rubbing at his nose. "I'm pretending to work. Let's sit."

136

He moves to two leather armchairs by the fire, drink in hand.

The room has a massive quality: it's paneled in dark wood, there's a rich Persian rug, and books line the walls, the fire glows; it's all a bit fake, Stephen thinks, like a room in a game of Clue. He moves toward the man holding out his hand to shake, conscious that his shirt is stained with sweat under his arms. I must keep my elbows down, he tells himself.

He shakes hands with his grandfather.

They stand at the same height; the old man must have been taller, once. His grey hair is light, slightly yellow. It could have been blonde, Stephen thinks. Probably was, like Pearl's. His skin is light and thin, wrinkles traced upon it.

They sit down, and the leather chairs squeak. Immediately the man rises again – "Drink?" and Stephen nods. "What'll you have?"

"What are you drinking?"

"Dewar's."

Like Pearl.

"I'll have that."

During the drive down, he imagined all sorts of things. He'd rejected the warm embrace and familial, even fatherly, concord almost immediately, and had proceeded through the sudden massive inheritance, and the meeting of a large and hitherto unknown family, to an image of cruel and disdainful rejection.

He'd forgotten about politeness. How polite they are being to one another. Stephen watches while his grandfather makes him a drink at a little chrome bar on wheels, tipping the last of the scotch out of the bottle.

"Ice?"

"Sure. Thanks."

The night before, he and Laura had been up talking until three in the morning. She'd initially resisted giving him advice, but really, she couldn't resist.

Do you think I should go down? he'd started.

What do you think?

I'm asking you.

I can't advise you, Stephen. How could I?

I just want to know what you think. What you'd do.

Well, I think I'd want to meet him. The truth shall set you free, etcetera. But as soon as I say that, I feel scared.

For me?

I don't know. Yes. Maybe. Scared for the little girl inside myself – if it was my situation, I mean.

You think he's dangerous?

In a way.

Come on, Laura. Pretend I'm one of your clients.

Well… okay, what do you want?

What do I want?

Yes.

To meet him.

So you have clarity about that.

I think so.

What's your greatest fear about meeting him?

That I'll like him. No, scratch that. That something will somehow…

It's okay. Take your time.

It's silly.

It usually helps to say it. And it doesn't matter if it's irrational; that's the point. What's your greatest fear about meeting him?

That Mom will die because I meet him. God. That's so… He'd paused. *She's dying anyway. So it's silly. And it's not like… but that's it. I'm afraid that the fact of me meeting him, even if she never knows about it, will kill her.*

They'd sat for some time without speaking. Stephen broke the silence.

So that's the greatest fear part. What's question number three?

She'd refused levity. *What's your greatest hope?*

His greatest hope. Talking with Laura, he'd thought he knew; now he's no longer sure.

The man sits down again, Stephen sips, and they look at the fire. They look at each other.

"How was the drive down?"

"Fine."

"How long does it take?"

Stephen has an impulse, quickly quelled, to say, *thirty years.* "A couple of hours, more or less."

"I'm glad you phoned me," the old man says then.

"I was drunk."

On the drive down, Stephen has decided he will play a clean and direct game.

The old man has drawn white – the accidental encounter with the lawyer granted him the first move – but Stephen can proceed as he wants. He can tell the truth.

"And I don't really remember what we said."

A blur high in the air, a bridge. A voice, tinny in his ear. A white piece

138

of paper with his own writing on it, fluttering through the air, disappearing into darkness below. A long walk home.

"Well, you told me who you were, said David gave you my number."

"The lawyer."

The man nods. "I said I'd like to meet you."

Stephen's longing to like this man is so strong it makes it hard to speak. His grandfather is wearing a white shirt, the fine cotton gleams in the firelight. He's a masculine man, a man's man, Stephen thinks. His clothes fit him well, and his physicality is direct, symmetrical. His hands are manicured, and hold the glass with a curiously mincing gesture. They are unlike the rest of him; they betray something.

"Mr. Lewis – "

"Call me Mitchell."

"Okay."

They eye one another.

"I think it... we might not..."

"I won't call you *grandpa*," Stephen says. The man shifts in his chair a bit. "Okay, Mitchell. My mother doesn't know I'm here."

"Really?" The old man stirs, a frown creasing, then leaving, his forehead. "How is she?"

Stephen dodges the question.

"I don't really know why I'm here myself. Curiosity, I guess. I just found out that you exist, you see."

"Yes. Likewise."

A smile lights up the man's face. It's an extraordinary smile, really charming; he's the sort of person you want to please, so you'd see that smile. The pink hands curl around the glass, the ice shivers.

"A coincidence. An extraordinary coincidence that David ran into you and my – you two. So, how is – "

"Is this the house that..." Stephen pauses. "Have you always lived here?"

"I was born here. And your mother."

Family house, this was his family house. Pearl had been a little girl here. Stephen could have grown up here, or grown up visiting the place, walking as a small boy down one of those winding streets, from some other big old house. Maybe one that looks over the ravine, the tangle of trees.

The carven mantel is lined with framed photos, a big one in the centre: the old man with a woman – big poufy dyed hair – tasteful though. Some younger people. Half-relatives? Had the man had other children besides Pearl during other marriages?

139

"Is that your wife?"

The man shifts. "That's Sophia. My second wife." He looks morosely at the photo. "Those are her kids by a previous marriage. We never... she's dead now."

Is he a widower? Stephen wonders, but the man continues, "Then came Della; she passed on three years ago. So now it's Gail. Me and Gail." He looks at Stephen. "Four wives, I've had. If someone had said to me when I was your age, Mitchell, you'll marry three beautiful women and lose them all, I'd have, well, I guess I'd never have had the nerve to marry at all. But I did. I did." He looks into the fire, a touch theatrically Stephen thinks.

"Do you have a picture of Gail?" he asks. Then he adds, not able to resist, "I take it she's not beautiful."

"What?"

"You said you married three beautiful women."

"Oh." The man takes a gulp of his drink, ice clatters against the rim as the last of the alcohol drains down his throat. "Well, that's her there," and he gestures at a smaller photo at the end of the mantel. "And now that you mention it, no, Gail is not beautiful." He smiles ruefully, and Stephen finds himself smiling back. "You caught me there, Stephen. She's going to look after me, though. That comes to mean something, at my age. When you're alone."

"Did Gail remodel the kitchen?" Stephen finds it difficult to reconcile the image of the devoted Plain Jane with those sunny yellow tiles.

"God, no. That was Sophia. Italian. God."

The old man shifts around in his chair, and Stephen knows as well as he knows it sitting with his mother, *he wants another drink.* He wonders if his grandfather smokes; the room doesn't smell like it. "Gail's away, visiting her mother; otherwise I'd love for you to meet her." If he had been a smoker he'd probably quit years ago, for his health. So he'd stay alive. The man digs absently under the seat cushion and his hand emerges with a silver flask. As Stephen watches he unscrews the top and tips the flask. It is empty.

"Ah." The man rises and checks the chrome bar, the emptied bottle. "Please excuse me, I'll just get another..."

Stephen hears his footsteps going down the hall.

It's hard to sit still; impossible. He goes to the mantel, takes a closer look at the photos. One from the early sixties perhaps – the old man, young here, with a woman.

Pearl's mother? Stephen's grandmother.

Her head's tilted back, looking up at her husband; she's smiling. Light hair. She's the kind of woman who looks like a child: pretty, small.

And there, in a frame but half-hidden behind, is another. The old man
– Mitchell – maybe fifty years old. And next to him, a teenager. She's wear-
ing little Adidas shorts and a stripy T-shirt, sandals. His arm is around her.
She's looking at the camera, her expression vacant. It's his mother, it's Pearl.

He's never seen a picture of his mother as a teen.

What's my greatest hope, Laura? he thinks.

I have to think about that, he'd answered last night. It was hard, like trying to scoop up mercury, the thoughts kept fragmenting. *I think I'm hoping that somehow he'll be able to help me understand why Pearl's so... why
she hates so much. Why she's always been so different from other mothers. I
know no one's normal, I know that. But she was always so... Younger, but
more than that. The drinking, boyfriends, the way she compartmentalizes.
Forgets. That's not normal. And she cut him off.*

Yes.

*But you know, I've been thinking. She cuts people off all the time. I re-
member so many friends of hers, people I kind of liked too, you know. People who babysat me and stuff. She excommunicates people. There was Judith,
who got cut off because she stopped letting people smoke in her house. And
Chandra, who moved into a fancier neighbourhood because her husband got
rich. Gone, like they'd never been in our lives. And Marianne – this was the
worst – Marianne got sick. She had a brain aneurysm. And my mother just
totally cut her off. She was with Marianne the day she had the aneurysm, and
she referred to it as "the time Marianne went all funny," with this disgust in
her voice. I used to call her Aunty Mary, that's how close she was. And Pearl
went to see her once in the hospital, and that was it. We never saw her again.*

That's scary.

*Yeah. I just don't get why Pearl... And so maybe if I can understand her,
I'll... Oh – oh God. I think that part of me thinks he'll be able to... not replace her. But make the fucking hole inside me when she's gone sort of... he'll
fill it a little. So I won't have to feel that she's gone.*

That makes total sense to me.

*But there's something else. Something vengeful. She can't tell me any-
thing about my father. A drunken teenage one-night stand, that's me. I hate
her for that.*

For not being able to tell you anything about your father?

Yeah. That, and everything else. On top of everything else.

*No wonder you're afraid she'll die if you meet him. If you're afraid you
are doing it out of revenge. But Stephen, I think you're doing it for yourself.*

And then she'd said:

I have an opinion, actually, about all this. Do you want to hear it?

Laura's opinion. He doesn't want to think about Laura's opinion.

Stephen walks back to his chair, photo in hand. She could be seventeen or eighteen here. Was this just before she got pregnant with him?

The man comes back in just as Stephen sits.

"Always have extra on hand, that's my motto." He pours himself a drink, remembers Stephen and gestures. "You?"

"No, thanks." Mitchell sits. Stephen puts the photo on the side table next to his chair, and looks up at the rest of the photos on the mantel. He thinks of how he'd feel if he were Gail coming into this room, the husband keeping pictures of his old wife up. With her kids, as if they were one big happy family. "How long have you been married to Gail?"

"Two years." He smiles again, blue eyes crinkling at the corners.

"We look a bit alike," Stephen says. "If I wasn't wearing glasses. I have your eyes." My mother's eyes, he thinks.

He glances at the photo next to him. His young mother looks at him accusingly with the eyes he now knows she inherited from her father. She's leaning slightly away from him in the picture. He feels a wave of guilt for his anger toward her: *drunken teenage one-night stand.* How can he be angry at her for that? For anything, now? *I hate my glasses too, Mom,* he thinks.

"So, Stephen, tell me a little about yourself. You're thirty. What are your interests? What do you do?"

"Ah..." Nothing he says will impress. "I work in a second-hand bookstore. I've been there almost five years now."

"So you like to read?"

"Oh, yes."

"What kind of literature?"

"Science fiction, mostly."

"Science fiction."

"Or speculative fiction, if you prefer that term."

It's evident the old man has never heard of speculative fiction.

Stephen imagines telling him about *The Hobbit* – that came first – then C.S. Lewis's Narnia. The ache inside him to have companions like the dwarves, or even siblings. To be able to press through a dark space and emerge into a world where there is magic and greatness. How sometimes he'd lie in the backyard with his eyes closed and wish and wish that when he opened them, he'd be in Middle Earth, or space. Battling evil single-handed, or being the scientist with hidden gifts, discovering how to use ESP to talk to the newly discovered intelligent species on a planet orbiting Barnard's Star.

"Any degrees?"

Stephen sighs. "I started English Lit at U of T. Ended up working for one of those companies that writes cheater essays for students." He sips his drink. "I didn't finish."

"Ah."

"And I play chess."

"Listen, I want to hear about your mother."

Check.

A bit reckless of the man. He is used to being obeyed. Stephen looks into the fire.

An opinion? he'd said to Laura. Thinking, not saying, *quelle surprise.*

Yeah, but I don't need to share it, unless you want me to.

Okay. Yeah, I want to hear it.

Your mother acts like a classic sex abuse victim.

What? Oh, come on.

I'm not saying for sure. I mean, it could be psychological incest, that has a real impact too. And if she's queer, that could be very damaging in the culture of the household, depending on how they dealt with it. And I'm guessing they wouldn't deal with it very well. But still...

What makes you think she was... had... like what?

There's lots of research into this stuff. We can look it up. She'd started a search on her laptop.

Wikipedia? You've got to be kidding.

It's a good place to start, actually.

And now the man wants to hear about Pearl. How she is.

Stephen shakes his head, very slightly.

"I don't have her permission."

Check.

Those hands; they remind Stephen of something, but he can't think what.

The silence grows in the room until Stephen's grandfather speaks. He can't bear silence, Stephen realizes, has to break it. "You're my only grandchild," he says. "My only blood. You and your mother." His tongue darts across his lips. "Pearl."

"You didn't have any other kids?"

"No." The man rises and walks to the window. With his back to Stephen he says, "All right, you don't want to talk about your mother. I respect that. That's her wish, I gather."

"I think so."

The man turns back.

"And she doesn't know you're here?"

"No."

"So you're pretty independent, Stephen."

"I… I guess so."

"Good. That's good. A man should know his own mind." The man perches on the corner of his desk. "That's always been my strength. Decisiveness."

"Well…"

"Your mother, she's decisive." The man smiles. "What a kid she was. Always running off on her own, insisting on everything her way. Fearless! What a kid."

Stephen wonders what kind of trouble his mother used to get into. Drinking young, that's for sure. Boyfriends, promiscuity. Lot's of dangerous stunts. She's alluded to being sent off to some private school to straighten her out. *It didn't work,* she'd said.

"She's told you stories, of course."

"Not really."

"No? That surprises me."

"She told me about an island."

Stephen won't tell the man that he's been there.

"The island! Yes, we had great times there. Happy, family times."

Stephen sips his drink.

"But your mother was always pretty dramatic. She used to make stories up. She still does, I bet. People don't really change all that much."

Stephen nods, not agreeing.

"She's probably told you some tall ones about me. She'd have to justify keeping you a secret from me all these years. I'm very glad we've made contact now." The man comes back to sit in the chair, elbows on knees, eager. "Very glad indeed."

"I am too," Stephen hears himself saying. Maybe this will work, maybe he can forge a relationship. Carefully, taking it slow.

"I'll bet you had an interesting childhood, with my Pearl as your mother."

Stephen laughs.

"See? I knew it. She's still trouble, isn't she?"

"I guess so." It won't do any harm to say that.

"Trouble with a capital T. She ever get married?"

"Umm…."

"Sorry, I don't mean to pry. It's just I miss her so, and…" The man turns his face away, jaw clenched. "I never understood why she estranged herself from me. From everyone."

Yes. Pearl does that. The man's jaw clenches, Stephen feels it as if it is his own.

"As you say, she's pretty dramatic."

It feels disloyal to say this. But it's such a relief to talk to someone who knows Pearl. Really knows her. Maybe knows her better than Stephen himself does.

"Dramatic!" It works, the mood lightens, the man's face lights up. "That's it exactly. That's the word. She'd take the smallest thing and... well, anyway, I don't mean to pry." Ice rattles in the old man's glass. Something changes in the room. The man looks back at Stephen, all hint of smile gone.

"I haven't seen or spoken to my daughter in twenty-five years. I want to know how she is!"

"Thirty."

"What?"

"You haven't seen her in thirty years. Since I was born."

The blue in the man's eyes brightens. "She came to her mother's funeral. And to the celebration for my wedding with Sophia."

He hadn't known that. He won't show it. "Did she talk to you?"

By the look on the man's face, Stephen knows Pearl didn't.

"Your mother was rather inebriated on both occasions. I don't think it would have done much good to talk."

Stephen keeps his gaze level, says nothing.

"Did you drive all the way down here just to get a look? Or are you going to say something?"

The man's voice sharpens; it's unexpected.

"What do you want me to say?"

"Pearl's – your mother's..." Stephen watches the man gather himself. "She makes things up." He takes another sip, he leans forward. He chuckles. "I remember once, when she was a little girl, she told her aunt I kidnapped her."

"Really?" He's fascinating, the way snakes are fascinating. "Why would she say that?"

"She was about five years old. Summertime. She was supposed to be in her bath but she ran out of the house, naked. What a kid. I'm in here and I see her in the garden – which had just been sprayed with pesticides..."

The man gestures at the window and Stephen looks out onto a winter landscape of shrubs, soft mounds where in summer there might be flowers. He imagines it, the little girl running outside into the snow garden. She is naked, she shivers, confused.

"Well, as soon as I saw her, I ran outside and swept her under my arm.

She yelled and screamed, she cried. She kicked me. I mean, someone seeing that, not knowing about the pesticides. What would they think?"

He's looking at Stephen as if he expects an answer. The story is strange, the details vivid yet irrelevant. "They'd think she was terrified of you."

"Yes," the man muses. "That's what they'd think. So you see how things can be misconstrued." He gets up and pours himself another drink. "And then she made things difficult for Sophia. We had the wedding over in Italy. Pearl didn't come, and – "

"She refused?"

"She wasn't invited. She, well…" The man looks over at Stephen and smiles, a sad smile. "She'd already cut me off."

"I see." Stephen sips his drink. Something goes cold in his belly. "I see."

"But we had a big celebration at this end. I managed to track her down; her aunt knew where she was… of course she was invited to that event."

"What aunt?" Is there some relative Pearl trusts and likes, someone he himself could meet?

"Her mother's sister. She's gone, now."

"Oh." He stifles his disappointment. "When was the, uh, your second wedding?"

"About a year after… after my first wife died."

"I see." He himself would have been four or five.

"But she came here, drunk as usual. And you couldn't imagine what she did there in the middle of our celebration."

"No, what?" Stephen looks at the photo again. Is his mother pregnant with him in the picture? The man's hand around his mother's waist, it's not really around her waist. It's around her ribs. High up, right under her breast. Touching. She leans away, her eyes blank.

"In front of everyone. She says, raising a glass, *Well, Sophia, I hope you're prepared to go down on your hands and knees, because that's the way Mitchell here likes it.*"

Stephen freezes.

The man doesn't notice, he's on a roll, feeling the drink a little.

"Your mother, she used to drink a lot as a young woman." The man sips, his eyes brighten. "Does she still drink a lot, Stephen?"

And now it's clear. Stephen is certain. In that moment, he is certain.

Laura had typed in "childhood sexual abuse"; it came up in Wikipedia as "child sexual abuse."

"*…Adults with a history of sexual abuse often present for treatment with a secondary mental health issue, which can include substance abuse, eating*

146

disorders, personality disorders, depression, and conflict in romantic or interpersonal relationships... revictimization in the teenage years, a bipolarlike switching between sexual compulsion and shut-down, and distorted thinking..."

What's revictimization? he'd asked.

A tendency to seek relationships or situations that are familiar – abusive if you've been abused, for example, or –

Stephen cut her off.

I don't know, Laura.

Did she have abusive boyfriends when you were growing up?

No. Yeah. This one guy for sure. She denied it but... But are you saying it's because her father abused her?

I don't know what happened. I really don't, Stephen. I don't mean to upset you.

I'm not upset.

There had been one of those pauses.

Okay, yeah, I'm upset.

I'm sorry...

That revictimization thing could describe maybe her drunken teenage hookup. Could describe me.

No, Stephen, no, it doesn't describe you! Whatever choices your mother made when she was eighteen... that doesn't change the fact that you're wonderful... and she loves you.

I'm the result of some "revictimization" complex.

We don't know that. Unless your mother comes out and tells you.

Fat chance.

Another pause.

Look, Laura, it's possible but I just don't see it. My mother is so... she's half nuts. She cut him off, sure, but she cuts everyone off. I mean, the guy sounded reasonable on the phone.

Your grandfather?

Yeah. My grandfather. And the symptoms aren't conclusive. They could describe anything. They even say it: "A specific characteristic pattern of symptoms has not been identified."

Yes.

So what does any of this tell me? Should I visit the old man or not?

She'd taken his hand, but didn't look at him. He thought it was because there were tears in her eyes that she didn't want him to see. *I think you know what you want to do. And for what it's worth, I think you're right. I think you need to do this, Stephen.*

147

"Pearl? She's a survivor," Stephen finally manages.

"Survivor?" The man gives a light laugh. "Of what? A loving father?" He looks around the room. "See what I gave her? This privilege. Stephen, whatever your mother has said… take it with a grain of salt."

"She doesn't speak of you."

The blow lands harder than he expects. The man snaps his mouth shut in a fury. "You drink a lot too, don't you? Like your mother. You should be careful."

It sounds like a threat. "I don't drink so much. Anyway, seems to run in the family."

Stephen puts down his half-finished drink and stands up. He hears the hush of his shoes over the carpet. He is backing toward the door. His body is taking him out of here, away.

"You're leaving? Don't be ridiculous."

Stephen plants his feet and looks squarely at the old man sitting in his chair, drink in hand. The firelight, the wood paneling, the way his hair and shirt glint with light in the dark room. He looks totally assured.

The disgust which has been rising in Stephen crystallizes, turning into something clear and hard.

The man stands. "I'll be in touch."

"No." It comes out with more force than Stephen intends. "No, I don't think so. Goodbye, Mitchell."

On the drive home the road gets blurry and headlights scream toward him. Wind is picking up, whining, nosing at the car. The sky darkens with cloud. He starts shaking uncontrollably and has to pull over at the Fifth Wheel. Same place they'd stopped before it all started, he and his mother. He swerves into the parking lot and stops the car, shuddering, hunched over and gripping the wheel with it. Is he crying? Something struggles up his throat.

He imagines his mother as a kid. He's seen photos, a few, Pearl doesn't have much of anything from her childhood. A little blonde girl, blurry, hard to connect that with his mother. The old man.

The storm hits and snow comes down in a fury. This is where it happened, the "stroke," God it seems years ago now, because from here his whole life is looking after Pearl in the hospital, Pearl with her radiation treatments, bringing her gum and dressing gowns, finding her outside smoking or in the hospital bed, laundering her underwear, bringing cigarettes and new books. Rubbing her feet. That's everything in the world, it's hard to remember he's ever done anything else.

What has the pink-handed monster done to Pearl?

Details don't matter. It happened. It happened until Pearl became the sort of person who cuts herself off from her whole life, who hides her son from her family, and smokes and drinks herself to death.

Those hands – and then he realizes what they remind him of. The hands acted, *decisive*, where he himself hesitates in inverse proportion. The hands are the negative of his own body, his cringing apology ready to turn to rage in a split second. That's why the man's hands looked so familiar.

Now he knows where he comes from. Stephen's breath shudders in his ribcage, he bangs his hands on the wheel, accidentally hitting the horn and making himself jump.

The man looks so good; it's only the hands that betray. Generations of pain in the curve of a hand. Whereas he himself tells the family story with his whole body.

But he hasn't done anything; he hasn't even known until today. Now he knows. Now he can feel it, make sense of it all.

Laura's waiting for him in the kitchen when he gets home.

"I was worried."

He shakes the snow off his coat. "Took me three hours to get from the Fifth Wheel to here. It's a bad one."

Laura nods. "I saw the forecast online. Hey, Cheryl called."

"Who?" He feels like he's emerged from a trip to the Arctic.

"Cheryl. You know. Sit down, I'll make you some tea. She says it'll cost eight-fifty to fix her car."

Stephen sits. "I don't have eight hundred and fifty dollars."

"Well, that's what she said." Laura puts on the kettle. "What's that all about?"

"I clipped her car with the Honda. Didn't even know it was hers; I left a note on her windshield." He takes off his glasses, rubs his nose.

The gesture is identical to that of the old man.

Stephen puts his glasses on the table. "I slept with her, Laura. With Cheryl. I didn't tell you." He hears Laura stop moving behind him. "It doesn't matter."

"When?"

"A while ago. Well, not that long ago. But it was before you and I were..." He gestures across the table, trying to represent their relationship since the photos at the riverside. "This."

"Oh. That's pretty, well, it's kind of funny." She sits; a little furrow creases her brow. "She's sort of tacky."

"She's not that bad. She's trying. Lonely, maybe."

"Yeah."

"You're the one she fell for," Stephen points out. "And now I owe her almost nine hundred damn dollars."

"You look exhausted." Laura starts to reach for his hand, pulls back. Stephen takes hold of her fingers. Then the shaking starts again. He hears himself apologizing and Laura climbs into his lap, twines around him, rocks him with her body. The storm roars and rattles outside; the kettle boils and boils on the stove.

Abruptly the crying stops.

Laura rises to take the kettle off, brings the teapot to the table.

"It's not just about meeting him," Stephen says. "It's... everything. Mom's coming home tomorrow."

An image, a white piece of paper flying into deep darkness and water, and then the shaking comes back.

"I'm sorry," and he puts his head down on the table, lets himself go until it passes. He sits up and wipes his face with his sleeve. "Ah, Jesus. Ah, God. Laura, I think I was thinking about killing myself." He covers his eyes with his hand. "No, that's not like me. I don't know." Laura's eyes are wide. "Can a person be suicidal and not even know it?"

"Oh, sure. Don't do it, though," she says. "Stephen."

They sit. Laura pours the tea.

"No," he says into their silence. "I need time." He thinks, *I need to live a really, really long time.* He smiles at Laura, a twisted smile and sad. "He's... he looks like Pearl. He lives in a huge house in Rosedale, family castle, really. He kept asking about Mom and I just didn't tell him. I'm pretty sure he... something about how he... and of course Mom is..." He takes a breath. "I don't want to have anything more to do with him."

They sit, and sit.

Laura stirs. "You've got enough on your plate. Let's just get your mother home."

Let's just get your mother home. She sounds unlike herself, the bounce is gone. She's being saintly. Was that because of dealing with him, his instability, his problems? Stephen thinks of his grandfather, of how he's gone through women just so he wouldn't have to be alone. He's used them up, three of them have died. Four wives. And then of course there's Pearl. And he himself – detritus – wreckage from the force of that man's huge need.

Stephen remembers a little clearing in a wood. No, not a wood – a small stand of trees, on the edge of a playground. He's about six years old, Grade One. At lunchtime he eats his sandwich (the sandwich he made himself that morning, sugar and margarine on white bread); then, when the teachers kick them out of the building to play, if he doesn't feel like playing with the others he goes to this little grove of trees. He goes there a lot. A big pine, towering, and some birches, pretty. He sits on a rock and imagines things, things he's read about in his books. He imagines different places, Neverland, away from here. He's alone, it's familiar. Now, it's almost the same. Each day, visiting his mother, going to work, even the drive down to Toronto to meet his grandfather, taking refuge in his head. Alone. He does things alone. He's still in that grove of trees.

"Laura," he says, "you and I... I don't think..." He takes a breath. "It just doesn't..." He looks at her – is he hurting her? He doesn't want to hurt her. "What do you think?"

She looks at him blankly.

"It's not that I don't care for you," he goes on. "I feel... confused and it doesn't seem like a good time to be trying to start, and I hate how I... This isn't going well." Shit, that sounds like he's been planning to break off with her. "I haven't been planning to break it off," he says. "I just... what do you think?" Shit.

"Stephen, do you think your mother's a dyke?"

"What?"

"She was flirting with me." She stares down into her tea. "Did you notice?"

"Oh. Yeah, I guess I did." He tries to follow Laura's change of tack. "She's always been weird with anyone she's met. She flirts with all my friends – guys, I mean. I just stopped bringing friends over to the house after a while, it was too embarrassing." He remembers one friend, they'd been about fifteen and he'd found Josh and Pearl making out in the kitchen. "Although sometimes... mostly they liked that Mom would get them drunk. As for girlfriends... I don't know. I never really introduced anyone to Mom before you. Figured she'd eat them alive."

"Well, I wondered if she was playing for the team."

"Did you introduce boyfriends or girlfriends to your mother?" he asks, curious.

"God, no. You kidding?"

"Yeah. I guess not."

Laura nods. "You could analyze our relationship in terms of our shared experience of role-reversal. Mothering our mothers..." She stops. "Our relationship."

"Ah, shit."

"No," Laura says slowly. "It's okay. I've been losing my boundaries with

151

you too… Maybe you're right. To break it off." She looks at him. "You do things alone, don't you, Stephen? It's how you do things."

She understands; it's such a relief. "Yes. I don't know how else to do it."

"And for us… It's hard to see where we'd go. I think. We're damaged in too many of the same ways."

He's not sure he agrees with her reasoning, but she smiles and it feels better to be friends, now.

Tired, they're both tired, but it's okay.

Later that night, as he lies in bed, he hears a phone ring; after a bit, he hears Laura go out. He gets up, stumbles to her room; the bed's empty. He puts his hand on the tangled-up sheets – still warm – it smells like her, sweet and a bit musky, nice, a nice smell, a bit warm-animal. The clock beside her bed says "11:11." Something about that makes it seem special. He shouldn't be in her room – he backs out, but he doesn't feel guilty. He's just saying goodbye.

Stephen books Tuesday off work. He drives to his mother's house to see that all is ready: puts fresh sheets on the bed, turns up the heat, makes sure there's toilet paper. The first home care worker is coming at 4:00 p.m., plenty of time for him to get Pearl home and settled. He runs out to the corner store and buys a carton of smokes and some magazines: *Vanity Fair*, she'll like that, make fun of all the beautiful people. He searches the house for the biggest ashtray he can find and brings it to the bedroom.

He stands in the room, feeling the silence of the house.

Soon he'll be here with Pearl, with nurses, waiting for her to die. He tries to picture what this will be like. Maybe she'll be lying in the bed, will slip away in sleep. He'll be there, holding Pearl's hand, telling her he loves her, because he knows that even when people look unconscious they can still hear; everyone says that… A surge of panic rises – maybe he can't do it – maybe it's too much.

He pushes this away. No. He'll just have to wait and see.

At the hospital Pearl is sleeping. It's a watery-sunlight sort of day, a leaky-yellow winter day. He drags a chair around to the right side of the bed so he'll be able to hear her properly when she wakes. She lies on her back, breathing through her open mouth. She's lost a lot of weight; her face is so drawn that her lips pull away from her teeth like pictures you see in magazines of starving people, elsewhere. It changes her face: a different Pearl with those sharp cheekbones and sunken eyes. Her breath stinks.

152

I was invincible. He remembers her saying this, describing her fifteen-year-old self. *I was invincible. Where the hell did you come from?* She was teaching him to drive, saying he'd better learn young; if you wait until you're older you get to the point where you realize that you're mortal, and then you're too scared. You turn into one of those people, she said, who never learn to drive.

Stephen at fifteen was so aware of his own mortality that the feeling of his blood moving through his veins would sometimes keep him awake nights; sitting behind the wheel of the metal monster was terrifying. It didn't help that Pearl gave the instructions all backwards; she was a terrible teacher and he told her that: *You're a terrible teacher, Mom.*

Shut up and do what I tell you. The brake. I said the brake, *not the gas, the brake's on the left. No, don't use your left foot, Jesus...* and they hadn't even left the driveway. Finally she got him to pull shakily away from the house, going about ten kilometers an hour, his teenaged body just soaking in sweat and miserable terror; she rolled down the window and lit a smoke, they went around the block a few times. She told him how to signal and turn, she flicked her butt out the window. *You're doing great,* she said, *just fine,* and then a truck came barreling around a corner, right towards him, he just couldn't see how there was room for him and this thing on the road, and without thinking he jerked the wheel sharply to the right and crashed into a tall wooden fence. Didn't hit the brake either; he revved on the gas and the car crashed through, jolting horribly, splintering wood. *Brake, brake!* screamed his mother and he did, with his left foot, and they stopped. He just sat there, foot jammed down on the brake, shaking. She reached over and put the car into park, then turned the key so there was blessed silence.

He was sure she'd be mad. But instead, after a shocked silence, she'd thrown back her head and laughed and laughed. *It's all right,* she said, *that was fun.* She lit a smoke and offered him one, like she sometimes did – *Smoke?* – she thought it was funny because he always said no. *Whoooo!* she said, fanning her hand in front of her face. *That was a rush. Wow!* They got out and looked at the car – no damage, a miracle. Then Pearl eyed the house in front of them, in whose front fence they'd just made a car-sized hole. *It's that asshole, Jeremy, Mister Big, whatever. Doesn't look like anyone's home.* She got into the driver's seat and started the car again, throwing it into reverse. *Let's go.*

Aren't you going to tell him? Stephen asked, standing by the open passenger door.

That guy walks around like he owns the neighbourhood; I'm not giving him the satisfaction. Get in the car, let's go to a parking lot. We'll practice there.

But… But he'd meekly gotten in and they'd gone off to the mall parking lot and she'd gotten him doing stops and turns until the sun started to go down. *Whoo-hoo!* Pearl yelled as she drove them home. *That was the most fun I've had in months! Way to go, Sir Stephano!* He still feels guilty whenever he walks by that fence. But his mother was right. That guy Jeremy is an asshole.

Pearl sleeps. There's another memory surfacing now, an island, was he nine? It was late fall, he was supposed to be in school but she took him away on a whim – a beautiful jewel memory. He'd been there before, but he'd been a little kid and barely remembered: there was something about drowning; in fact at nine he hadn't realized that it was the same place. The pieces only fall into place now and he sees that they'd visited this island twice. A cottage on a private island, with a great big house they never went into, all shut up. It belonged to the old man. A family cottage, and they went in fall so the man wouldn't be there.

He looks at her sleeping face. The line that's always there between her eyebrows deepens; she stirs, sinks again. She must have really loved that place, he thinks, to risk going there twice. Visiting her birthright.

They took a boat stashed in a marina. Pearl sang, passing islands with houses like castles. Her voice was high and sweet; he loved it when she sang. A song with a slow, steady beat that she pounded softly on the console with her palm, something about being able to drink a whole case of you and still be standing up… It's that Joni Mitchell song, a famous one, he realizes now. A song beautiful enough to make you weep.

They stayed only two nights. First night he'd been scared, hadn't known that a river becomes a giant lapping animal, and trees rub their spectral bones together like hands. He lay there getting more and more afraid until something actually tapped at his window, scraping down the glass like a fingernail and he yelled in fright.

It's okay, his mother said, coming in to him where he sat bolt upright on his damp little bed. She sat on the edge of the bed, got him to lie down again, stroked his forehead; it felt so nice. *This island is full of noises, sounds and sweet airs, that give delight and hurt not.* She was saying things from that magic play she liked to read him sometimes. She smoothed his hair over and over – he was too old for this but it soothed him – his eyes started to close but he tried to stay awake, tried to keep hold of his mother's voice. *It's a magic place, this island. There are spirits here, maybe fairies? Elves. Like in that book you like,* The Hobbit – *yes, elves, that's right. I've heard*

154

things, here. A thousand twangling instruments would hum about my ears, and sometimes voices, that, if I had waked after long sleep, will make me sleep again. She stroked his head, he felt sleep coming. *And then in dreaming, the clouds methought would open, and show riches ready to drop upon me, that when I waked, I cried to dream again.*

What riches? he asked sleepily, and she named a bunch of things she knew he liked: a crystal chess set, an elfish cloak that makes you invisible, a sword with jewels on the hilt, one of those exciting new Game Boys. He giggled, but sank back into sleepiness.

Remember the sunset? He did, red clouds over the water, at the end of the dock, red like watermelons and gold and purple too. *I used to dream of clouds like that, when I was little. It was so beautiful that when I woke up I cried.*

Why? He was almost asleep now.

Because I wanted to get back to that dream.

Pearl moves a little under the hospital blanket, settles. He puts his hand on her forehead, strokes his hair. Pearl stirs under his hand, opens her eyes, sleepy. She smiles.

"Is this not Stephano, my drunken butler?"

"That's me."

"Am I going home today?" Her face brightens a little.

"Yes."

She yawns widely without bothering to cover her mouth, like a little kid. She lets her eyes wander about the room, and he keeps stroking her forehead. "That feels nice." Then, "There's someone I want you to call."

Stephen sits back in his chair, heart leaping. "Who?"

"It's someone you've never met – oh, no, once you did."

"Who?"

"Shoulda been your father."

"What?" He leans in, breath catching, not sure he's heard.

"She should have been your father. If anyone could have been."

She?

"Would've been a sight better parent than I was. But you'll meet her, if you can find her. Tell her to come here." She pushes herself slowly up the bed until she's sitting, and biting down impatience, Stephen arranges pillows behind her back. "Get my comb, will you?"

Pearl combs and combs her hair.

"Still not losing any, see?" She triumphantly brandishes the plastic comb; only a few stray hairs float in its teeth.

He nods. "Still not losing any."

"Let's hope not ever," she says. "Bad enough to be…" She hands the comb to him to tuck into her toiletries bag. She twists her hands together. "I want a smoke."

"Who is this person you want me to call?" Stephen flips open his phone.

"Oh, I don't know her number. But you can find it, right? On the net or something. Her name's Mouse."

"Mouse?" He vaguely remembers his mother mentioning this name before.

"Yeah." Pearl looks out the window. "I gave her that name. Long time ago. When she still loved me. Mandy Brown."

Stephen puts his phone away. Great; some old lover of Pearl's, suddenly invited to the deathbed scene. If this person really exists; he wonders if Pearl is getting weird in the head.

Then he remembers it doesn't matter. She gets to do this her way.

"Okay, her name's Mouse or Mandy. Do… does she have a last name? Where does she live, what does she do?"

"Brown is her last name, I told you," Pearl snaps, sounding more like herself. "She lives in B.C. I read something about her in a magazine; she co-founded some company with a bunch of women. Green investments, something like that." She looks out the window again, playing with her fingers. "She's done pretty well for herself." She turns back to Stephen, glaring. "For the love of God, get me out of here. Why the hell are you just sitting there like a damn lump?"

The switch takes him by surprise. He gets to his feet, mumbling apologies. Of course, he's sorry; he'll talk to the nurses right away, see if there's paperwork to be done, get a wheelchair… He's all the way to the door before she speaks again.

"Sir?"

He turns.

She's sitting up, one hand raised; she's quoting: "Bear with my weakness; my old brain is troubled. Be not disturbed with my infirmity."

He can't make out her face. The sunlight streams through the window and lights her from behind like a holy thing.

$\mathcal{I}$t's big. Goddamn it's big, this island. There's no substitute for driving across the place to feel the sprawl of it, the sheer, illogical, nine-hundred-kilometre expanse.

Mouse drives the Trans Canada from St. John's to Port aux Basques in one long tooth-numbing day. Port of the Basques: they'd known about the Grand Banks years before Cabot got that far, keeping their source of huge, fat cod a secret for generations, coming across the Atlantic in tiny boats year after year. Mouse can't picture it. She has trouble believing she's going to make even this, a drive across an island in a twenty-first-century rented car. Only on this godforsaken rock would a major highway be all hills and twists and no light. It's already after ten and she's supposed to be lining up at the ferry within the hour; it leaves at quarter to midnight and she hates being late.

The signs haven't come as often as she'd like. Placentia, Gander, Grand Falls, Corner Brook: familiar names loom up in the dark. There isn't much snow until she gets close to the west coast, and then it starts whipping across the pavement, sinister pale snakes in the headlights. The weather forecast calls for a storm; it originated in Texas, hit Ontario two days later and is heading Newfoundland's way, but Mouse had hoped to get to the ferry and ride it out on the crossing. The wind increases and the car begins to shake. She's north of Port aux Basques, where gales come howling down the eastern slopes of the Long Range Mountains. The Wreckhouse, they call it.

The name comes to her through some small neural pathway, hardly ever used now; comes to her as she struggles to keep the tiny rented car on the road, steering into the wind and watching the huge transport truck in front of her slew and shudder. The truck looks like it's tipping; Jesus, it's going over. The Wreckhouse. Silent under the force of this wind, the truck tips with an illusion of gentleness onto its passenger side, lying there like a downed animal.

She pulls over. No other headlights in sight – God, will her phone work here? Mouse struggles to open her car door and can't; against that wind she has the strength of a child. She scoots over to the passenger side and cracks open that door; it almost tears out of her hands. In an instant she's frozen; why hadn't she put on her hat and gloves? Too late now; she crawls out of the car and staggers, hunched over like an ape, toward the truck.

She's almost there when another transport comes crawling along the road from the opposite direction; with relief she sees it slow and stop. She changes tack and begins to struggle toward it, thinking, it'll take the two of us to pry open that downed truck. She gets there and the driver has his door open and is screaming at her, something whipped away by the wind: *"Get away, get back, I might go over!"*

Mouse staggers back and watches as the trucker maneuvers his vehicle alongside the tipped transport, shielding it from the wind. He gets out and together they clamber up onto the side of the truck. Mouse's fingers are frozen now, but she forces them onto the cold metal of the door handle, prays it isn't locked. It isn't, it opens, and with the trucker's help she gets it up. The driver inside looks up at them. *"Hello, I'm all right,"* he says. Yells. They haul him out by his armpits and together walk him to the cab of the other truck. The three of them fall into the seats – the trucker closes the door – and suddenly the scream of the hungry wind dims. They can hear their own breath, like sobbing.

"Thanks," the rescued driver gasps.

"Jesus, I thought you were a man," the other trucker says to Mouse.

She looks at him across the heaving chest of the rescued driver. "Well, I'm not."

"Sturdy girl," says the rescued man, and manages a grin.

After shaking hands all round, the second trucker walks Mouse to her car. She pulls out; her rental shudders, but stays on course. She can see the trucker, a wraith in her rear-view mirror, appearing and disappearing in the toss of blown-up snow.

It takes nearly half an hour for her fingers and face to thaw, and longer to stop shaking. She's nearly there. A line of cars comes roaring past – passengers off the ferry, she assumes; there's no other reason for a crowd like that, not out here. Damn, damn, damn. She hates being late. Headlights dazzle her; it's a relief when the last car finally passes, leaving her driving on in the dark, alone. The wind has let up some now that she's out of the funnel; there's less snow flying at the windshield. She speeds up. She isn't going to miss this ferry – there isn't another one for twenty-four hours.

Suddenly a shape lurches out of the darkness, something huge and pale in her headlights. She has just enough time to register the moaning shriek that comes out of her, the way her heart flies up into her mouth. She skids to a stop. The moose crosses the road and disappears, shadowy, a ghost in the woods.

Yesterday she'd been in St. John's, nearly through her annual ten-day visit with her mother. It had gone pretty well, this one – no fights, lots of TV. Thank Christ they both like the Home and Garden Network – it gives them something to talk about besides Clancy and his *terrible* wife and *adorable* children. Mouse is rather fond of her nieces and nephew, but Jesus, there's only so much you can say about a three-year-old thug of a boy and two distressingly princess-like twins. And she's sick of the alleged saintliness of Clancy and the terribleness of the wife. There's no changing the subject once her mother gets onto that.

Mouse wishes her mother would ask, just once, without being prompted, about Susan. She and Susan have been together over ten years: twice as long as Clancy's marriage.

It had been evening, her phone buzzed; she knew it was Susan. They speak every day while she's away, something to look forward to.

Mouse takes her phone out of the kitchen, too full with her mother and the ever-blaring TV, and sits on the stairs to talk. She hugs her knees and pictures Susan in their new condo, sitting on their new white couch in the hip new neighbourhood in East Van. "Are you in the living room?" she asks Susan. "On the couch?"

"Yes, and I'm wearing lacy black underwear and nothing else, what do you think?" Susan snorts when she laughs, makes Mouse laugh too. "How's your Mom today?"

"Fine. We baked cookies."

"That's sweet. Tell her I say hi."

Susan's visited St. John's a few times and Mouse's mother is very polite to her. Mouse has never told Susan that on her solo visits, whenever she mentions her lover, her mother gets quiet, sniffs, and changes the subject.

"How's your day been?"

They talk. Mouse cajoles Susan into waiting until she gets back before painting the bathroom, and then Susan says, "By the way, Beth called with a message."

Beth is Mouse's secretary. "Why didn't she just call my cell?"

"She wasn't sure if you'd want this message – she seemed to think it was a bit weird, wanted to know what I thought. It was a man. He phoned this morning asking if you could please call him back, it's important and it's about his mother. Left a number."

"About his *mother?* Weird."

159

Stephen, his name is. Something, maybe boredom, prompts her to dial his number immediately after hanging up with Susan.

He answers. His voice is deep, rather pleasing, but there's a hesitancy. Yes, he's Stephen, he says, he'd tracked her down by Googling her because his mother requested... sorry, he should have started by saying who his mother is, sorry.

Mouse sits huddled on her mother's stairs, phone to ear, halfway between the first and second floors of the cramped little house. Framed photographs of Clancy and his family – the kids, the wife – line the wall. There's a lone picture of herself from years ago, a university graduation photo. She looks the picture of young 'eighties dykedom, all spiked streaked hair and ear-piercings. Her mother wouldn't realize that; otherwise it wouldn't be on the wall.

His mother is Pearl, says the man. Pearl Lewis.

He mistakes her silence for incomprehension or offense. He rushes into more apologies and explanations.

"Slow down," she says. "Back up." It's been over ten years since she's heard from Pearl. A hand squeezes her stomach. What is it? Fear, maybe, but of what?

"She's, well, she's dying, I'm afraid. She's got terminal lung cancer."

Mouse stares at the photos on her mother's wall. A black and white one of her father on a hunting trip, smiling, a caribou at his feet.

"She asked me to call you," the man says.

"Lung cancer." That is her own voice.

"Yes." A pause. "I'm sorry to have to give you that news."

Pearl is dying.

"She told me you're friends from university. She wants me to contact you and..." Mouse senses him rushing in to reassure her; he's that kind of person, even though his own mother is dying. "So you see, I had to... I'm sorry."

"I know who you are." Mouse's voice sounds strange; she clears her throat. "I met you when you were a kid." Impossible to connect this voice to that skinny little four-year-old. She stands and makes her way up the stairs to the guest room, her mother's quilt-sewing room with a little cot shoved against the wall amidst piles of fabric and patterns. "Is she... is she close to death, Stephen? Is she in hospital?"

"She's at home. We've gotten part-time home care. Yes, I think she doesn't have long. Weeks, maybe. They say."

"Is she conscious?" Mouse sits on the cot, pushing aside her laptop.

"Oh... oh, yes, she's not that far gone. Yes, she's still talking and all

160

that, still… herself. But she wanted me to contact you. She… wants to see you."

Oh, God. Oh, shit. Oh, Pearl, damn you.

Mouse goes online and books a rental car; for some reason she feels she must drive to see Pearl. Red, how do you request a particular colour of car? She cancels her flight back to Vancouver. She calls Susan.

"But…" The incredulity in her lover's voice tells Mouse just how strangely she is acting, and cements her determination. "You haven't seen this woman in how long?"

"Over ten years."

"So she's hardly a close friend."

Mouse pauses. "We used to be."

"I see." Mouse hears the repressed jealousy in Susan's voice. Usually her lover's slight possessiveness charms Mouse. "But you've never mentioned her to me. Not once."

"Well, it *has* been ten years since we spoke."

"Since you met me," Susan points out.

Yes, that's true; she hasn't called or written Pearl since meeting Susan. She hasn't needed to.

"And why not fly to Toronto?"

I don't know. "Look, I just need time, baby," she says. "I love you. Okay?"

"Okay." What else can Susan say?

Her mother is also upset. "Who is this friend, anyway?" she asks. "What about Susan? How does she feel about this?"

Since when are you the defender of Susan? Mouse wants to ask; she sees it, the suspicion in her mother's eyes. If there's one thing worse than a married lesbian, it's a free-ranging lesbian with a girl in every port. "Pearl," is what she says. "A friend from university."

"Well, *I* never heard of her."

"She's *dying,* Mom."

At that she subsides, but she can't believe Mouse is just canceling a flight like that, what a waste of money. "I can afford it," Mouse says. She bought her mother a trip to the Caribbean last year, a new car; she's good with money, it's her *job* – but then Mouse sees what it is. "You're mad because I'm leaving early, aren't you?"

"You can do whatever you like, sure," her mother sulks.

Mouse wraps her arms around her mother and hugs her.

"And don't think you can buy me off with hugs," her mother sniffs, laying her head on Mouse's shoulder.

"I love you too," says Mouse.

She leaves before dawn the next morning, driving a cherry red car.
She makes it to the ferry.

It's a relief to stand up, to get out of the car and walk across the parking deck. The immense space cracks and booms; it's cold. Mouse squeezes between parked cars to a door, climbs narrow staircases. Eight decks, a big cafeteria, a lounge, a bank machine. Mouse finds her cabin and washes her face in a tiny sink. She feels strangely wide awake. The engines shudder and announcements blare: they are to expect high seas, passengers are to use caution. Loneliness engulfs her. She'll call Susan now, in case they lose the signal on the open water. Four and a half hours earlier, in Vancouver.

Susan is so worried by the incident with the moose that Mouse doesn't tell her about the Wreckhouse.

The crossing is supposed to take about six hours but they take nine, with the bad weather. Mouse wakes at dawn and pulls clothes on, goes in search of breakfast. On the way she meets a blind woman with a seasick guide dog. "He's that worried," the woman says, "because he knows he can't take care of me properly," and the blonde dog looks up at her and cries. Then she finds a woman curled on her side in the washroom, sick as that dog.

Mouse goes along halls until she finds the on-board doctor, and leads him back to give the woman a Gravol injection. "You might want to see about that guide dog, too."

Other women come in, one wearing fuzzy slippers.

"You've come prepared."

"Oh, yes, my dear, I takes this ferry too often. Got to have me slippers."

The other women fix their hair, brave the pitch and roll and attempt to put on makeup. Mouse looks at herself in the mirror. *I look pretty good for forty-eight,* she thinks, then laughs out loud. Pretty good.

Breakfast is served by two cheerful Newfoundlanders: "And my lovely associate will serve you the eggs!"

"Why, thank you, me love! Bacon, dear?"

Mouse takes a pass on the eggs and featureless meat, settles on All Bran in a box, a plastic cup of no-fat yoghurt, an inedible muffin and coffee like battery acid. She eats and drinks it, all of it, looking out the window at the greying horizon. Spray flings itself against the glass; the ferry heaves. She's enjoying this, she realizes. She hasn't traveled alone for years, not since meeting Susan, excepting for annual plane rides to visit home, which she fills up with work on her laptop. She forces open a door onto the deck. It's cold, cold; she thinks she can make out a dark mass of land, Cape Breton coming up in the spray. She sidles along the deck past a few huddled smokers under a metal staircase, and rounds a corner. The full force of the wind hits her and she's taken across the deck. She washes up against the rail and whoops into the wind, her breath torn from her lungs. She whoops again, like a kid, laughing.

Too bad it isn't summertime. It'd be good to see more of Cape Breton. She drives off the ferry into grey daylight, drives as fast as she can in that cherry red car. The storm has passed, leaving clear skies. South Gut/St. Ann's, Big Hill, St. Patrick's Channel, Aberdeen. Off Cape Breton Island and across Nova Scotia: Antigonish, New Glasgow, stopping for fast food outside Amherst. She isn't sure how far she'll get in one day – she's pushing it – in New Brunswick now, approaching Moncton. She's always found New Brunswick confusing – so like and yet unlike the rest of the East Coast – those big *farms*. But she loves this highway; in places the red, oxidized dirt stains through the snow, reminding her of the rosy shorelines of Prince Edward Island. Her father had a particular rant about P.E.I.: how in the Ice Age the glaciers scraped over Newfoundland and took the topsoil with them – then upon their retreat, they dumped all that rich, red stuff into the Gulf of Saint Lawrence. *And so formed Prince Edward Island,* he'd finish. *Those Green Gables bastards got our topsoil! The Rock, they calls us, trying to be cute. I'll give 'em rock.* She still smiles, thinking about her father. She still misses him.

She gets to Fredericton later that night, drives into the first motel she sees on the outskirts, a shoddy affair with a pool, covered for winter, outside her door. She has to lie on the bed for half an hour before the feeling of motion subsides. ·

"It's just so unlike you."

Mouse mutes the TV, but she keeps her eyes on the flickering figures. "What do you mean?" she asks Susan.

"It's impulsive. You're such a planner."

"I've got a plan. I'm driving to Ontario, and I'll fly back to Vancouver from Toronto once I'm done there." Mouse hears the slight whine in her own voice and immediately wants to apologize.

"And when will that be?"

"I'll know better once I get there, I guess."

Mouse looks at the dancing figures on the silent television, the incomprehensible dialogue. Only Pearl could induce her to commit such acts of recklessness, of abandon.

Later she calls Stephen. "I'm tall, with short dyed-blonde hair. Um, my jacket is red Gore-tex... The rental car is red."

"Well, I'm not tall, my hair is neither here nor there, my coat is an indeterminate shade of blah..."

His dry tone pulls a laugh out of her. They arrange to meet at the rental-car outlet, where she can leave the car and he'll drive her to Pearl's house. Brown hair, five-ten, grey wool coat, glasses, thirty: this is how Pearl's son describes himself. Thirty years gone by.

Mouse's dreams that night are of driving, past rivers and islands. Pearl is at the wheel, and Mouse cannot say a single word, no matter how hard she tries.

She sees the slender young man approaching her across the frozen pavement of the parking lot.

An adult, a man. Those cheekbones, the lips, and behind the glasses, those startling eyes. Pearl's son has gone from that little swimmer on the island to this. He's holding out a hand to shake.

"Mouse?"

And before that – before that – the recklessness of Pearl, faint scent of Old Spice, her self-absorbed and irresistible madness.

She takes his hand. "I won't tell you how much you've grown."

He ducks his head and purses his lips. He's tired, she thinks.

"I've got a car here – it's a bit of a beater – this way..." He leads her toward a battered grey Honda. "How was your trip?"

Can she see any of Pearl in him besides the physical similarities? He's like a negative, she thinks; he effaces himself.

"Fine. Long."

He realizes she's carrying luggage. There's a comical moment where they actually engage in a tug-of-war over her big bag. She lets him win.

"It's heavy – careful."

He carries it easily. They load the bags into the car – "It's my mother's, it's Pearl's," he says – then head to the office so Mouse can do the rental-car paperwork. The little glassed-in office is crammed by a family of about twenty, it seems, and it takes a while to get to the agent to pay. As they walk back to the grey car, Mouse breaks the silence with the first remark that comes into her head. "They were Iranian."

164

"Who?"

"That family. They were speaking Persian." She hears something almost smug in her voice, a kind of urban B.C. drawl in her vowels. Is she trying to impress him?

When he turns the ignition key, music blasts, and he hastily hits the *off* switch on the battered CD player, apologizing.

"What is it?" she asks.

"The music? *Yield*." He swings the car out and around the corner.

"The band's called Yield?"

"No." He clears his throat. "Pearl Jam. A bit mainstream of me."

Mouse looks out the window; the sun has disappeared behind the horizon. Grey, Ontario is grey, the outskirts of the town are lined with strip malls. She wonders how his driving will be, him being a seemingly hesitant person; she fears either aggression or equivocation, but his driving is surprisingly competent, smooth and a little fast. They speed along. Traffic isn't bad.

In the silence there are too many questions. She wants to ask him what kind of mother Pearl has been, is she still so self-absorbed, did she take care of him? Of herself? Did she grow up? Does he love his mother, who is she, when will she die? – all stupid questions, impossible questions rising up because there is silence. Mouse breaks it. "Put it back on if you like."

"What?"

"The music."

"No, it's okay."

"No, really. I'd like to hear it." When he reluctantly presses play (turning the volume down first) she thinks the song is vaguely familiar. It's a list song, a wish song. The voice is masculine, blurry around the edges but it cuts through. She recognizes the sound – that nineties Seattle scene.

"One of the soundtracks of my teens," Stephen says.

"I like it." She does. It's full of longing.

They drive, the song ends. Stephen ejects the CD.

"You've traveled a lot," he says.

"Hmm?" She looks at his profile. Strange how he looks like Pearl – with more jaw to him, more masculine – yet so unlike. And that hesitation, that isn't Pearl at all.

"The Iranian family. You've traveled a lot." He glances in the rear-view mirror, signals, changes lanes.

"Oh – yeah, I have. Work, holidays. But the Persian thing, I just know that because my girlfriend's half Persian. Susan. We've been together ten years." Might as well get that out of the way fast.

"Oh, yeah. Guess she's glad not to be living in Iran just now."

"Sure." Mouse pauses. "They're not too fond of lesbians there."

"Were you and my mother lovers?" He glances over at her, suddenly direct, blue eyes gleaming.

She is surprised by how much the question throws her. "No, I wouldn't call us..." She adjusts her seatbelt. "It was... we were young..." Why is she feeling so embarrassed?

"It's okay. I don't care or anything. You don't have to talk about it if you don't want to."

This is ridiculous. She's as out as anyone – she organizes the annual ride of the Vancouver Dykes on Bikes, for God's sake. "No, it's okay. It wasn't serious between us, I guess." God, that's a lie, what a liar. "Okay, well, I was, she was the first girl I ever fell in love with. But it was short. It ended badly."

"With me," Stephen says.

She stares at him.

"I figured out the math. " He keeps his eyes on the road. "When you knew each other and all that, from what Mom says."

"She talked about me?" Mouse clutches at the seatbelt again with her hand, pulling it away from her throat. Why is her heart squeezing and squeezing, up her throat, into her mouth?

"Well... it must have been something, for her to want you to come now." He glances at her again. "Thank you, by the way. For coming. I haven't thanked you. It's very kind of you, and it means a lot to her."

"How... is she?"

"She's on steroids to reduce the swelling of the tumours, so she's pretty, um, she can be kind of irritable."

Mouse imagines Pearl on steroids. "I bet."

They drive.

"She's at home, you said?"

"Yes. Pretty much stays in bed at this point. Needs a bit of help to get to the bathroom and all that."

"You have nursing care?"

"Saint Elizabeth sends someone for a few hours each day, to wash her and stuff." His voice flattens, he sounds tired, now, talking of this.

"How are you holding out?"

"Okay. I thought I'd be able to keep working during the week and look after her nights and weekends, but she doesn't really sleep at night. So there goes that idea. I got a couple of weeks off work. I don't know what I'll do after that."

"Well…" Mouse doesn't know what to say. "You said she doesn't have long, right?"

Stephen stares at her.

"I mean, not to connect your work schedule with her – " She cuts herself off, looks out the window again; it's nearly dark, now. They are, she thinks, getting close to the centre of town; it's hard to say, things have changed so much. She curbs a wild impulse to promise this young man that she'll stay until the end, look after Pearl for him. She can't do that, she is a busy person, and she can't leave Susan alone for weeks on end for some teenage love who actually hadn't even really been a lover. Who had, really, ruined a part of her life.

"Yeah," Stephen says into the silence, his voice neutral. "Well, I'll work something out."

Streets look vaguely familiar, but she's making that up; she only lived there a few weeks and that was on campus, thirty years ago. Red brick houses, pretty with white trim and porches. Snow gleams under street lights.

"She's a bulldog," he says finally. "The doctors won't say anything. But the nurses, they talk about that stuff. They say it's amazing she's hung on this long. She's stubborn, they say."

"They got that right," Mouse mutters, then catches herself. But it's okay – Stephen's smiling. She lets out a laugh, and they grin at each other. His teeth are crooked, unlike his mother's perfect smile, but it's appealing. *Pearl's perfect pearlies* springs into her mind – what she and the others in that play they worked on together called Pearl's smile. Mouse realizes that things she had seen as a sort of emanation from Pearl the person – hair, skin, teeth, clothes that were unostentatious but fit just right – were markers of wealth; realizes that she's now come to be able to identify a person, just by looking at them, as coming from wealth. Most of her clients are wealthy: the rich with consciences, the ones scared by all the storms and rising sea levels, the economic crash and climate change.

It strikes her how strange it is that Stephen is so shabby – and this car. He doesn't have the bearing of one used to entitlement. And those awful glasses. Has Pearl's evil father died, turned out to have less money than they'd all thought? A sombre group of suited lawyers, an imagining of mahogany tables and hidden creditors: *He was living far beyond his means,* they're saying, *we're sorry.* Pearl takes the hand of a small boy and walks away. Some other family owns the island now, a rich family with nice children, all of them with perfect hair, skin and teeth.

When her father died there had been some debts, she remembers. The

167

car, and something else that her mother wouldn't talk about. Mouse guesses it had something to do with the other woman, the cheat, the lover. Anyway, it was over now.

"At least you have time," Mouse hears herself saying. "Time to be with your mother."

Stephen accelerates past a minivan. He turns his eyes on her again. "Time," he repeats.

"Before she dies," Mouse clarifies. "My own father died very suddenly; I didn't get to see him."

"Yeah." Stephen looks back at the road. "Yeah." It's a bleak word, it's enough to hurt you just listening to it.

As they pull into the downtown, Mouse's heart beats faster. She tells herself to brace for it: sickness, age, difference. Pearl may be unrecognizable to her, a wreck, a shadow; it is this, she tells herself, that is hammering away in her chest. She feels a guilty flash for Susan.

"I gotta call my girlfriend." She rummages for her phone. It rings and rings. She'll leave a message. "Hey, Susan, it's me. I've arrived and I'm okay. Call you later. Or you call me, love you, 'bye." She wishes Susan had picked up; why hadn't she picked up?

Stephen passes a police station that looks like a fast-food outlet with a drive-through, turns a corner, and slows onto a quiet street. Street lamps illuminate things in waves: more pretty red brick houses, and some that look like old farmhouses. He pulls into a bumpy driveway outside a small house. It is perhaps old, but clad in ugly aluminum siding, white and mint green, dirty. Someone has carved a large modern window into the front; uneven curtains cover it. Stephen cuts the engine. "We're here," he says. "Mom's house." It is the shabbiest house on the street.

He pulls her luggage from the back while Mouse steps into the drive, struck by the feeling of dry cold in this place, so different from the wetness of Newfoundland or the mildness of B.C. She zips her coat, stretches.

"Let me get that," she says, relieving Stephen of one of her bags. She follows him up the icy drive.

"Sorry, the porch light is burnt out and I haven't replaced it yet," he says. "Watch out, it's slippery here. Should put some salt on that."

The porch floor sags a little, creaks, and Stephen holds open the front door for her.

The smell of cigarette smoke hits her in a wave. The front hall is small, with a staircase ascending just inside the door. A woman's coat hangs over the newel post; a few coat hooks on the wall are loaded with hats and coats.

There's a poster on one wall, Picasso's *Don Quixote*. The black and white lines, the cheer of Sancho's roundness, seem so unlike what Mouse is feeling that she turns away.

"Hello!" Stephen calls up the stairs. He puts the bag down, and Mouse hears footsteps overhead. "There's a nurse here," he says to her. "I didn't want to leave Mom alone. Here, give me your coat." A young woman comes down the stairs wearing a generic health-worker's uniform. She looks too young to be a nurse.

"She's sleeping," the young woman says with a smile at Stephen.

"You're kidding," he says, "really?"

"Yup. Dropped right off."

"What'd you give her, Deb? Be honest, now." He takes Mouse's coat. "This is an old friend of Mom's. Mouse, Deb, Deb, Mouse."

"Mouse?" falters the nurse, and Mouse nods, shakes hands with her. It's interesting, seeing Stephen talking with this girl. He seems to gain stature as he talks, and the nice young woman – Deb? – seems to like it. "Nice to meet you, Mouse. I didn't give her anything." She lowers her voice. "She was hitting the scotch pretty hard, though." She giggles.

"That's you," Stephen says to Mouse. "She was really excited you were coming. Well, she can drink if she wants to, right?"

"I'm not supposed to condone it, but, yeah," says the nurse. "Well, I'll see you tomorrow."

"Tomorrow? I thought you weren't on again until Wednesday." Stephen helps the nurse into her coat.

"Yeah, well, I like you guys. Your mom's a riot. I'll see you tomorrow," she says, switching white sneakers for boots and heading out the door. Stephen goes after her.

"Hold on, it's slippery..." He looks over his shoulder at Mouse. "I'll just be a second." He lets the screen door bang behind him. Mouse hears his voice and the nurse's goodbyes, footsteps leaving the porch, grit hitting ice – Stephen's salting the drive.

Slowly, she sits on the stair and takes off her boots. Then she walks farther into the house. The hall gives way to a serviceable little kitchen. A small living room off that, with wall-to-wall carpet and a low table with a big, square, dust-free spot where, she guesses, a piece of furniture used to be, perhaps a TV table. Stephen probably moved it upstairs for his mother. No photos. Mouse goes back out to the kitchen, sits at the small table. It's ugly, this house.

She hears the front door open and shut, and Stephen removing his snow boots in the hall.

"I'm in here."

He comes in rubbing his hands together. "Cold tonight." They look at each other. "Um, I got my old room ready for you. Please make yourself at home. I don't know how long you... Um, would you like some tea?"

"Love some," she says. "Well, should I go visit Pearl or something? Let her know I'm here?"

He moves to the stove. "Are you kidding? She's asleep. This is gold. She hasn't slept in, I don't know, days, apart from a few hours here and there." He fills the kettle with tap water and puts it on the stove. "It sounds like I'm talking about a baby, doesn't it? Don't worry, she'll be awake soon enough."

While the kettle boils and the tea steeps, she and Stephen argue about the fact that he'll be sleeping (she ferrets it out of him) on the couch, while she herself has his bed. "Look," he says finally, "it's a very comfortable couch. I've slept on it lots. Really. I am not being a martyr."

Mouse goes out to the hall for her bag, rummages through it for the stupid gifts she bought on the Newfoundland ferry. Hand-knit socks for Stephen. She's touched by his evident pleasure: his face lights up and he puts them on immediately, walking around the kitchen and exclaiming how comfortable and unsurpassingly warm they are. "You sure are fun to give presents to," Mouse says dryly, but she's pleased.

"What'd you get Mom?"

She reaches into her bag, pulls out the bottle. "Screech."

Posters cover almost every inch of wall in Stephen's old room; the interstices reveal baby wallpaper, and the bedding is red and black. "It's clean," Stephen says apologetically, "even though it still smells like goats."

"Goats?"

"What Mom calls it. That teenage boy smell." He shows her the bathroom. The toilet has one of those plastic seat-things to raise it up, and Stephen shows her how to take it off. "It's there for Mom – she hasn't the strength to get up from the normal height." There is a bathtub with a plastic bench in it so Pearl can shower.

She wants so badly to see Pearl, now – it is frightening not to. "Can I look in on her?" she almost begs.

"Sure. Sure. She's just across the hall." He walks softly out of the bathroom and opens a door. Mouse follows him.

The room smells strongly of cigarette smoke and that faint scent of illness. A bedside lamp is on, casting a warm glow across the bed.

"She likes the light on," Stephen whispers.

So thin. Her hair straggles across the pillow, still blonde, no grey in it that Mouse can see. The blanket rises and falls, rises and falls as Pearl breathes. Her face is drawn. It doesn't look like her, no.

"Is she in pain?"

"No." He's looking at the woman in the bed with longing, with fear, or is that her, is she seeing herself in him? She forces herself to look away from him, to focus on the figure in the bed.

"God, she's changed." She cuts herself off, the banal remark.

"More than you have?" he whispers. A faint question.

She doesn't know the answer. "Let's let her sleep."

But Pearl stirs, small limbs moving under the blankets. Aren't the blankets too heavy for such a small creature? Pearl opens her eyes.

When she sees Mouse and Stephen standing side by side in the doorway, her mouth opens and her eyes get wide, wider. It starts as a natural expression of surprise but the eyes get larger and the mouth drops open until it's like a cartoon, Mouse thinks, it's unbearable. She feels her own face stretch into a fake smile, but terror presses behind the bones of her skull, anyone could read it.

The covers thrash a little and a thin hand emerges. Pearl pretends to shut her own gaping mouth with her palm.

"Mouse. You're here."

Two hours later the Screech is half gone ("You know I despise rum, Mouse, now open that thing. Stephen, get us some glasses. Coke. And ice!") and they are singing Marianne Faithfull at the top of their lungs. It collapses in laughter and Pearl has a coughing fit.

"Remember how old that used to seem? Thirty-seven."

"Fifty seems old to me now." Pearl gets her coughing under control, lights another cigarette.

"Look," Mouse says, clearing her throat against sudden tightness, "if you're going to keep polluting yourself that's your business. I'm opening a window," and she stands unsteadily to crack open the bedroom window.

"I'll catch my death of cold." Pearl lets out a raucous laugh. "And my ending is despair, unless I be relieved by prayer."

Mouse sits on the sill. "I can't believe you remember that. Those lines."

"Oh, I've got a fabulous memory. I remember everything." There's a pause, grim and sad it feels, then Pearl says, "'Now my charms are all o'erthrown, and what strength I have's mine own. But release me from my bonds with the help of your good hands.' That means I have to go to the can, and you have to help me walk there." Pearl pushes at blankets, and

171

Mouse helps her. "Look at my legs," Pearl says. "Jesus, just look at them. Sticks." And it's true, they're so thin. "Get your shoulder under there, that's right, and… one, two, three, up!"

When they stand there's an anxious moment while they sway, a little too drunk, Mouse a little too unused to this, but they get their footing and sway together out the room and across the hall, each holding an outstretched hand against the doorframe of the bathroom.

"Just how much help do you need?"

"Hike up my nightie. Yeah. That's right. Okay. Yeah, the underwear down too, thanks. Okay, lower me down. I'll yell for you when I'm done."

Pearl sags on the toilet, holding herself up with one hand on the sink. Mouse hesitates, worried that Pearl will fall.

"Go, go. I'll be okay."

Mouse shuts the door and leans against it. Too much rum, God, she'll feel like shit tomorrow. She hears Pearl mumbling, singing. "At the age of thirty-seven, she realized…" A long silence. "Hey, I'm ready!"

Mouse opens the door, crouches down to help Pearl pull up her underwear. Pearl's snatch has a jaunty little curl of blonde hair over it, like a wave. Her skin is thin, it's awful, those legs not meeting at the hips, the jutting hipbones, but Mouse puts a good face on it, isn't going to cry, and then, "You're crying," Pearl says and it's true, she is.

"Sorry, sorry. Okay, let's go." Mouse swipes tears away and they stagger out into the hall again. "At the age of thirty-seven," Mouse howls, and Pearl comes in, "She realized, she'd never ride…"

"Could you two keep it down? I'm trying to read!" Stephen calls from downstairs, joking, and the two women smother giggles.

Then Mouse starts crying again, and it takes a while to get Pearl settled back into the bed. She needs the pillows behind her back and head just so. "God, not like that, you're almost as bad as Stephen. I mean, look at me, you got me laid out flat as a corpse." A hospital bed would be just the thing, Mouse thinks, she'll look into that tomorrow.

"You know, Mousey." Pearl's breathing hard. "Hey, hand me that inhaler, will you?" She breathes through the thing, holds her breath, then lets it out with a wheeze. Her breath seems easier after that. "You know, Mousey," she says again, "it was you who gave me the idea to cut off the old man."

"What old man?" Mouse sits back in a chair.

"Dad." Pearl's eyes brighten, her mouth hardens. "Dear Old Dad. You said it to me. Why do you take his money if you hate him so much?" She gestures at the air, a memory. "An' I said – It's what he loves best. I'll take every damn penny I can."

172

Mouse remembers. She remembers the island. "Yes."

"But then afterwards, I was thinking." Pearl whispers. "And I was pregnant too, right? And I thought, this baby. He can't ever get near this baby. If I don't do anything else, I'll take care of that. So I cut him off. The old man." Pearl slaps her hand down on the covers. "I've been a terrible mother, Mouse." She looks down at her hands and Mouse wonders what she'll say if Pearl goes into a confessional, an exposé of her inadequate mothering. "But I did one thing."

Pearl's head droops; she's passing out.

"Your father's still alive?"

Pearl's head jerks up. "He's still alive." She lights a smoke, reaches for her glass, movements performed a thousand, thousand times. "He's a monster. A Frankenstein. All these different parts he stole from people."

"You haven't seen him since... since we were on the island?"

Pearl pins Mouse with her bright eyes. They're too bright, Mouse thinks, it's the cancer in her shining through. Something's happening in the room, like everything is very far away and clear, yet close and pressing on her at the same time. Mouse feels like she can't move in her chair.

"I went to my mother's funeral, didn't talk to him. And I went to a party celebrating my mother's fucking replacement, the new wife. I thought about... you know, the big confrontation. Tell everyone. *Everyone*. His friends, my uncles and aunts and cousins." Pearl closes her eyes and slides down until her head is on the pillow. Mouse feels the light dim, the room is murky, too hot. "But it didn't work. I'm all talk, Mousey." The eyes open again and they're just Pearl's eyes, blue, blue eyes. "It works in movies, maybe. The big confrontation. Me, I'm still scared of him." The head on the pillow twitches. "No, actually. Not now, not anymore. I'm not afraid." Pearl looks at the wall. "He can't do anything now."

Her eyes are closing. Mouse will stay there until she sleeps, then gently take the cigarette from between her fingers and put it out.

$\mathcal{G}$reen. Stephen wants it over him, around him. Waving over his head.
He's had this dream before, several times. But this time it's different.
Usually he wants to fly, his arms suddenly music – that song his mother
used to sing with the slow steady beat – climb ringing green bells toward the
laughing faraway blue. But this time he stays down by the great, vast river.
He steps forward, water washing chill.

Step. Step. And it closes in, stones shifting beneath thin soles. The
same song, but rich and strange. The high sweet voice, *in my blood like
holy wine.* Music walks laughing through his ears, singing careful syllables,
a guitar.

Step. Thighs green under the water. Green brown, that sound. Waves
contract.

Step. Eyes and ears go under, fear creeps in.

Step. Crashing under, vanishing, black. Sound, mumbles, something
like talking. He sees a big fish. Pale, this fish, slimy blue, freshwater dolphin. And he hears a deeper noise, hollow, confused and cold, like...

Step. He doesn't want to now, he'll drown. He looks up. Light, the sky
– look – humming above. Follow the sky. But instead he plummets, cold,
into the singing.

This is the tune of my catch, he thinks. This is the tune of my catch.
Listen! He can touch the music, protect everything, even his sweet pale
joyful dolphin. That's where it is, he thinks. It's in the music.

Stephen wakes with a crash on the comfortable ugliness of the couch.
He scrubs at the side of his face, feels a waffle imprint where its brown weave
pressed into him. Joni Mitchell's dulcimer chiming in his head. He props
himself on an elbow to get his phone for the time. Six. Mouse will be up
soon for her morning run.

The dream stays with him, an echo of joy.

It's strange having this old friend of Pearl's in the house. Three days now
and she's already made herself indispensable. She rented a hospital bed for
Pearl – it's coming today, Stephen remembers – and she's found a thousand
ways to make herself unobtrusively helpful: buying groceries, getting juice
and drinks for Pearl, doing laundry. Having her here means he can leave the

174

house for more than short snatches; yesterday he even had a bit of an evening out. It's all good, and yet faint resentment curls in his chest; he feels it and dislikes it about himself. She bought an expensive coffee machine her second day here – "I will not, simply *not*, make it through without decent coffee," she told Stephen laughing – which seems like moving in, and yet still he isn't sure how long she intends to remain.

He suspects she doesn't know either. Coming home last night, he walked in on the end of a phone argument between Mouse and her girlfriend back in Vancouver. "I'm staying until I'm not needed anymore, that's how long," he heard her say. "Oh, come on, Susan. No, of course not; she's at death's door, you're being ridiculous…" Stephen backed out and made a lot of noise re-entering the front door.

He rolls onto his back. It was a good idea to hang out with Dieter last night; he feels almost human now. He'd met Dieter at the East Wind and then they'd gone on to another bar.

"How's it going?" Dieter had asked, and Stephen felt the push in his throat, reminded himself not to be irritable with the question; no one really knew what to ask or how.

"Better, now this old friend is here. She's really helpful. In fact she's so goddamn helpful I might have to kill her."

"That's good, man, that's good." Dieter nodded and smiled, showing his perfect teeth. "You'll let me know if I can do anything, right?"

"Sure. You can start by buying me this beer."

Dieter threw back his head and laughed. "The night's on me."

Stephen told Dieter the edited version, making a story of it. Occasional visits from Pearl's friends, daily visits by personal care workers.

"Any of them cute?"

"Well, yeah," Stephen said. "There's a couple of really nice ones. So I play the dying mother card, you know."

Dieter snorted.

"At this rate I'll have dates lined up until next year."

"So you and Laura are…?"

Stephen took a long dive into his Tiger. He felt the alcohol begin to take hold, relaxing him. His hand reached convulsively for his phone and he checked it, making sure it was on.

"Your mother?" Dieter asked, an anxious look on him.

"No, just checking… Yeah, we're pretty much splits. I mean, we're still friends and all that, but…"

"Will you have to find another place, you think? Because if so, you're welcome to stay with me, man, you know that. Any time."

Stephen looked down the bar, at the light streaks gleaming on beer taps, people leaning over to order, bartender wiping hands on a towel, the normalcy of that. "I haven't gotten to thinking that far."

"Yeah, yeah. Sure."

They drank together simultaneously.

"Don't you start going with her, though." Stephen pretended to glare from under his eyebrows.

Dieter waved his hands in surrender. "No way, no way."

"So yeah, it's been a pretty weird time. Pretty weird," Stephen said. Through the crowd he glimpsed someone with blonde hair at the far corner table, her back to him and Dieter. Laura? He craned his neck but the crowd was too thick to see through. "Just after I got Mom home from the hospital, this old friend of hers shows up with crystals. Fucking crystals, Dieter."

"Crystals?"

"You know." Stephen mimed dangling one from his fingers and Dieter choked on his beer. "I never met her before in my life, and she shows up the second I get my mother home from the hospital. Stayed for three goddamn days. Total space invader." He'd thought Pearl would kick the woman out but soon realized, to his dismay, that she sort of liked having this person around. "She was a suggestor, too."

"A suggestor?"

"Full of terrific ideas. Always prefaced by, *You know what you should do?* And she expected me to cook dinner for her every night. *You know what you should do? You should move Pearl's bed into the northwest corner. And your stove is really in a bad place in the kitchen.*"

"You're kidding."

Stephen shook his head. "And then she kept asking me what parts of Mom's body had the cancer, and finally I just said, Look, her body's riddled with it. It's all through her. And then she began to fucking *cry*. Said the feng shui was all wrong and *you know what you should do?* We needed to adjust the *relationship corners* in all the rooms. Turns out the main relationship corner in the house is Mom's booze cabinet. And upstairs, the toilet's there."

"What does that mean?" Dieter asked.

"I don't know, but it's bad, really bad."

The two of them hunched over laughing. "As if you don't have enough to – "

"Yeah, it's been a trip. So anyways, this Mouse person is a saint compared to Crystal Dangler."

"Hey, so, is your Mom like, a lesbian?"

The girl in the corner caught Stephen's eye again – it *was* Laura. His throat tightened; did he want to see her tonight? "Um, I suppose so. Well, no, she dates men too. Dieter, you know, really, my mother's a slut."

"Aw, come on…"

They hunched over laughing again.

"Well, she is. Was. I mean, I found out – did I tell you this?"

"What?"

"While she was in hospital she told me that she doesn't even remember my father's name. Never knew it, actually."

Stephen saw the smile go dead on his friend's face – this was too heavy, he realized, for this, for now.

"Wow, that's… wow."

Stephen shrugged. "It's the way it is," he said. "It's not like it really changes anything. Look over there – is that Laura?"

Dieter looked and Stephen felt the relief of turning the conversation.

"Yeah, it is. Wanna go somewhere else, or…?"

"Naw, it's okay."

Dieter ordered two more Tigers and some beer snacks. The place was filling up; it was a Thursday night, the preweekend crowd, the just-one-more crowd.

"So…" Dieter said, and stopped.

"What?"

"I gotta tell you something, man. You're different, somehow. Like, I know you've got a lot going on, but it's more than that. You're bigger or something." Stephen stared at his friend, then cast a look down at his own belly. "No, no." Dieter looked earnest. "There's something… I don't know how to say it. Bigger. More substantial about you."

A faint chill walked up Stephen's spine. "Laura said that… something like that too."

Dieter's hand went heavy on his shoulder; a friendly squeeze. "You're going through so much, man. But it's like you're coming into your own. Sorry, I'm not making sense."

Stephen looked out the window at the street. Cars hissed by through the slush; a group of people came out of the restaurant across the road: dad and mom and two teenaged children and an elderly couple – grandparents. "Look at that, Dieter."

"What?"

They watched in silence as the group talked, arranging who was going in what car or something; you could imagine it. Old man held old woman's arm; dad person talking in a hurry; mom person lingering with the old couple. One of the teens flipped open her phone, quick fingers. "Family," Stephen said.

Dieter held still; he understood, Stephen knew. He got the strangeness of this for Stephen. The family across the road said their goodbyes, going off in two directions down the street, passing from sight.

"Listen, I met my grandfather," Stephen said.

Dieter's head whipped around, his eyes widened.

"My mother doesn't know I tracked him down. She doesn't want me to have anything to do with him. He lives in Rosedale. Old money."

"Rosedale? Your mom's from Rosedale."

"He seemed to want to get to know me but…" Why was he telling Dieter this?

"But what?"

"He's… there's something wrong. In the past, with him and my mother. And now, with him, there's something really… wrong. In the end I told him I didn't want anything to do with him."

"What do you mean, something wrong?"

Stephen poured his beer from the can into his pint glass. "Imagine something that would make a daughter cut her father off forever."

Dieter slowly nodded.

"So I said no." Stephen's body began to laugh, deep shaking, and he put his hands over his face and scrubbed, ran fingers through his hair. "Ah, it's been strange, a fucking strange time, I can tell you."

Dieter poured his own beer, and Stephen felt his shaking subside. They drank.

"Rosedale, eh?" Dieter said. "My old man probably knows him. They all know each other, those guys."

"Maybe we would have grown up around each other as kids or something. If things had been… different."

Dieter raised his glass. "We know each other now," he said. "And that's good enough for me."

As they got close to finishing their pints, Laura caught sight of them. She waved and walked up the bar toward them. Dieter excused himself and Laura climbed onto the stool next to Stephen.

"How's it going?"

"I never know how to answer that question," Stephen said.

"Sorry, I'm sorry, that's banal."

He felt pleased, then bad. "No, it's okay. Um, I'm doing all right. You?"

"Yeah, I'm okay."

He could smell her, the scent of her, familiar. He could remember the feeling of the nape of her neck under his lips, pulling her small body to his. He leaned away and took a sip of his drink. "One of Mom's exes is staying now," he said. "Someone from before I was born."

"Male or female?"

"Female. Mom said she should have been my father."

"That's a weird thing to say."

Stephen nodded. "I gather they were together when my mother conceived me with the nameless stranger."

"Talk about full circle."

Stephen nodded, reflexively checking his phone for the time. "I should go soon."

"It's nice to see you, Stephen." Laura reached out and took his hand.

Stephen stiffened, then his initial wave of desire faded. Warmth flooded him and he leaned in, kissed her cheek. "It's nice to see you too."

He wanted to be back at the house in case his mother needed him, in case she died and he wasn't sitting there by the bed, the way he'd pictured it, the way it had to happen.

He wants to be there. He wants to hold her hand.

He lies on the couch and waits to hear Mouse stirring upstairs, or for his mother to ring the bedside bell he's given her to call him with – whichever comes first. But all remains quiet. It's still dark outside, this time of year – will be for a while. No birds.

He remembers walking in on his mother – she was on this couch – with some boyfriend or one-night stand. It was late at night and Stephen had woken up to something. He can't remember how old he'd been – young enough that he was scared when he looked into his mother's bedroom and saw she wasn't there. Not home yet from going out with "a friend" – and now someone was breaking in. Terror. But he'd handle it, he could do it. He'd unplugged a lamp from beside his mother's bed and crept down the stairs with it, like he'd seen in a movie. The light in the kitchen was on, he could see into the living room. And there on the couch was a man with a naked butt, on top of his mother. Stephen remembers yelling his head off. He knew what was going on – he knew about fucking at that age – but still, it was scary. He'd thrown down the lamp and run back up the stairs, still yelling.

He remembers hearing voices, his mother's raised in anger, then the door slamming. A pause; his mother's footsteps up the stairs. "Stephen?" But he'd pretended to be asleep.

179

Stephen gets up and finds his glasses, pulls a sweater over his T-shirt. Colder than it should be – he shuffles to the kitchen and turns up the heat, his mother likes it hot now. Drinks a glass of water. He goes softly up the stairs. Pearl, when he looks in, is sleeping. He tiptoes in and sits by her bed.

A few days later he'd brought up the man on the couch. "Did you make him leave?" he'd asked.

"Who?" his mother had said.

Her breath rises and falls. He reaches out and straightens the edge of the sheet. The certainty falls softly around him like wings. She hadn't been trying to deflect the conversation the way other parents did. She actually did not remember that Stephen had walked in on her fucking some guy.

As he'd gotten older, Stephen explained other incidents to himself with her drinking.

He remembers the aftermath of the first fight with his first real girlfriend. He'd been living in Toronto. Morning had come, he'd woken up with a sense of uneasiness. But went about his day, called her that evening to make plans as usual. He'd been taken aback to find that she was not only still upset by their fight, but wanted to talk about it. He remembered saying, bewildered, *But it's done. What's there to talk about?*

He'd learned that most people don't expect you to forget fights.

It's falling into place, into lines like the ugly plaid of the couch, the fact of where he comes from. Pearl is a survivor, she's always behaved this way. The keeping of monstrous truths in careful airtight compartments so that the little bright objects and habits of daylight don't fly apart like a bomb – this is survival. And he's been part of her survival, come from this and he's never known why. He's always thought that his strangeness, his lack of comprehension – *But it's done. What's there to talk about?* – were indicators of his own fundamental wrongness.

Pearl stirs under the blanket, curls onto her side, and Stephen watches her. Something is working in her body, a mysterious malignancy, and soon now that will be done. And what will there be to talk about?

From here it feels like it will never be over, this dying, this need to figure it out. Stephen looks at Pearl and she is like a little girl, and this is familiar, this feeling that it is he who is the older one. He mentioned this to Laura once. She'd said that made sense given his mother's Peter Pan personality, and her narcissism. He'd thought that was glib. Now he sees his mother dressed in green, green like a leaf and laughing. She stands up high in a tree, one hand on the gnarled trunk and she's laughing. She looks so young.

A sound from his old room and it's Mouse, waking up. Immediately

Stephen is aware that he needs to piss, and resentment flashes through him because he'll need to leave his mother's side right now to make sure he gets the bathroom before the guest does. Resents it even more because he knows Mouse would always be polite about it, defer to him if she knew. She's so capable and kind, it makes him twist up inside. And there's something else, about the way she seems to know his mother better than anyone else he's ever met. It's hard, he realizes, to share Pearl.

Later that day he wants to eat his morning thoughts. The hospital bed is delivered; Pearl is enervated by the event. She tries to engage the men delivering the bed, speaking from her pillows: "Thank God you're here. My son's been trying to kill me, leaving me flat on my back all the time." She laughs, lights a smoke. "So, do you two come with the bed?" One smiles, but the other ignores her so she turns on Stephen. "Stop hanging over me!" she snaps. "Christ. Go get a glass of water or something." He moves away from her but stays in the room. The two men pick up the old bed, Pearl and all, and cram it against the wall; Pearl gasps with jolting and her eyes roll back with pain or shock. Stephen begins to move to her but she says, "Get off me, I said!"

Mouse stands in the doorway and he doesn't want to look at her, but she's watching him with a look in her brown eyes – he can't tell what it is – censure... no, compassion? More detached than that. She's taking it all in. The men quickly assemble the bed; Stephen can smell the new mattress, a high note in the stuffy smokiness of the room.

"Need help getting that old bed out of here?" the nice one asks, but Stephen shakes his head. Mouse follows them out; she's pretended to Stephen that she'd found some way to get the bed covered under OHIP, but Stephen knows she's lying and is paying for it herself. He's keeping his mouth shut, for Pearl.

He gets linens from the hall closet and starts to make up the new bed. It's got controls on the side and he brings the top part up – it moves insect-like, a creature folding itself into an L – "Look, Mom, it works."

"Of course it fucking works. Don't leave the pillows all over like that; stack them up for God's sake." She gets her legs out from under the covers and sits up at the edge of the old bed; he can feel her irritation at her own slowness.

He sits next to her. She's hunched over, her hands on the mattress next to her hips. Her bare feet graze the floor; he notes that the distending fluid has left them, they are shapely again; strange. She lifts her head and looks at him, then to his surprise she smiles. "Okay. Let's get this forty-nine-year-old carcass over there."

181

His throat constricts; gently he places her arm across his shoulders, encircles her waist, and slowly they walk over to the new bed. It's too high for her to get into and she tries to steady herself on it while Stephen fiddles with the controls to lower it; she cries out and almost falls when it finally sinks. She's in; he moves the blankets over from the old bed.

Next he's tucked the sheet too tightly over her feet: "Are you trying to mummify me? Jesus you're rough! And you haven't moved these pillows."

"Oh, for heaven's sake, Pearl. That's enough," comes Mouse's voice from the door.

Stephen looks at Mouse, startled.

"Oh, okay, okay," says Pearl. "You're right. This is great. This is a great bed. Look, I'm happy." She plays with the controls. "Up! Down! Fold in half... whoops!" She is genuinely delighted; she makes them all laugh.

After a time she tires, nods off. Stephen and Mouse retire to the kitchen.

"Thanks," Stephen says.

"You're very patient."

Stephen sits and puts his feet up on the table, just like his mother hates; then he takes them down again. "I mean for the bed. Thanks. It will make all the difference."

They sit in silence for a time, his deflection of her sympathy hanging in the air.

At last Stephen says, "It's just because she's sick. You know."

"Yes." She gets up, pours herself a coffee from the expensive machine. "Mind you, Pearl always did have a talent for mobilizing an army of servants."

He barks out a laugh. "Even when she was eighteen?"

"You better believe it." Mouse grins at him. They smile, but a chill descends over the room, filling it like blue, like water.

Stephen speaks into the coldness. "She gets mad about the pillows and the sheets and all that because she can't control the big stuff."

Mouse bites her lip and looks down at her hands. "I still say you're a kind of saint."

At that Stephen really laughs. He puts his feet up on the table, stretches his arms behind his head. "I'd catch it if she could see this."

Later when Pearl awakens they move the old bed down to the living room. Pearl sits with the hospital bed as high as it can go, directing traffic with her cigarette and complaining that they are damaging her furniture. The old bed is a piece of shit from the Salvation Army, Stephen thinks, why does she care? They move it down to the living room, and Mouse insists that she will sleep there, giving him his own room back. He accepts. He likes being closer to Pearl. It makes it easier when she needs help in the night; that's what he thinks, and can't quite admit that he is terrified of missing the moment when she dies.

Days pass, and the electric blue inside of Pearl sinks, subsides. Often, now, she sleeps, sailing high on her new bed. Sometime she almost seems to be hallucinating; she talks about boats, water, sometimes there's a storm coming and she worries about it. Stephen tells himself it's because she's between sleeping and waking. He can't stop thinking about the tumours, how they fill her chest, her lungs, her heart and brain. Every time she seems confused he wonders, is it her brain? Deb and the other nurses, when they come now, look at him with pity in their eyes.

He and Mouse fall into a routine. She gets up early and puts on coffee for both of them; he, a tea drinker, takes to coffee; the jitters seem part and parcel of this experience, this hallucinatory unfolding. Then Mouse goes for her daily run, scrambling fearlessly on ice, coming back an hour later bruised and breathing hard, elated. He hears her leave for the run and that's when he gets up, checks on his mother, starts breakfast. Once Mouse is back they eat in Pearl's bedroom with plates balanced on knees, chatting, the women teasing each other if Pearl's alert. She isn't eating much. Newspapers are read and lampooned, the TV's on. Late morning the personal care worker comes and then Stephen and Mouse vacate the room while Pearl is washed and settled. Lunches, dinners they take turns cooking. Days pass.

One evening he sits by Pearl as she sleeps, reading. Mouse comes into the bedroom.

"She sleeping?"

"Yeah."

Mouse sits across the bed from him, gently takes Pearl's hand where it lies outside the covers, palm upright like she is waiting to receive something. Stephen watches Mouse run her fingers gently over his mother's palm and wrist. They must have been in love, he thinks; maybe they still are. In the lamplight the faint white bars of Pearl's scars gleam a little, and Mouse looks more closely. "These..." she whispers.

"Yes."

"Are they... what they look like?" Mouse puts Pearl's hand down gently. Pearl stirs a little, settles.

"Well," he whispers, "sort of. It was one of her attempts."

"God, Stephen, *one* of...?"

Her brown eyes look at him; she is appalled. Stephen wonders if they should go downstairs for this, then wonders how much he wants to get into

183

with Mouse. He feels the familiar dull dread settle over him. "I guess it was hard on her, being a single mother and that. I wasn't the easiest kid. We fought a lot."

Mouse looks down at Pearl's face and there's a long silence, so long that he flips open his book again. The words are swimming. His guts slide inside him, clenching in pain.

He's about to ask Mouse if she minds sitting with Pearl for a while, excuse himself for a walk or something, when she speaks. "Stephen, I don't mean to... this might sound invasive, but... you don't imagine that her self-destructiveness was your fault, do you?"

Heat rushes through him, he feels his armpits prickle, his palms sweat. "Oh, of course not. Psych one-oh-one and all that; kids always think it's their fault, don't they?"

She looks into his eyes. "But... you have to know she was like that, long before you. I can tell you that. I *tell* you: it's always been in her. Not her fault. But there."

He hears her words and thinks, maybe later I'll take this in, maybe it will make a difference, later. He hears himself talking. "The wrists were when I was fourteen, and she threatened to take a bunch of pills once. When I was seventeen she actually did; that was the most serious one. I had to call an ambulance..." He remembers the lurch and slide, the terror of that evening. He'd moved out by then, and if he hadn't happened to drop by she probably would have succeeded. "I walked in just as she finished off a whole bottle of Paxil, plus a bottle of Tylenol and God knows what else."

"She was on antidepressants?" Mouse asks.

"Almost killed her. When they pumped her stomach her lips were black."

"She slit her wrists *and* took pills?"

Stephen looks at his mother to see if she's registering any of this, but her breath rises and falls, faintly rattling, even. "Well, the wrists just, they didn't do much. You have to cut this way," and he demonstrates a cut lengthwise between his tendons, "and she went across. It was messy, but she didn't lose too much blood." He closes his book. "The others were more like stunts, you know."

Mouse nods.

"She's sort of like a teenager in a lot of ways," he went on. "Tries to be totally obnoxious and you're still supposed to love her."

They sit for a while. Stephen reaches over and smoothes a strand of his mother's hair across her forehead. "Still not losing any from the radiation treatments."

"She's so pleased about that. I think she's pointed it out to me every day." Another silence, then Mouse says, "That's a lot for you to be dealing with at fourteen, seventeen years old. And now you're what – thirty?"

The comments come at him like a black bull might, and he flips the pages of his book, turns words like a matador. "Funny thing is, what nearly killed her was a vacuum cleaner."

"A...?"

"Yeah. She was carrying a vacuum cleaner up the stairs – I was supposed to take it up for her, and I hadn't, and it sat in the hall for three days and finally one night she takes it up herself in a drunken rage. She gets to the top of the stairs and then falls over backwards, right down the whole flight. Doesn't let go of the vacuum, though. She lands on her back and it smashes down on her ankle." Mouse has gotten a quiet fit of the giggles. "They had to pin it, and then in the hospital she got c-dif and almost died."

"C-dif? That superbug?"

He nods. "Only responds to, I think, two antibiotics and only one of those worked for Mom. Man, she was mad." His hand goes over his mouth; Mouse's squeaky attempts to stifle her laughter are as infectious as giggling in church. "Drank like a fish, smoked like a chimney, and had pretty much eliminated food from her diet, but somehow it was all my fault for not carrying that fucking vacuum up the stairs."

The two of them wheeze like a pair of broken concertinas until the laughing fit subsides. The room fills again with Pearl's breath, the faint rattle in her lungs. He feels another silence coming on, can't bear it.

His phone vibrates in his pocket. It's a relief; he can look away from Mouse and his mother. It's a Toronto number. "Excuse me," he says and takes it out into the hall.

"Hello, Stephen. It's... me, it's Mitchell Lewis." The man mistakes Stephen's silence for incomprehension, clarifies: "Your grandfather."

The pause that follows is infinitesimal, and during it Stephen's imagination leaps. He is an adult male who has a grandfather. Some nice old man you were taken to visit as a kid, who came through with presents on birthdays and took you to the zoo; and then gradually you grow up and find yourself enjoying the odd self-directed visit. The old man springs for a big graduation gift, and later, offers to pay for the tombstone of one's dying mother.

He leans against the cool plaster of the wall, feeling it firm against his back, stares up at the ugly hallway light fixture in the ceiling. "I told you not to call me."

The man pauses. "I know, I know. I apologize for... invading your privacy." This makes Stephen think about what the man did to his mother.

Someone like this does not know what it means to invade someone's privacy – other people's privacies are only resistances to be broken. He is going to hang up but then the man says, "I thought I'd give you time to think things over. Surely you can't..." The smooth voice is rising a little, and the man stops talking and clears his voice. When he continues it is pleasant again, modulated. "Surely you can't cut me off without even trying to get to know me."

"Yeah, well, maybe you don't know so much about me." It sounds childish, and Stephen winces.

"I'd like to change that." A pause. "Your mother doesn't have to know."

Stephen wishes it could all be different. He wishes everything could be different and he always has: crouching in the miserable little kindergarten library, flinching from bullies on the bus, escaping to university only to flunk out while writing essays for other people's money, working amid the dust of the bookstore, hurting Laura, playing bad chess, sitting in this smoke-soaked hallway and hearing his dying mother's breath rattling high in her chest.

"It's all so fucking hateful."

"What is?" the man asks, then pushes. "I want to help you, Stephen."

"But it's what I've got." Stephen won't be derailed. "What I am. You can't call me, ever again. Do you understand?"

"Don't talk like that," says the man, confusion under the smoothness in his voice that is, Stephen realizes, an expression of his clear expectation of winning.

Stephen takes a deep breath. He repeats himself, separating and emphasizing every word. His voice is raised, he doesn't care; he notes with surprise that he has slid down the wall and is sitting on the floor. "*Do... you... understand?*"

Another pause. "It doesn't have to be this way," the man says.

"It does." His mother's breath, in, out. His own, a little ragged. "Goodbye, Mitchell Lewis." Stephen turns off his phone.

He won't let himself feel regret. He will trust his mother, the liar, the drunk. He will trust her because she has tried to love him the best way she knows how. She brought the terrible poverty of her heart to him; she had nothing else to give him, no other way to protect him. His body is grown into the negative shape of that twist in her, like two trees twined together. The rift between them is small now, very small. He will not wrench apart from her.

He scrubs angrily at his face, drops his phone. "Fuck," he says softly, then wants to laugh at the terrible inadequacy of that, of everything. He's forgotten anyone else is there, is startled when Mouse comes out into the hall.

"You okay?"

Stephen looks up at her; he doesn't care if she sees he's been crying. "Yeah, I think so."

He gestures at her to follow him downstairs. In the kitchen he automatically puts on a kettle for tea, leans against the counter. "That was my grandfather. Pearl's dad."

Her eyes widen. "I thought so. From the bits I could hear of your end, sorry." She looks away. "You know him?"

Curiosity rises in Stephen. "Do you?"

Her hands start arranging and rearranging the objects on the kitchen table: a newspaper, a pencil, a salt shaker. "Only in as much as I knew Pearl when she was eighteen. I... didn't like what I saw. Of him in her."

"Sounds about right."

"Does he know about... her? Now?"

"No." Stephen takes his phone out again, looks at it. "I am going to get my number changed."

"Oh, good!" Mouse bursts out, and Stephen stares at her. "Sorry, it's none of my business but..."

"But you have an opinion anyway."

She has a worried expression on her face, like someone who likes to order things but knows that right now, she can't.

"I met him once," he confesses. "Mom doesn't know and she doesn't need to. He's... basically trying to bribe me to get to know me. Getting sentimental in his old age."

"You think so?" Mouse asks.

"No. Actually, I don't. I think the only thing he knows is power. I'm a chance to get one over on Pearl. Not to mention a new challenge in and of myself." The kettle is rattling; Stephen puts a teabag in a mug. The adrenaline of the encounter over the phone is draining from him now; he feels very tired. "I just wish... why can't everything be different?" He hears the childishness of this. "Oh, shut up, Stephen."

"I'm sorry. I'm so sorry." Stephen is startled to see tears in Mouse's eyes. She gets up; she's not going to try to hug him, is she? But she stays where she is. "Listen, Stephen, I can't do much. But I can stay here with you. Until you don't need me any more. If you want me here that is. Just... let me know." The look on her face is open, clear.

Two days later the weather changes. It's been iron cold but something comes from the south maybe, from over the mild Pacific. It gets itself, by some meteorological miracle, east of the Rocky Mountains, across the vastness of prairies and the rocky icy Shield, and all the way to this Ontario town – thawing ice – making high banks of snow soft and punky like the inside of a tree still standing yet long ago struck by lightning. In the morning Pearl seems to respond to the weather; she perks up, watches some TV, picks on Stephen for his clothes (*For God's sake, why can't you wear something other than grey or black? Even some navy fucking blue would enliven things, Christ!*) and Stephen sends her into a dangerous but worth-it coughing fit by dressing in some terrible collection of Pearl's own shirts, pink and red together with a canary yellow toque.

Now it's nighttime. Pearl is sleeping and Stephen and Mouse are sitting, again, by her bedside.

Mouse says, "My father died of a heart attack when he was about the age I am now. It's a genetic thing."

Her face is neutral; Stephen isn't sure why she brings this up. "Can you get tested for it?"

Mouse shrugs. "I think about it sometimes. But I'm not sure I want to... anything can kill you." She meets Stephen's eyes. "He died while I was on that island with your mother. I was seventeen. I left university after that, then lost my mind and went to B.C." She swallows. "Sometimes I wonder if I've ever come back."

"From B.C.?"

"From that insanity."

Pearl breaths in and out, in and out.

"Sometimes I think," Mouse says, "that part of me is still on that island. The place your mother took me." She flushes, looks away. "You know how it is when you are young."

That last part is an excuse, he thinks. It isn't the truth. "You didn't stay in touch," he says.

"Not really. The odd phone call over the years, letters. Email now and again. Not for a long time, though. I was surprised that she wanted to see me now." She stirs like she's going to get up, but doesn't. "That's where I met you."

"Where?"

"The island."

Pearl stirs beneath her blankets. She sleeps.

"You were a little kid," Mouse whispers. "Maybe three, four years old. You had these really cute yellow swimming trunks, and you liked ducks." Stephen sees tears are swimming in his mother's friend's eyes, and for some reason this calls up an answering tightness in his own throat. "I don't really like kids, but I liked you."

"Thanks."

Mouse sniffs, wipes her nose with the back of her hand, flashes him a quick boyish grin.

Stephen's dream from days before floats back to him, the music under the water, the fish. There had been a fish, he remembers, under the dock – he lay on the warmth of the wood and saw it swim under, a big one. And when he'd been wading he'd been afraid that the fish would hear him and come out and bite his cock. And he'd fallen under, and… He sits up. "You," he says. "You were the person, the other person on the dock. You saved me from drowning."

She stares at him. "You slipped over the drop-off. I remember that."

He sits back. "Good thing you were there."

"Your mother would have gotten you out if I hadn't been."

Stephen can't answer. He can't speak. There is no certainty inside of him that his mother would have noticed his disappearance.

"She could always swim better than me," Mouse said, an accent coming out in her, reminding Stephen that she is from Newfoundland. "She was just paralyzed for an instant. She was scared, sure."

She's convincing herself, Stephen thinks. Trying to. It's not working.

"Mouse, do you mind if I go for a walk? I think I need some air."

He's about to leave the house when Mouse comes down the stairs. Urgency in her face.

"Stephen. All that stuff she put you through – she was already like that."

Dull anger rises in him, more like resistance than any kind of rage, and even in the midst of it he has an impulse to laugh at himself. Stephen doesn't want to hear any criticisms of Pearl from anyone else. Only he is allowed to criticize his mother.

He makes his face a neutral mask. Mouse is a decent person, he reminds himself. A nice person, from a family where parents loved her; she almost lost her mind when her father died, that's how much she loved him. He can picture her as a young woman. She's earnest, organized, direct. Pearl, at eighteen – Stephen can see it – must have raked her through and through.

But Mouse surprises him; she doesn't need his pity. "I wish I could show you." She puts her hand on Stephen's arm. "You were the best thing that ever happened to her. And she knows that."

Stephen walks out into the winter's night. The strangely mild air flows past his face, his hair like dark water. It is worse that Mouse tries to comfort him, tries to jolly him out of his guilts, doubts and agonies. He sees these tortures as little devils flying about his head, a picture he saw once, an old engraving – the opposite of cherubs and just as smug, baby demons with tiny lethal pitchforks. His pricking lifelong companions.

His feet move, he feels tiredness in his bones. This whole thing is aching within him; his bones, his muscles aren't accustomed to the burden of grief. He feels his legs moving, he is walking, his feet make noise on the half-melting slush and still-icy ruts on the sidewalk, and he can't think of a single reason why all this should be so, why the houses should stand as they always have, why the bare trees wave in the wind, why the river down hill should still be flowing under the ice. His feet take him to the footbridge, he walks across, footfalls making a deeper noise, hollow, cold. The obsidian water strikes the dam, forced, rolls over as writhing whiteness.

There's a light on the other side of the bridge, up what in summer is a smooth grassy slope, glass-green, like water. He is walking toward the light. The roaring at the dam fades, the sumac of summer still raise their calyxes of sour furry fruit to the sky, red like tongues tasting the winter air, like hungry flames. He cuts across the snow-covered field, earth baked hard with frost, following trails cut by dogs. The light flickers, it's warm. It's high up the slope, he thinks, but as he gets closer he realizes it's in a tree, a pine. It sways in the gentle wind, the warm wind scented with the changes of spring, a golden circle of light cast around it, feathered with the shadows of many branches. Someone is sitting in the broad lower branches of the old pine tree.

Stephen feels that he casts shadow around him as he moves across the frozen earth, a circle of shadow.

He's always cast shadow. He remembers this: lying in his bed at night, frightened, eyes like saucers in the dark. If he could *see* the monsters coming, somehow that made it better. He lay there quiet, eyes wide as oceans to catch the menace in dark corners. Keep quiet and all's well. Light golden outside, leaking in around his closed door like sunshine, like safety. The light's always outside. He plays tricks with time to pass it, he can bend time, parse it. He masters the night in fragments. His small warm body is the centre of the night, he learns to people the dark with friends, a company of small fantastic heroes. Imprisoned in a hard bed frame by knotty twisted sheets, he keeps his eyes on the golden light, the magic circle of light that's always outside him, and he bends time.

He's close enough to the tree now to see it's an ancient white pine, glorious. The person in the branches is a girl, a young woman, the one with the baby. She holds a bundle in her arms, a blue blanket. Stephen can't see where the light is coming from.

"Hello," he says as he approaches up the slope, not wanting to startle her. "Nice night."

The girl looks down at him. Her feet kick just above the ground; the branch on which she sits is gracious, sweeping low. Her pale hair is uncovered, delicate as sunlight swimming over her shoulders. Her eyes are large, her face white. She joggles the silent bundle in her arms.

"Haven't seen you in a while," Stephen says. A faint rush of wind comes up and pushes at Stephen's back, mischief in it like a dark smile. The trees sway, branches full of sorceries. "He's quiet, isn't he."

"Yes," the girl answers. "He never cries."

She looks down again at the bundle and sadness knots her face. Stephen stands there, doesn't know what to do.

The wind comes up again, stronger this time, the rush of it rocking the branches. The tree creaks and then inside that sound, another. It threads the night like a golden needle. The baby's crying. Faint at first, growing to a real yell, and Stephen and the young woman look at each other, she up in her tree branch, he down on the ground.

Delight blooms in his chest. The girl joggles the baby and the baby cries and the girl breaks into a smile like the moon rising up.

The day Pearl dies is almost warm.

The weather changed the night before and when Mouse leaves for her morning run she welcomes the mildness; it reminds her of Vancouver. A little sound of pleasure escapes as she launches herself off the porch and onto the pavement. She loops north, along the old railway track that is now a trail, runs until the town is behind her and farms open on either side with those quaint rail fences they have in this part of the world. Going toward the university. Yellow gold grasses stick up from the snow, hissing in the wind.

Pearl's been sinking all week. She usually rouses herself for the personal care workers' visits, but other than that she seems to sleep. She's not eating any more. It's a way of deciding to die, Mouse thinks.

She's seen a change in Stephen too. Something has softened, she thinks; he's lost the hurt, perpetually kicked look; it's melted into something clear, resilient as water.

She's three times now pushed unwanted commentary on Stephen. Mouse hates herself for it. Her feet pound, she runs hard, tries to run the feelings out of herself. How can she be so tactless; she, who prides herself on her restraint? She asks herself if it's leftover resentment that's taken shelter in some harbour of her own heart; does she still love Pearl, is she looking for some kind of vindication? It's pride and folly, to think that she can help Stephen, fly into his life unannounced and make everything better. She's wondered if Pearl summoned her here for that purpose: to explain things somehow, be a surrogate parent and take care of her son.

But that's too straightforward for Pearl. Mouse will never know why Pearl called her in. Just that she's here now and she wants so badly to help, to be of use.

She runs until she feels like she's halfway to the moon. Her legs don't tire; she could run until the land stopped, run west to Susan if she wants. Her lungs open and close, clean, her feet pound. The air slaps her face, a relief after the close air of Pearl's room and Stephen's dogged caretaking. She runs and runs. It's hard to turn back. When she gets to the street of Pearl's house she puts on a final burst of speed, sprints the whole way and practically tears the door off the hinges when she opens it. The house stinks of cigarette smoke, the sulphur of eggs, burnt toast. "Hello!" she hollers as she comes in, adrenaline bursting from her throat. "Hello!"

"Up here." Stephen's voice comes from above, and she hears it right away, the tight panic. She takes the stairs two at a time, heart pounding clean blood through her. She gets to Pearl's room and they're locked together, the two of them.

Stephen's face is terrible, brave.

Pearl sinks, he sinks with her. He tries to give her breath. Again and again he breathes into his mother's body while Mouse cries.

It's just like Pearl, she thinks later, to put on one last burst of chaos like this, no matter how carefully they've prepared. When it comes to that final moment, she fights, she struggles with death. She fights barefoot, her feet are bare, her beautiful feet.

Stephen and Mouse go to the island. It is spring, too early for cottagers, too early for the old man or anyone else to be there.

It's been nice seeing Mouse again. Her face is tanned from running outdoors in the West Coast spring. They go first to the marina where Mouse remembers stealing the Lewis family boat, but of course it's still out of the water from winter.

A burly grey-haired man is working on an engine. Mouse and Stephen introduce themselves, ask if he knows anyone who could take them to the island.

The man looks sharply at Stephen then, and straightens up, wiping his hands on his trousers. "Lewis, you said?"

"Yes." Stephen wonders if he should have used his real name; will his grandfather be alerted now to this visit? "I'm Pearl's son."

The man is still for a long moment. Then he nods. "I can see her in you."

"You knew her?"

"My name's Floyd Lachambre." When Stephen says nothing – not knowing what to say – the man goes on. "I'm caretaker on the island. I knew her when she was a little girl."

"I remember her talking about you," Mouse bursts out, smiling. "She had very fond memories of you."

"She's…" The man, Floyd, clears his throat. "She's gone, isn't she?"

Stephen swings his backpack off his shoulder, heavy with the urn. He takes it out, finds himself holding the lacquered wooden container out to the man. "She's here."

He takes them across the water in his boat.

The island looms, the dock.

"Water's high," Floyd grunts. He helps Mouse onto the dock, clears his throat. "I'm going up to the big house to check on some things."

"We won't be long," Stephen says.

Floyd looks at him from under the beak of his baseball cap. "Take your time." He walks up the slope and disappears behind the great gabled house.

Stephen walks the length of the dock with the urn under his arm, feel-

194

ing the slap of water against the wood. It's chilly, and the water's disturbed and grey; it's hard to imagine wanting to swim. The dock, towering in memory, is small, really.

"Want to look at the cottage?" Mouse heads up the path toward the smaller house.

Stephen gazes out at the blue grey line of the horizon. He'd thought maybe the place would seem familiar but it doesn't; it's a foreign land, this island. He turns and follows his mother's friend up toward the cottage.

"Wow, it's practically the same." Mouse cups her hands to peer through an unshuttered window. "Even the cushions. And that little bear rug."

Stephen sees a luxurious, old-school cottage interior. Little squares on the mantel that must be family pictures; Stephen wonders if there are any of Pearl there. He hopes not.

Mouse drops her hands. "Do you want to go in?"

He shakes his head. "Let's walk around the island a bit."

They take a rough path to a little cove. A circle of stones, overgrown; it would be a nice place to make a fire, sit out at night. They wander up through a wooded area, come around again to what used to be tennis courts.

"Where do you want to...?"

"The dock."

The wind is picking up, there's a smell of rain on it. They stand together at the end of the dock. Gulls wheel, crying overhead. Stephen crouches and takes the lid off the urn, removes the plastic bag that contains his mother's ashes. It's so strange that this is Pearl. This reduction, this collection of pale fragments, has even less to do with his mother than the body that lay under his hands while he and Mouse waited for the paramedics. He remembers seeing it, that change, awful: she went from being his mother – so thin she could hardly walk but still vital, still trying to order events – to a sort of flatness. All the theories and ideas he'd been throwing around for a month to try and prepare for what was about to happen – that the soul weighs such-and-such, that beings are reincarnated, even an attempt to believe in heaven, a place where the spirit can rest – fell apart in the face of this, the smallness and deathly stillness of his mother's body. Yes; she looked, he remembers, flat. And naked, somehow; it had been painful to have the paramedics look on her.

Stephen stands up. "Let's each remember her as she was, alive."

"A favourite memory?"

"Yeah, if you like."

Mouse nods. "That's a good idea. Okay. You scatter the ashes."

"Let's each do half."

She looks surprised. "You sure?"

Stephen hands the bag to Mouse. "You first."

His mother's friend takes the bag and steps forward to the very edge of the dock. She rips a small hole in the plastic and then stands there for a long time, eyes closed. Stephen backs away to give her space. He wonders what memory of Pearl she has chosen; something from when they were young, here together, he imagines. Finally breath comes out of Mouse in a ragged sigh, and she looks down at the bag. She enlarges the hole and reaches in, takes a handful of the ashes, and throws them into the air. They rise over the dock in an ashen column, blow back a little, disperse.

Mouse turns to Stephen. "I hope some of those went into the water." She sort of smiles. "Every time I've been present for the scattering of some-one's ashes they always blow back into your face. Always."

"The last joke," Stephen says, and steps forward to take the bag. He closes his eyes, senses Mouse backing away.

It's a week or so before Pearl dies. Stephen is sitting next to her bed; he's been sitting there for a long time.

She wakes a couple of times, needs a glass of water, some juice. He fetches the things and sits there, and he must be nodding off because suddenly he snaps to with a jerk, head going over sideways.

"Caught you." Pearl's looking at him with her head turned on the pillow, warm in the lamplight.

Stephen rubs his eyes. "Guess I should go to bed," but he doesn't move.

One of Pearl's hands is outside the covers and she begins to reach out, whether toward him or to her own face he can't tell; then she drops it back onto the blanket, palm curled upward. Stephen reaches over and takes her hand.

"Hey." She smiles at him. "You know you never cried as a baby?"

"I know."

Then she yawns widely, like a little kid. "Gosh, I'm sleepy."

There was a moment, he thinks, thirty years ago, when his mother gave birth to him and they knew each other. Pearl gave birth to Stephen and he sits by her as she dies. Their history – pain and hurt they would inflict or had inflicted – all of that, it sweeps above them like a great northern wind bending green and hopeful trees.

The two spirits greet each other.

Stephen watches his mother being born, and she holds him dying in her arms.

"I love you," Stephen says.

196

Her face is trusting, even hopeful. "I love you too." She closes her eyes, opens them again. "Stephen."

It all falls into Stephen's body in a great whoosh. He is there, he is alive with her, with his mother. His heart beats with it. It could almost break him, this love. It is love.

So they hold hands. They sit like that, together.

He fills his palm with ashes and sends them over the water.